NO HALO
REQUIRED

Travis Casey

Written by Travis Casey

All rights Reserved 2020©

ISBN-13: 9781795316705

For my good friend
Eric Beal
Thanks for all your support—
in literature and in life.

Cheers to my editing team:
Carolyn Lee of Proof to Print editing, Angela
Wiechmann, Julie Conrad,
and Mary Leffler.

Cover design by Mich Fisher
from ArtfulCover.com

All the very best and a heartfelt thanks,

Travis Casey

Chapter 1

Isaiah Hightower was as dark as the night he walked through. The warm June evening escorted him in unannounced obscurity toward Dark Alleys—his second favorite place on earth.

The soles of his loafers landed softly on the ground as he crossed the parking lot. Anticipation grew with each step that took him nearer to the door of decadence. His nerves tingled with excitement, but there was also sadness accompanying his visit. Yes, he was going to see Alicia—but this would be the last time he'd ever see her. That was his vow.

Isaiah walked past the etched glass doors of the Player's Club to a barely noticeable set of stairs tucked on the far side of the building, obscured by evergreen trees. There were no signs or lights drawing attention to the steps that led to a door below street level.

Isaiah looked right, then left. No one was around. He hurried down the steps and out of sight. A rustic oak door at the bottom of the steps guarded the club's happenings against the outside world. A low wattage bulb barely illuminated the entrance. Hightower rapped on the door twice—then paused exactly two seconds before delivering four more sharp raps.

A wooden flap that served as a peephole opened just enough to allow an eye to peer at the visitor.

"Yes?" the voice behind the door purred inquisitively.

"Hickory dickory dock, the mouse is on the block."

Hinges squeaked as the door opened. The voice behind the door remained hidden from view. Isaiah stepped in and turned right, heading toward a dim light peeking out from around the edges of a dark blue velvet curtain. The low-level rays invited him to join the activities on the other side. Soft music barely outranked mumbled conversations. Sweat collected on his palms as he reached for the drape. His blood warmed as eagerness raced through his veins. He eased the textile barrier to one side and stepped through.

A dancer arched her back as she held the pole with one hand and completed a 360-degree strut around the brass rod, ensuring the entire audience got a view of her tight, rich brown, naked body from every angle. She stopped, resting her back against the pole, then pushing her breasts out further, enticing patrons to throw a few extra dollars on the stage for her effort.

It worked. They did.

His excitement rose.

Alicia was on stage, looking more delectable than ever.

Isaiah's smile widened. He sat at a vacant table just behind the front row.

A waitress stopped and took his order, returning moments later with his root beer. He slipped her a couple of extra bucks for her trouble. She smiled and readjusted her top, offering him an eyeful of cleavage—which he appreciated.

He managed regular visits to Dark Alleys—the very private and discreet gentlemen's club. All members had a lot to lose if their visits ever found their way into the public domain. They trusted the "honor among thieves" philosophy, applying that attitude to recognizable businessmen, politicians, judges, celebrities, and of course, men of the education system.

If lust wasn't enough, gambling was also included on the menu of sin. But sin was an ugly word that should be reserved for degenerates and those with an evil heart. Isaiah was neither of those. He was not driven to Dark Alleys by an appetite for depravity. Rather he was invited to join by a man of impeccable public standing—a city councilor for Savannah, Georgia. When Isaiah was duty-bound to expel the councilor's son for selling marijuana on school property, the councilor invited Vice Principal Hightower to join him at Dark Alleys to discuss alternatives to expulsion. The alternative turned out to be membership to a club that opened doors to meeting influential men who had as much to lose as Isaiah. But "business" was secondary to partaking of manly pleasures in a discreet environment.

Isaiah looked around at the clandestine gathering. Although the room was dim, he noticed some familiar faces. Reverend John Theis sat in the front row as usual. Isaiah had discovered he was quite the pervert when he saw him pleasuring himself in the men's room shortly after Alicia, of all people, had left the stage one night. The quarterback for the Atlanta Falcons football team sat toward the back, trying unsuccessfully to disguise himself with a Green Bay Packers cap and all too dark sunglasses. Isaiah had previously shared a joyous conversation with him about his team winning the Super Bowl. He, in turn, had acknowledged that he knew Isaiah and his work for Ebony Evolution. There seemed to be an unspoken mutual ransom in his acknowledgement of Isaiah's work that they would both be wise to adhere to the confidentiality and non-disclosure agreement all members signed.

Isaiah was going to miss this place, but after nine years at Savannah High School—six years as the head of the English department before being appointed as Vice Principal—he was moving on. He had accepted a job as the principal of Hilton Head High School in South Carolina. It was his turn to be the top dog. With his upcoming move to Hilton Head Island, he needed to dedicate himself to his new job. Not only that, he and his wife, Yvette, were committed to raising awareness for Ebony Evolution—an action group he founded five years ago that highlights racial injustices against African Americans and demands authorities answer to the public for their actions.

His new job and impending move presented the perfect opportunity for him to wipe the slate clean and start afresh. He needed to. He loved his wife and wanted to dedicate himself to her—and to God. He was led down an errant path for political favors, but with a new chapter about to open—one that Yvette pushed him to develop—it was time to re-establish his moral fortitude. Yes, one more night of sin to flush his soul of impurity and his new life would begin in earnest. Tomorrow.

Alicia sauntered off the stage and made her way over to Reverend Theis' table—shaking her boobs tantalizingly close to his face. That's all he needed. Isaiah would stay out of the men's room anytime

Theis wasn't at his table. The good Reverend slipped five bucks in her black and gold garter. She gave him an affectionate rub on the cheek with the back of her hand, then puckered her lips and moved on.

She turned, placing herself in front of Isaiah's table. Her eyes widened and she smiled. "Isaiah! I didn't see you come in. I didn't expect you for another hour yet."

He returned the smile. "Hello, Alicia." Isaiah's graying mustache and goatee added an extra air of authority to his already commanding voice. "I wanted to spend all the time I could with you—" He looked her up and down. "Or at least see as much of you as I could before I go." He chuckled at the innuendo.

She grabbed her breasts, giving them a seductive squeeze. "You wanna spend time with me or with these?"

He studied her breasts, enjoying the twitch in his trousers Alicia always triggered—and the thought of what would follow when she finished her shift. "It's a package deal, isn't it?"

"Of course. What do you have booked for us tonight?"

"I thought we'd go back to that Guests of Georgia motel just outside of Port Wentworth. You like it there, don't you?"

Alicia sighed. "No, but you do. It's our last night, Isaiah. Can't we go somewhere special? Like the Marriott or something?"

He shook his head. "No, sorry, but I do have a special surprise for you."

She slipped her hand under the tablecloth and clutched his manhood. Her lips brushed his ear as she whispered, "Granted, this is special, but it's no surprise."

His lips grew into a smile. "You wait. I think you'll be pleased."

She gave his crotch an extra squeeze. "Well, you know me—if I'm pleased, you get pleased back."

"Then it's a win-win." Isaiah laughed. "What time do you finish?"

"Now that you're here I can cut my shift short and finish after this dance, but I'll get off sometime after you check me into the Guests of Georgia motel." With silky grace, her hands caressed the sides of her breasts before her fingertips ended up on her nipples, giving them a gentle pinch.

His twitch hardened. "In that case, I wish you had picked a shorter song."

***

Isaiah checked into the Guests of Georgia motel while Alicia waited in the minivan. When he came out of reception, he motioned to her to join him. They walked side-by-side up the outdoor staircase to the open-air walkway of the second floor. Isaiah took several scouring looks around as they made their way to room 229. He didn't see anyone, just a dog sniffing around a garbage can.

He opened the door and breathed a sigh of relief when they entered. As far as he could tell they made it in undetected. Escorting his mistress always made him nervous—but it also heightened his sexual desire for the forbidden fruit—and he couldn't get much more forbidden than Alicia Saunders.

She looked around the room. "No champagne on ice?"

He shook his head. "No, not tonight."

She moved in and wrapped her arms around his neck. "But this is our last night together. I thought you had something special planned." Her face lit up. "Unless you brought me here to ask me to move to Hilton Head with you."

Isaiah's heart rate spiked. Even in jest that was a ridiculous thing to say. She worried him when she talked like that. She was youthful and fun, but hardly matrimony material, even if he wanted to get rid of Yvette—which he didn't. He sidestepped the suggestion like a matador in the bull ring. "Don't talk crazy talk."

She unwrapped her arms and shrugged. "Okay … no champers … no ring … what's the surprise?" She rolled her big brown eyes. "Oh my God. You're not going to make me do that thing again, are you? You know, pretend I'm Oprah?"

He smirked. "Not unless you want to …"

"No—I—do—not. Honestly—"

He took her hand and led her to the bed. "First of all, don't take the Lord's name in vain. A simple no would suffice." They sat down, Isaiah holding her hands in his.

She looked at the floor. "Yeah, sorry, I know that bugs you."

"It's not me you should worry about upsetting." He took a purposeful look at the ceiling—and the Man above. He readdressed Alicia. "I know you want to go to a community college and get a degree. I'd like that too. You're a smart girl, Alicia, you don't need to strip—"

She jumped off the bed and stood over Isaiah, looking down at him. "Yes I do, Daddy! I told you. If I'm going to go to college and get a *respectable* job, I need a car to get me from school, to work, to home. I can't be taking the goddam—the blasted bus!"

Isaiah reached in his jacket pocket, pulled out a neatly wrapped wad of cash. "Surprise!" He handed Alicia her future. "Here's three thousand dollars. I want you to get yourself a little run-around, get a job that will suit your schooling, and get your degree so you can make something of yourself."

Her eyes widened. "Really?"

He nodded. "Yes, really. It's my going away present to you. And since I won't be around for you to entertain anymore, you don't need to parade that hot naked body of yours in front of sickos and perverts to make a buck. You're better than that."

"Do you really think I could make something of myself?"

"Of course you can. Teasing men with your nudity can only lead to trouble. You need to finish your education and get into a long-term career. Do you have any idea what you'd like to be?"

She walked over and picked her purse up off the desk and pulled out a pair of fuzzy handcuffs, twirling them by one cuff around her finger. "How about a cop?" Her smiled broadened. "First thing I'd do is a strip search. Then I'd cuff you. Then I'd fuck a confession out of you."

"Do you have to use—"

She grabbed his face, halting his words. "You have the right to remain silent, Hightower." She pinched his face harder. "Now, get it off, convict." She stood back and watched.

Isaiah couldn't keep the grin off his face as he stripped. "I never thought getting arrested could be so much fun. I think you'd make a great cop."

"Now, spread 'em," she barked. She pounced on his naked body to begin a three-hour carnal session.

Chapter 2

Isaiah walked up behind his wife, wrapping his arms around her waist while she stood at the stove cooking his breakfast. He nestled his mouth into the crook of her shoulder, nibbling her neck. "How's the most gorgeous woman in South Carolina?" he growled between playful bites.

Yvette Hightower giggled. "Feeling radiant knowing the most handsome man in the South finds me attractive."

"Don't sell yourself short, darling. After church I may just take you to the promised land?"

"Denny's?"

He teasingly sunk his teeth into her jugular. "Our bedroom, baby."

"On a Sunday?"

"I know it's supposed to be a day of rest, but you're looking too fine not to unwrap."

Yvette experienced a belly flip. After fifteen years of marriage, he still did it for her. And judging by his mood, she still did it for him. Their move to Hilton Head was the best thing that ever happened. Perhaps it was Isaiah's new position as the man in charge of the high school—which she insisted he apply for—but his sexual appetite had certainly increased since they left Savannah. But then again, his stress level had been reduced considerably. Bossing around a bunch of rich white kids had to be easier than dealing with teenagers coming from the broken homes of inner-city Savannah.

Yvette tried to keep her focus on the eggs, but her husband's advances were nothing less than a major distraction, not to mention a source of erotic tingles. "Then I hope Reverend Goodstone doesn't get too long-winded—or preach on the evils of sex outside of marriage."

Isaiah dropped his arms and stepped back. "What's that supposed to mean?" His face went through an array of expressions, but only behind Yvette's back.

She turned around with a glean twinkling from her large, perfectly round eyes. "Because maybe that promised land belongs to the principal and one of his students. Say, the head cheerleader. Maybe Principal Hightower needs to discipline a certain cheerleader. Maybe even give her a spanking."

Isaiah's face grew stern. "That's ridiculous. I would never have an illicit encounter with one of my students."

Yvette grinned. "Of course you wouldn't. That's what's fun about it. It's a sin without actually sinning, and certainly without guilt."

Without guilt. Those words readjusted his heartrate from a nervous tempo to a happy beat. A smile spread across his face. "And why would this cheerleader need a spanking?"

"Maybe for having impure thoughts about the principal's pecker."

He cast his head back, looking toward the ceiling. "Oh, sweet Tahiti. If I hadn't promised Reverend Goodstone I'd greet the congregation before church I might just ask God if He minded if we played hooky today."

11

Yvette nodded toward the table. "Sit down, Hightower. Breakfast is ready—and you're going to need your energy for when we get back from church, so don't be giving God all your halleluiahs—save a few for me."

He punched his fist in the air. "Halleluiah!" he shouted.

***

Yvette enjoyed the ride to church. What she relished even more than the passing green scenery were the sly glances Isaiah threw her way "checking her out." He had complimented her over breakfast on how nice she looked in her brown and white dress. The brown was the same color as her skin making it look as if she simply wore white strips covering her modesty. The look excited her—and obviously Isaiah too. A million bucks, he compared her to. She was pleased she could still wear horizontal stripes without looking fat. Not all women could do that at forty-one. She was anxious to get to the church and tell Gloria Huntington she still had what it took to get her husband to acknowledge her as desirable. And while in church she'd pray that the good Reverend would keep his sermon short—assure the righteous of their passage to heaven, damn the sinners to hell, and get the heck out of there so she could get back home and screw the principal's brains out.

They pulled into the parking lot where Isaiah parked in one of the six spaces reserved for deacons. Yvette waited for Isaiah as he walked around and opened the door for her. He didn't do it all the time, but church was one place where he *always* opened the door for her—Sundays and special occasions—that was their arrangement.

Yvette got out of the car, gave Isaiah a smile and a pat on the cheek, and then headed for the church. She bounded up the stairs to the white wooden chapel in three-inch heels in search of her friend, leaving Isaiah behind to shake hands with other parishioners.

Gloria Huntington stood at the entrance of the Hilton Head Evangelical Free Church waving a Japanese paper fan in true Southern Belle style— with short, rapid strokes—each stroke barely covering a two-inch span from start to finish. Despite her fanning vigor, the South Carolina humidity threatened to penetrate her makeup base. That would be unacceptable. God and Maybelline would have a lot to answer for if her superior good looks melted on the steps of the house of the Lord.

They first met when Gloria was fighting to clear her husband's name of murder charges, crimes she insisted he didn't commit. Isaiah donned his shining armor and raised the profile of the case. He loved bringing national attention to injustices against people of color. Yvette and Gloria became friends and both were delighted when the Hightower's moved to Hilton Head, making it an even closer friendship.

Following Gloria's lead, the two women air-kissed, leaving Gloria's makeup intact. Yvette admired her spirit to use such a rich red lipstick to compliment her light-brown skin. Large red and gold earrings dangled prominently over her shoulders ensuring she would be seen as a woman of daring—and style.

"Darling," Gloria purred. "How delightful to see you. I must say, you look adorable."

Yvette stood back, opening her arms and smiling—showing white teeth worthy of a TV commercial. "He noticed," she boasted.

"Darling," Gloria eyed her up and down, "Stevie Wonder would notice you in that."

Yvette slid her hands over her hips. "I do work hard to make him proud."

"And you succeed. The man appreciates his wife. How wonderful is that?"

Even through her dark skin, Yvette blushed. "You're too kind."

"Not kind, observant. After all, you married a significant cog in the education of our children, a champion of the African American community, and a deacon of this very church. You have every reason to be proud of him. And isn't he up for the Citizen of the South?"

"Yes, I nominated him for the COTS award and had the Chief of Police in Savannah second it. Isaiah is the most wonderful man I've ever known—and so driven."

"Yes, and, girl, I bet he's driven you to some places most of us can't even imagine."

Yvette play-smacked Gloria on the arm. "Stop it. You're so naughty." She stepped closer and whispered. "And yes he has. He's driven me to some places even God doesn't know about."

The women giggled.

Yvette straightened her posture. "But when the lights are on, I'm honored to hold the title as Mrs. Isaiah Hightower."

"Of course you are."

Isaiah stepped between the women. "Good morning, Gloria." He attempted to deliver an affectionate peck to her cheek but she pulled back, protecting her makeup. She puckered her lips and simply kissed the air in front of her.

"Isaiah," she greeted him. "Slain any dragons lately?"

"I can't say that I've disposed of any mythical creatures recently, no."

Yvette draped her arm over her husband's shoulder. "But what he has done ..."

He held a victorious beam. "Well, only if you consider the Hilton Head Town Council a dragon."

"Oh?"

"I've persuaded them to close the Bare Trap on Madison Street."

Gloria smiled. "I can understand with a wife as beautiful as yours you have no need for strip clubs, but why would you invest your valuable time in such an insignificant crusade?"

"Insignificant? It's hardly that. We need to protect the children."

It was barely noticeable through her packed foundation, but Gloria's face creased. "Isaiah, why are you worried about strip clubs? As immoral as those places may be, they have checks in place to ensure they are kept as a visual orgy for adults; whereas all the children of today's world have to do is jump on the pornographic gateway known as the internet and they can see all the nudity they want—and heaven knows what other kinds of debauchery."

Isaiah shook his head. "It's too near the high school. Young girls see the strippers arriving at work in Corvettes and Mercedes and will give up their education to make money the easy and uneducated way. No, God has spoken to me. He asked me to shut down this particular playground of sin, and I answered. The council has accepted my arguments

and the Bare Trap was closed down two days ago."
He thrust both arms in the air. "Halleluiah!"

"And that's your dragon?"

Isaiah dipped his head. "No halo required."

"And they did it on that argument? Your students may become strippers one day?"

"I may have mentioned that a sophomore student was already a dancer there."

"What? At sixteen? Was she?"

Isaiah shrugged. "It's possible—one day ... maybe."

Yvette stepped forward. "And statistically, the ratio of minority dancers to white ones was grossly out of proportion. The place is not only immoral; it discriminates against people of color."

Gloria looked at her friend. "And you researched this, did you?"

Yvette nodded. "As you mentioned, Isaiah is a busy man. I help where I can when discrimination is involved. Out of twenty-three performers at the Bare Trap, twenty-one were white, one African-American, and one Native American—I believe she dresses up as a squaw."

"I see." Gloria continued flapping her fan. "And you want to see more people of color taking their clothes off?"

Yvette frowned. "No, you're missing the point—"

Isaiah patted her hand. "Not to worry, darling. Those Jezebels won't be taking their clothes off for the underclasses of Hilton Head anymore."

"Thanks to you," Yvette congratulated him, then turned to Gloria. "He's one of God's angels."

"No halo required," Gloria echoed.

Yvette looped her arm through Isaiah's. "Let's go give God the thanks He deserves and get the heck out of here. My pom-poms want shaking."

They entered the church—Isaiah's favorite place on earth.

Chapter 3

Isaiah parked the Chrysler Voyager in the space designated for *Principal Hightower* and paused at the front of the building. The smart façade with its cream pillars and *Hilton Head Island High School* proudly spelled out in bold blue letters never failed to excite him. Potted palm trees stood on each side of the entranceway of the single-story building.

What continued to impress him was the absence of graffiti on the building and the pristine, unbroken terracotta pots holding the palm trees.

With just a few months left in the school term, he reflected on his time at Hilton Head compared to his tenure in Savannah. The brutality of violent fathers, if they were present at all, had been replaced by soccer moms wearing Dolce and Gabbana sunglasses to protect their eyes from the sun—not to hide bruises. Schools personified and it was a case of Jekyll and Hyde.

His brown wingtip shoes clicked on the polished floor as he walked to his office. He crossed over from the hall tiles to the blue and gold carpet of the principal's office. His secretary was at her desk.

She stood up when he walked in. "Howdy, Mr. H. Here's your java." She picked up a Starbucks cup on her desk and handed it to him as he passed by.

Isaiah smiled. "You're an angel, Betty. Thank you so much."

"I need to talk at ya once you get hunkered down, Mr. H."

He liked Betty, but her grammar drove him crazy. Perhaps she was hired as a token promoting affirmative action, but a person in the education system should speak properly. Nonetheless, she brought a lot to the table in return. She had been at the school for over twenty years and didn't put up with any shenanigans from the students. She ruled them with an iron fist. Although most of the students were white, and Betty was dark brown, many of the students identified with her as a grandmother-type—the kind of grandmother that raised them instead of their parents and they wouldn't dare talk back to her. He was certain she dealt with more than fifty percent of the discipline problems herself and he never had to see them.

Isaiah raised his coffee cup. "Just let me court this caffeine beauty for five minutes, then I'm all yours."

She dipped her head and wiggled her full figure back into her ergonomically-friendly red chair.

He passed through the door labeled Principal Hightower and took a seat behind his large oak desk. He peacefully sipped his coffee while he congratulated himself. He had nearly completed his first year and had been nominated for Principal of the Year by the South Carolina Board of Education. Not only was he a powerful force in the education system, he was also a deacon of the Hilton Head Evangelical Church. His religious achievements made him as proud as his scholastic successes. Coupled with a profession that allowed him to shape young minds, he also helped mold souls for the greater good. He relished his role as Deacon Hightower every bit as much as his profession as Principal Hightower.

As a result of his hard work and Yvette's diligence, and he was up for Citizen of the South—an award bestowed upon the most significant man south of the Mason-Dixon line—never awarded to an African American before. He could be the first. He was satisfied. He did it. He made it to the top.

At forty-nine, life was everything he hoped it would be.

A knock at the door gathered his attention. "Yes?" he called out.

Betty walked in carrying a notepad.

"Yes, Betty. What are we doing today? Resolving crises or praising someone's achievements?"

A quick smile revealed the large space between her two front teeth which sometimes created whistling when she spoke. Suzy selling seashells would bring a whistling tsunami. "Does the name David Marsh ring any bells with you?"

Isaiah tapped his upper lip with his finger. "David, Marsh, David Marsh ..." he mumbled as his mind trawled his memory bank. "Sounds familiar. Should I know him?"

"He wasn't no dummy and graduated from here last year. The boy could play some ball and got himself a scholarship to Chatham College in Savannah."

"Of course!" He clicked his fingers. "He was the white quarterback playing at Chatham. The only white guy on the field, as I recall. Yes, now I remember. There was a lot of press coverage on that in Savannah. How's he doing?"

"Not too good. He done got gunned down in a drive-by shooting—on the campus at Savannah no less. Two bullets to the head."

Isaiah's head slumped. "Oh, sweet Jerusalem."

Betty opened her notepad. "The college is holding a memorial for the boy. And they done asked if his former principal could attend."

Isaiah looked up. "I wasn't his principal."

"No, but Principal Durham from last year will be in Europe that day and won't be able to be there. They done asked if you'd take his place."

"When is it?"

"In two weeks. April 22nd."

Isaiah looked in his diary and shook his head. "That won't work. I promised my wife I'd help her with a fundraising project."

"Dadblangit." She drew a breath, looking agitated that her work on the matter hadn't ended with their conversation then and there. "I guess I'll have to go find Vice Principal Becker and send him. I know how he just *loves* this kind of upheaval to his schedule."

Isaiah nodded. "I'll say a prayer."

"For who? Becker or David Marsh?" She faked a smile and left.

***

Isaiah turned into his sweeping horseshoe-shaped driveway. Mature shrubs bordered the herringbone laid brick drive that came off the most idyllic tree-lined street where replica gas lantern lights illuminated Vista Oaks Drive each night shortly after sunset.

He parked the minivan in front of the garage and headed for the front door. He stood at the entrance looking through the clear glass of the Georgian panes that allowed an unobstructed view straight through the house, across the wooden floors, and out the back of the patio doors that led to expansive and uninterrupted views of the Atlantic Ocean in the distance. The house came with a price tag that was $50,000 over budget. Isaiah could have resisted the five bedroom/three and a half bathroom split level dwelling, but Yvette loved it and vowed to keep it as a spotless sanctuary for Isaiah to retreat to after a hard day.

"Yvette," he called out as he walked through the door. He set his briefcase in his office just off the entranceway. "Yvette," he shouted.

"I'm in here," she answered back.

Isaiah followed the voice trail to the living room. She was stretched out on the couch in a blue tracksuit watching *Real Housewives of Atlanta.*

Yvette sat up and turned the TV down. "How was your day?"

"Interesting. They wanted me to go to Savannah but I had to turn it down."

"Why?"

"Chatham College is holding a memorial for David Marsh, the white kid who played football there. He got shot on campus and they want a principal from his high school to attend the service."

"So why aren't you going?"

"It's the twenty-second. We'll be marching for African Americans against Alzheimer's that day."

"Oh, forget that."

Isaiah's eyebrows peaked. "Excuse me?"

Yvette waved a dismissive hand. "I didn't mean it like that."

"Don't worry, I'll send Becker."

Yvette erected her posture. "Now you really have to go."

"Why?"

"You're going to send a white guy to an all-black college to commemorate another white guy? And the college gets a Hilton Head flunkie instead of the man in charge of education of the most prestigious island in all the South?"

Isaiah chuckled. "I think you're overplaying my importance—"

Yvette stood up, her hands finding firm placement on her hips. "You are going to Savannah, Principal Hightower, and you are going to do your school proud. Do this boy proud." She stepped in and cradled his head. "Do your wife proud."

"Do you really think it's that important?"

"As important as winning Citizen Of The South. This will look good on your résumé of achievements and caring for the community. Besides, I'm sure there will be some important people there. It won't hurt your profile."

Isaiah wrapped his arms around his wife's slim hips. "In that case, come with me, baby."

"No, I can't."

Isaiah sweetened the pot. "I'll take you out for a romantic dinner at the Black Pearl. Surf and turf."

"Sorry, baby. I can't let the organizers down. I promised I'd be there."

Isaiah was genuinely disappointed. "Are you sure you can't come? I'd like you to be there with me."

"I'd love to come, baby, but I can't. Next time, I promise." She kissed the side of his head. "Hey, you're going to a Historically Black College. Make the most of it. You never know who you might see."

"A memorial." He let out a deep breath. "I'm sure I'll have a great time."

Chapter 4

Isaiah displayed the faculty parking badge that Chatham College had sent him in the window of the minivan. It hadn't been a bad drive from Hilton Head—only forty-five minutes. It felt natural being back in Savannah, but also strange. Like he had moved on—up the ladder, even. Savannah reminded him of the hardships he had endured before he got where he was today. But now he had the perfect life in Hilton Head. It was worth the struggles. This was a good grounding excursion for him. It fell in line with his belief that one should never forget their roots. So a visit to the past now and again would remind him what a lucky man he was.

Isaiah ran his hands down the front of his suit as he made his way to Cougar Arena. A few years earlier, as vice principal of Savannah High, he had visited the campus on a reconnaissance mission. He made it his business to have some knowledge of all the local colleges so he could help guide students who wanted to stay in the area—not that a lot of his students were in a financial or mental position to attend college—but he stayed abreast of the possibilities all the same.

Conversations buzzed incoherently as he entered the auditorium. Many of the 5,000 blue seats were empty, but there were still about 1,000 people in attendance. He walked across the wooden gym floor making a beeline for the seats at center court. A tall African American man stood in the middle of the front row wearing a black and red regalia with a gold medallion hanging around his neck. Isaiah recognized the garb as something the dean of the college would wear.

Isaiah stood in front of him and looked up into his gold wire-rimmed spectacles. He extended his hand. "Dean Fuchs? Isaiah Hightower. Principal of Hilton Head High School, David's alma mater."

The dean took his hand firmly and smiled. "Principal Hightower. How good of you to come. I'm sorry we have to meet on such a sad occasion."

Isaiah bowed his head respectfully. "As am I, Dean Fuchs. I'm afraid my presence and my prayers are all I can offer, but I gladly give them both."

Fuchs smiled. "Thank you. If you'd like to take a seat behind me, the service will start in about ten minutes."

Next to a vacant seat behind the dean's chair sat Lionel Webster—the Savannah Chief of Police and Isaiah's long-time friend. "Lionel … What are you doing here?" He extended his arm and they shook hands.

A sheen of perspiration glistened off Chief Webster's shiny face. His robust, circular frame likened him to that of a well-crafted snowman—with a deep African tan. His cartoon appearance wasn't consistent with being the kingpin of Savannah justice, but he had the gold bars on his shoulder boards to prove it. "Hello, Isaiah. Sadly, it happened on my watch." He looked across the auditorium. "Did Yvette come with you?"

He shook his head. "No, she had to march for good causes elsewhere."

"Too bad. Send her my regards, will you?"

"I certainly will. So what happened? With the Marsh boy?"

Webster pulled out a handkerchief and mopped his brow. "A drive-by. The boy was walking with a mixed-race girl. We're not sure if it was racially motivated or just a tragic random loss of life. But when a white kid gets murdered on an HBCU campus we have to assume race played a part."

"Any suspects?"

The chief nodded. "We have two in custody, but the mayor is all over my ass. That Marsh boy gave Chatham their first winning season in eight years. He was collecting icon status after only one year. The mayor loved him. I gotta come up with something soon or I'll be looking for another job."

Isaiah rested a comforting hand on his friend's shoulder. "I'll be praying for you."

Webster cocked an eye at him. "You got anything better than a prayer?"

Isaiah ignored the sacrilegious comment and looked around the crowd. He spotted a few familiar faces—probably from Ebony Evolution events. Maybe an odd student from Savannah High had made it to the campus on a sports scholarship. Looking at the crowd, he wondered how David Marsh had coped at a Historically Black College and University. It was a nearly all-black campus—eighty-four percent by all accounts, with only four percent white and the further twelve percent coming from other minority backgrounds. It couldn't have been easy, but the kid would have had guts. Isaiah admired that.

Dean Fuchs stood up and walked to a podium set up at center court and began speaking. As expected, he announced what a great athlete and human being David Marsh was—and of course a credit to Chatham College.

As the dean continued, Isaiah's eyes roamed the auditorium. He noticed a pastor sat in the seat next to the dean's chair, no doubt he was the eulogy grandmaster. He looked down his row and noticed some black faces wiping away tears—big black faces—David's teammates he assumed. He looked to the front row. Two girls sat comforting each other as they sobbed. *Wait a minute. That's not two girls ... That's a girl and Alicia!*

Isaiah nearly jumped to his feet before he realized that would make a spectacle of himself. He quickly replanted his butt firmly in the seat. His unrest drew a noticeable look from Chief Webster. Isaiah briefly covered his face, trying to hide—but from whom? He gathered the nerve to peek again, craning his neck, looking down the first row. It was. It was Alicia.

His palms beaded with sweat while his mind raced. *What was she doing here? Was she a student? Why would she be in the front row?* Dean Fuchs's words turned to mush as Isaiah's mind churned out question after unanswered question, drowning out any other noise that may have been existent. Then he realized, in the middle of his befuddlement was an undeniable excitement. Yes. Seeing Alicia excited him. But why? He did have unsolicited thoughts of her several times over the past ten months. She would simply appear in his consciousness bringing a host of impure thoughts that he would have to pray away. Sometimes he'd have to pray harder than others. She was a drug he couldn't have—no—a drug he'd didn't want and no longer needed. He had

27

kicked the habit. He had reformed! He took another gander at her. Behind the tears was a beautiful girl.

He ignored her, focusing on Dean Fuchs's comments of compassion. *Blah, blah, blah.*

He stole another glance toward Alicia. Thankfully that episode of his life was over.

Isaiah focused on the dean, nodding in agreement. *Yes, poor David Marsh. What a tragic loss.*

He looked at Alicia again. His excitement wouldn't dissipate. Or was it was curiosity? He wanted her to better herself. Perhaps she did. She must be a student at Chatham College. Yes, of course. His guiding influence had yet again saved a lost soul from wickedness. His three thousand dollar gift helped her better herself and saved her from the flames of hell. *Halleluiah!*

Yvette proposed he may meet people he needed to. Yes, that's why he was there. To share in Alicia's joy of her new beginning. He would talk to her after the service and offer her praise for transforming her life. God sent him to Savannah to see the work he had accomplished in turning a young life around. He looked forward to seeing her after the service.

***

Dean Fuchs, Chief Webster, the pastor, and Isaiah stood in a circle on the gym floor reliving the eulogy and accolades and agreeing on what a wonderful young man David Marsh had been. Despite the moment of sincerity, Isaiah kept one eye on Alicia. She still sat in her seat, wiping away tears with her friend. *Why all the grief?* Finally, she moved. She got to her feet and walked arm-in-arm with her friend toward the exit. He kept a close eye on her and waited until they were nearly out the door.

Isaiah interrupted Dean Fuchs. "If you'll excuse me, gentlemen, there's someone I must speak to." Without further explanation or waiting for any response, he hustled after Alicia.

The two girls walked along the sidewalk with Isaiah jogging after them. "Alicia," he called out.

The girls stopped and turned.

Alicia's face lit up when she recognized him. "Isaiah? What are you doing here?"

"I was going to ask you the same thing." His eyes roamed her body. *Oh, disciples of delight.* His gaze zeroed in on her breasts. Her enlarged breasts! He shuddered when he realized he was perving, but it was amazement that made his eyes stop where they did. He re-engaged her eyes. "Can we talk a minute?" He glanced at Alicia's friend, shooing her away with his look.

Alicia looked at her companion. "Can you excuse us a minute, Tanya? I'll meet you in the car."

"Okay." The girl turned and walked away, still wiping tears from her eyes.

Isaiah pointed to a picnic table sitting on the green grass. "Shall we?"

They walked over and took a seat.

"What are you doing here?" he asked.

Alicia nodded toward her friend. "That's Tanya, David's girlfriend—except what do you call a girl who's been widowed out of wedlock?"

He shrugged. "I don't know. Are you a student here?"

"No, but Tanya is. She's pretty tore up. I don't think she'll ever get over it."

"So you knew David?"

She shook her head. "No, not really. Only what she's told me about him. Tanya and I are Facebook friends. We don't really know each other personally, but we chat all the time. A lot of her friends disowned her for going out with a white guy, so she asked me if I'd come with her. I was crying for her, not him."

"I see. Yes, it's tragic," Isaiah sympathized. "But I heard he was with a girl when he got shot. So it wasn't her? That Tanya?"

A faint smile broke the sadness of her face. "No, that was Gwen. They were study buddies. David was having trouble in some law classes and she was helping him."

"He was studying law?"

She nodded. "Criminology, I think. If he didn't get a football contract he wanted to be a detective."

His eyes found their way back to her breasts.

She caught him. "You like what you see?"

He broke out of the trance, embarrassed. "My memory hasn't gone, has it? I mean, you weren't like that ..."

She smiled. "No. Don't be mad, but I didn't get the car with the money you gave me. I got implants instead."

His manicured eyebrows arched.

"I figured if I got implants and stayed at Dark Alleys another year, I'd get better tips with bigger boobs. Then I'd be in a better position financially to pay for college—and I could get a car too." She pointed to her left boob. "Toyota." Pointing to her right breast, "tuition. I'm what you call 'a thirty-four double T.'" She giggled.

Isaiah grinned. Although disappointed in her disobedience, he appreciated her ingenuity. "So you're still at the club?"

She nodded, but in a shy manner. "I will better myself one day, but I don't want to rack up huge debts trying to get a degree."

Isaiah bowed his head. "I thought maybe you were in college here." He glanced at her from the tops of his eyes. "One day ... maybe?"

"One day," she conceded.

"What would you be studying?"

She shrugged. "I don't know." She leaned in and whispered. "But a certain someone did tell me I made a pretty good cop." She laughed.

Isaiah smiled. "I'm pleased to hear you haven't given up on bettering your future. I wish you every success." He took another sneaky peek.

"Can I see you again?" she asked.

"I don't know if that's such a good idea."

"We were always good together, Isaiah, and I'd like another rendezvous with the best lover I ever had." She patted his knee and stood up. "Besides, if I gave a girl three grand, I'd like to see how she spent it."

She looked at her breasts.

So did he.

"You can see your investment any night at Dark Alleys except Tuesdays and Wednesdays. I miss you. I want to see you again."

He shook his head. "I'm a new man, Alicia."

She cupped her breasts "And I'm a new woman. Come see for yourself." She winked and walked off toward the parking lot to find her friend. "Come see me, Isaiah. I mean it."

Chapter 5

Isaiah hung his pressed slacks in the fold-over garment bag. He moved to the dresser and selected a pair of socks and underwear.

Yvette stood by the bedroom door watching her husband pack. "Tell me again, why do you have to go to Savannah?"

"Chief Webster wants to canonize the boy. We're going to discuss how to best commemorate him."

Yvette stood with her arms across her chest. "Can't you do that from here? I mean, he was a student at Hilton Head."

"But he got killed in Savannah. Their scars haven't healed."

"I still don't know why he should get so much attention. Black people get gunned down all the time and the only mention of that is on the crime statistics page. We're only given a number, not a statue."

He let out a frustrated sigh. "Then just pretend I'm doing it for Chief Webster. The mayor wants something special or Webster's out. I'm helping our friend."

"Will it raise your profile?"

"It's not about me."

"But if you're going to be Citizen Of—"

Isaiah stood straight and gave his wife a reprimanding glare. "Yvette, this is not about me."

"Well, I don't see why it shouldn't be about you. If you're going to help the chief of police solve a crime then Isaiah Hightower's name should be up in lights. And those lights should be saying Citizen of the South."

Guilt pricked his conscience for the first time in ten months. Yvette was the perfect wife for his public persona: loyal, dedicated to him, driven, and supportive of his causes. So why was he running off to Savannah to reignite a fling with a stripper? Was it her youth? Her fun-loving and irresponsible nature? Her hot body that he donated $3,000 to enhance? He badly wanted to insert his "I" between those double T's—but why? Yvette would do anything for him if he asked.

Alicia is young, fun, and sexy. Yvette is grounded and mature. That's what I need in my life. Wait—am I talking about the former or the latter?

Yvette's voice derailed his train of thought. "Do you really have to stay overnight?"

"You know what? No." Isaiah shook his head. "No, I don't have to go at all. It was a stupid idea. I left Savannah behind—I mean, Chief Webster will have to figure this out for himself."

Yvette stepped in, her fingers traced the tip of his shirt collar. "I don't know, maybe you should go. Lionel is your friend and needs your support. And it won't hurt getting your name out there."

Isaiah shrugged. "I don't know … I probably shouldn't go … You know, the kid was white—"

"No, you should go. It was on an HBCU campus. Do it for the other students … and for Lionel."

Now he was being urged to go. Whether he wanted to or not. He glanced at heaven. Was this a sign?

"Any ideas what you and Lionel might work on?" Yvette asked.

"We never discussed a plan. In fact, we don't have a plan."

"Then perhaps you best stay the night, as you suggested. Why don't you stay at the Marriott?"

Isaiah pulled a face of disbelief. "Not the one on the riverfront?"

"Yes, that would be the one."

"But that's—"

Yvette's stance firmed up. "You're the principal of the school honoring a dead student. You're going out of your way to help the boy, his family, and Chatham College, not to mention the chief of police. You deserve a little luxury. Besides, you earn a six-figure salary. We can afford it. And, since it's school business, it's a tax write-off." She smiled.

"Well, when you put it like that …"

Yvette pursed her lips to one side. She held her head down while she looked at Isaiah from the tops of her eyes. Her big round eyes held a devilish look. "I did promise I'd come with you the next time you went. Should I be packing?"

Isaiah silently chuckled. The luxury was not intended for him, but he was going to take it nonetheless. He had resisted the temptation and said no, but God was talking to him through Yvette. It was her lips but God's voice. He could say no to his wife, but not to God. He had to go and go alone.

Isaiah stood tall and took a deep breath. "I would love for you to come, darling, but I'm going to be busy. It might be a late night."

"Busy doing what?"

Although now growing impatient he tried to remain calm. "I don't know. That's what Lionel and I have to discuss. Maybe he'll want to raise money for a David Marsh sprinkler head on the fifty-yard-line. I—don't—know."

Yvette's face brightened up. "I'm pretty good at fundraising. I did raise over two thousand dollars from a bake sale alone for your Ebony Evolution campaign when Darvill Thomas got gunned down by the police in Atlanta, remember?"

"Yes, you did. But Marsh was white."

His wife's face crinkled. "What's that got to do with anything? Besides the obvious."

"It means..." Isaiah stepped over and took his wife's hand. "We don't want too many Hightowers who have a reputation for raising money for black people there. This could be a political powder keg if it's not handled properly."

"But this isn't about race, is it?"

"No, but the killing may have been racially motivated. We need to tread carefully."

She moved in and took his face in her hands, stroking his cheeks with her thumbs. "That's why I love you. You're doing something noble—although I'm sure there's more sympathy for a white kid getting shot than an African American, you still want to help."

"Thank you for your support, darling, but it would be best if I do this alone. We don't want this too high profile. After all, white or black, a young man did get shot. Chief Webster's taking it pretty hard. It happened on his watch, and you're right. I need to support our friend."

"Yes, you need to go. But are you sure I can't come?"

"I'd love nothing more than to come back to the hotel room and see my gorgeous wife waiting for me. But you know Chief Webster. That man can rabbit on about nothing for hours on end. Not only that, his soul needs comforting. I might not get back to the room until after midnight."

"I wouldn't mind waiting."

"Maybe next time."

"Is that your final word?"

He offered an apologetic smile. "Let me see how it goes this time."

Yvette stared at her man, starry-eyed. The passion she cast with that look gave him confidence that her admiration of him was deep-rooted. She would yield to his determination and let him drive the situation forward as he saw fit. It was time for her to take on her cheerleader role. It was unspoken Hightower karma. He knew it and she knew it.

Isaiah threw a box of cufflinks into the pocket of the garment bag and zipped it up. He grabbed the handle and jerked it off the bed, heading for the door. He stopped in front of Yvette and gave her a peck on her cheek.

"Are you sure I can't help—"

"I'll be back tomorrow," Isaiah said. "I'll call you."

Yvette stood at the bedroom door, her big eyes showing love, respect, and support.

Isaiah marched down the hallway; his hard-soled shoes echoing pronounced steps as he trooped across the wooden floor to the front door. The door opened, then closed with a distinctive click.

36

Isaiah strolled across the marble floor of the Marriott Riverfront Hotel making his way to the reception desk. The young man behind the pristine white counter looked up.

"Good afternoon, sir. Welcome to—" The boy's hazel eyes grew large. "Principal Hightower? Well, I'll be ... How are you, sir?" The boy's grin was as wide as the river behind them.

It took Hightower a moment to recognize him. "Josh McKinna?"

He nodded. "Yes, sir. In the flesh, and working in this fine establishment."

Isaiah looked around, admiring the lobby. Balconies from internal rooms lined the interior looking down on the lobby and seating area. Plate glass windows went from the ground floor to the top of the eight-floor building letting in a full heaven of light. Outside, a cargo ship sailed past with an entire rainbow of colors from the containers she carried on full display. "Looks like you've done all right for yourself, Josh. Nice environment to work in, but it's long hours in the hospitality industry, isn't it?"

The boy looked pleased to gain approval from his former vice principal. "Yes, sir, but I'll be moving into hotel security soon. I'm working the front desk until something opens up, but I keep an eye on the monitors in the back when I can. It's good practice and you never know when there might be a terrorist attack. You wouldn't believe how many cameras this place has. You can't be too careful these days."

"No you can't," Isaiah agreed.

"I'm off at six o'clock, so at least I have the night off. What brings you back to Savannah?"

"Business."

"Not a principal's conference by any chance, is it? You should have had a word with me. I could have gotten you a good rate."

"Josh, how many times have a told you—'got' serves the purpose, it need not be gotten." Isaiah drove his English students mad by banning the word 'gotten' from their vocabulary. His grandmother proscribed the word from the Hightower vernacular after she studied English at Cambridge and credited herself with learning the Queen's proper English. Her professor chastised her for using "a gross Americanism," as he described it, in his classroom. She never uttered the misused tense of 'got' again.

The boy bowed his head. "Yes, sir." Then eyed the principal after the appropriate amount of time for paying respect to the reprimand. "Is Mrs. Hightower with you?"

"Umm ... no. No, she isn't."

"Too bad. She's a radiant lady. I always loved hearing her sing in the church choir. She has the voice of an angel." Josh looked at the ceiling reflectively for a moment before readdressing the principal. "Are you still teaching Sunday School in Hilton Head?"

Isaiah stood a little taller. "Actually, I'm a deacon at my church."

"Really ..." Josh's smile showed approval. "I've always admired your dedication, Mr. Hightower. To God and the education system."

"Thank you, Josh. Now—is my room ready?"

"Certainly, sir." The young man feverishly punched the keypad of the computer, a ginger lock of hair falling over his eyes as he worked to accommodate his guest. A moment later he handed Isaiah his room key.

Principal Hightower made his way to his room overlooking the Savannah River. He pulled a small bottle of mineral water out of the mini-bar and poured it into one of the glasses sitting next to the ice bucket. He sipped his five-dollar drink as he stood at the window, looking down at the Savannah River as a red and white paddle boat pushed past carrying its cargo of gawking tourists.

Yes, he conceded, Yvette would have loved the view. And the king-sized bed. And the his-and-hers sinks. There was no doubt that she loved him and wanted to help. Maybe she loved him too much. She could do with the break from him he rationalized. It must be hard work idolizing someone every waking moment.

***

Isaiah had arranged to meet Chief Webster at six o'clock for a drink. Webster telling Isaiah he needed to do something for the Marsh boy provided the perfect reason to come to Savannah. Then Yvette pushed him to network with "the right people." Alicia may not have been the "right" person, but he couldn't ignore the signs—or perhaps it should be classed as opportunity. The Lord works in mysterious ways, but even Columbo would have his work cut out for himself trying to figure this one out. But Isaiah was a servant, not a sleuth. He had to just go with it.

He hadn't realized how much he missed Alicia until he saw her again. He had dismissed her as an indulgence, but now accepted he had a responsibility to guide her to a better life. Knowing her as he did, he knew how to get her to respond. He was her mentor. She was his shiny mid-life Corvette.

He had time to kill before his meeting with Webster and sat in the lobby with a coffee watching ships as they sailed down the river. He found it captivating and discovered a certain peacefulness the way boats of all sizes glided down the water effortlessly. After finishing his coffee he wandered into the gift shop—not looking for anything in particular, but hoped he could find a little token for Alicia to celebrate their reunion. Wooden shelves lined one wall. At eye level were a row of stuffed animals. A bear caught his eye. He picked up the brown stuffed animal and examined it. The bear had a big smile and wore a t-shirt proclaiming "Daddy's Home." His smile stretched as big as the bear's. He took it to the counter and paid the $25 in cash. Alicia would love it.

***

Isaiah sat in the back end of a mock ship in the Buccaneer tavern. He didn't like meeting in a public bar. Simply being in a place that served up drunkenness as a matter of routine could direct people to the wrong conclusion. But Lionel insisted that after a rough day fighting crime he needed a whiskey. Isaiah sipped his root beer as he waited.

The head crime fighter of Savannah showed up a few minutes after six in civilian clothes. "Isaiah." Chief Webster walked in and sat opposite Hightower with a whiskey in hand.

"Hello, Lionel." He cocked his head to one side looking at Lionel's drink. "Is that your cape removal kit?"

Webster laughed. "I guess you could say that. So what brings you to Savannah? Are you putting a cape on for some Ebony matter, or is this a social call?"

He slowly nodded. "I'm thinking about what you said. You know, something to secure David Marsh's legacy, which would, in turn, save your job. I'm here to help."

"Look, I've had plenty of run-ins with the mayor. He gets a bee in his bonnet and then it blows over. It's not really a big deal."

"Well, I'd like to help."

"Doing what?"

"I'm not sure, that's what I was hoping we could discuss. Let's bounce around some ideas."

Webster leaned back. "You're taking this rather seriously, aren't you?"

Isaiah gave a sympathetic shrug. "Just trying to help a friend."

"It might be easier to sweep this thing under the rug. If we go highlighting racially motivated killings we'd have to come up with something pretty good."

"Good is what I do, Chief." His lips curled into a grin.

"I'd rather hide it under a bushel. What were you thinking?"

"I don't know. I've always been good at raising money. Maybe something to commemorate his time at Chatham?"

"What? A plaque?"

"I could probably do something bigger."

Webster leaned back and folded his arms across his chest. "You've done a lot of fundraising for Ebony Evolution, haven't you?"

He nodded. "Yes, yes I have."

"And you know the two suspects we have in custody for David Marsh's murder are black, right?"

"So?"

"Do you see any problems with a prominent black leader raising money for a white kid killed by black gangsters?"

Isaiah's brows knitted together. "Lionel, I'm incensed. He was practically a student of mine. I do what's right because it's right—not because of a person's color. Victims or perpetrators."

Chief Webster raised his hands in an attempt to calm Isaiah down. "Okay, okay … I'm just asking." Webster took a moment to think. "Well, money's always good. If you'd like to raise some money to donate to the college in David's name, I'm sure that would be welcomed by the college and the mayor's office."

Isaiah gave a single sharp nod. "Consider it done."

"How much do you think you can raise?"

"How much do you need?"

"How should I know?" Webster snapped. "This was your idea. I don't even know what you're raising it for."

Isaiah closed his eyes, nodding. "Okay. I'll get the college a thousand dollars or two. Maybe they can rename an end zone 'Marsh Madness.'"

Webster shook his head. "He played football, not basketball."

Isaiah smiled. "A grand's a grand, Chief. They can do what they want with it."

Webster pointed to Isaiah's near-empty glass. "Got time for another one?"

Isaiah glanced at his watch. "No, I better take off. I told an old friend I'd look them up next time I was in town."

Webster nodded. "Fine. Give Yvette my regards, and next time you come to town bring that lovely woman with you."

"Sure thing, Chief."

Isaiah left the Buccaneer and got into the Voyager. Sweat had collected on his palms as he took ahold of the steering wheel and aimed the vehicle for Dark Alleys.

He couldn't wait to see Alicia's Toyotas in waiting.

Chapter 6

Isaiah stood at the familiar oak door, reciting his favorite rhyme. "Hickory dickory dock, the mouse is on the block."

The large wooden door squeaked open and Isaiah entered his playground. There could only be one reason God made women so beautiful—and this was it.

Isaiah pulled the velvet curtain to one side and walked through. The song "Cherokee Nation" provided a fitting accompaniment for the dancer who snaked herself around the brass pole in the middle of the stage, wearing only a Native American headdress—feathers from the end of the headgear tickling her bare, firm buttocks. Her tongue glided effortlessly and seductively across the underside of her top lip. Subdued swoons of approval purred from the men gathered around. Isaiah appreciated the climate of businessmen sipping Manhattans and mineral waters humming subtle praise for the dancers as opposed to servicemen and drunken rednecks hollering to "Get it off, honey," that invariably lowered the tone of other establishments of the same ilk.

Isaiah slid into the vinyl-covered chair at a table for one near the back of the room, ordering a sparkling mineral water from the waitress. He focused on the dancer. A small smile crossed his full lips. As a public speaker himself, he appreciated the energy she delivered to the audience. Art was art—in depravity or in righteousness.

The chief finished her routine to courteous applause.

His water arrived just as the next dancer stepped onto the platform. There she was. Alicia took the stage. Desire crept into his core.

He wanted to watch from the back this time. Observing other men lusting over what they couldn't have. At the end of the night, she would be leaving with him. He could never allow Yvette to excite other men with her nudity. A wife's nakedness is sacred. But Alicia … she was a toy of excitement. Her profession allowed her to use the genes she was blessed with to arouse men in a non-committal way—that's why she could never be his wife—and although various men would vie for her physical attention, Isaiah was the chosen one. That made him special. A man to envy. The Adonis of consensual lasciviousness.

He leaned forward, resting his elbows on the table, drawing himself a good eight inches closer to the action and getting a better look at Alicia. She peeled off layers of clothing in a way a concert maestro would conduct an orchestra—with graceful elegance—accentuating the right note at the right time. And the girl certainly hit all the right notes.

She dropped to the stage floor and rocked on her hands and knees directly in front of a member, pushing herself forward until her lips were but an inch from his ear. She whispered something to the man. Isaiah clenched his fist, willing her advances to stop.

She crawled to the next patron and repeated the whispering routine. Isaiah decided to let his presence be known. The poor girl probably had a lonely night with an extra cheese topping pizza planned. Wait till he told her she'd be spending the night at the Marriott with him. He wanted her excitement to grow as she sashayed that hot naked body on stage for all to see, but only for him to touch. Her own nudity seemed to turn her on as much as it did her audience. Isaiah wanted to use that to his advantage. She'd be so horny by the time they got to the hotel room his simple touch would send her into an orgasmic frenzy.

Isaiah moved to the edge of the catwalk, settling himself into the last chair left on the end. He pulled out a five-dollar bill and laid it in front of him. It caught Alicia's attention and she was there within three ticks of the second hand.

She looked at the benefactor who placed it on the stage. Her eyes widened as she smiled. "Isaiah! I didn't see you come in. What a surprise. Why didn't you call and let me know you were coming?"

He returned the smile. "Hello, Alicia. I wanted to surprise you."

She grabbed her breasts, giving them a seductive squeeze. "How do you like what you bought me?"

He examined her newly implanted D-cup breasts. He approved. "Very nice indeed. Do they come with a private showing later?"

"Of course they do. You didn't come down here to just perv out and leave, did you?"

"Are you kidding? This is my appetizer. The main course is back at my hotel. Are you hungry?"

"The hotel? I suppose that means we're going to that Port Wentworth dump, huh?"

Isaiah leaned in to whisper in her ear. "How would you like a night at the Marriott? On the waterfront."

Alicia squealed. It was unprofessional, but the unexpected excitement hit her like a random hiccup. "Really? The Marriott!"

Isaiah raced his finger of hush to his lips. "Shh ... It'll be our little secret."

"Oh, Daddy, I can't wait," she gushed.

No, me either. That was the reaction he craved. Technically, what just happened was foreplay—for both of them. *And when she sees that "Daddy's Home" bear sitting on the pillows the girl's panties are going to melt on the spot.*

"What time do you finish?" he asked.

"I should be able to get off early, but the tips do get better after ten." She placed her hands under her boobs. "And since I got these babies tips are up twenty-five percent."

Isaiah ignored the jolt in his trousers and looked at his watch. It was shortly after eight. "You're not suggesting I pay you to leave earlier, are you? That would be immoral." He grinned.

She smiled back. "I'm not a prostitute or chasing the decadent dollar for selfish indulgences. I'm just a girl trying to make a buck to better myself. You should know that."

He nodded. "Yes, of course. But perhaps I could offer you some compensation for leaving work early."

"Compensation?"

Isaiah dipped his head. "That would be fair. Far be it from me to steal your tips."

Alicia brushed her nipple across his lips, then delivered a devilish grin. "Doesn't Oprah stay at the Marriott?" She winked.

Mother of talk show billionaires. He upped his goal to raising three thousand dollars for the David Marsh fund—that would take more time—and more visits to Savannah.

***

Yvette Hightower walked across the lobby of the Marriott hotel. She wore her baby pink ASOS pipe down high heels that tied around her ankles offering a soft bondage entreaty. They were Isaiah's favorite. She felt her shoes were the showpiece. She complimented them with a tight-fitting pink dress that showed off her slender frame. The clicks of the heels across the white marble floor announced a picture of class and elegance was in the building. If the truth be known, deep down she felt like a high-class hooker. That thought secretly excited her. If she could get her husband to play the game, ecstasy was on the horizon.

She stood at the front desk. A young man had his back to her placing some papers in a tray. She cleared her throat.

He spun around. "Hi, welcome to—Mrs. Hightower!" The boy looked her up and down. "What a delightful surprise."

A smile graced her pretty face. "Well, Josh McKinna. Imagine seeing you behind that desk—and looking so handsome as the man in charge."

He straightened his posture. "I'm not really the man in charge, but sometimes I do feel like I'm running the place. We had a sick call this afternoon, so now I'm here all night." He shrugged. "What are you going to do, right?"

"I'd say you're definitely management material."

He took a moment to look pleased with himself. "What brings you here? As if I didn't know."

"I thought I'd surprise Isaiah." She looked at her watch showing 8:05 p.m. "Do you happen to know if he's in his room?"

Josh picked up the phone and punched in some numbers. "I know he went out a little after five. I haven't seen him come back yet, but he may have slipped past when I was away from the desk." He stared into space as Isaiah's room phone rang, stealing stealth glimpses of Yvette when he thought she wasn't looking. He put the phone down. "No, there's no answer. He must still be out."

"Any chance I can wait in his room?"

Josh threw his shoulders back. "Now I do feel like management."

Yvette's ears perked up. "How's that?"

"I have to make an executive decision. We're not allowed to let just anyone into guests' rooms. But since I know you, and Mr. Hightower, I can make an exception."

"That is so managerial of you, Josh." She tapped the side of her nose. "My instincts are never wrong."

Josh's blush was obvious. "I'll print you a key."

***

Isaiah walked around the corner away from Dark Alleys and waited for Alicia. Once she joined him, they walked several blocks before hailing a cab. Anonymity was assured inside the club, but once outside, speculation was fair game. Isaiah Hightower had been a respected pillar of the community while living in Savannah. And as he found out by checking into the Marriott, he was still recognizable. To be seen waving his arms for a taxi outside a nightclub could destroy his reputation. A prominent figure for the church and education system should not be seen around establishments that would lead to assumptions that he was engaged in activities that involved drunkenness or frequenting clubs which could erode one's moral integrity.

The yellow taxi pulled over to the curb. Isaiah opened the back door allowing Alicia to get in, then he joined her in the back seat. "The Marriott Riverfront hotel," Isaiah instructed. He hoped the driver was some stranger and not another former student that he guided to the upper echelon of the minimum wage plus tips scale.

"Si, senor," the driver acknowledged.

Gracias.

"Oooh, the Marriott." Alicia snuggled closer to him. "You really know how to treat a girl."

He leaned back and grinned. "Yes I do, Alicia. Yes I do." He let Alicia stay in his zone, hand on knee, as the taxi transported them to the hotel. He knew the closeness would rev her into a higher gear for the forthcoming encounter in the bedroom. Give a woman subtle comfort with her clothes on, and she would be wet clay in the potter's hand with her clothes off. They wore silent smiles as they made the journey to the Promised Land.

The taxi dropped them off outside the Marriott. Alicia slipped her arm through his on the way to the entrance.

He discreetly pushed her arm off. "Wait until we're in the room."

She squeezed her lips in a pout.

They waltzed through the revolving door in separate cubicles, Isaiah leading the way. His excitement grew with each step. He couldn't wait to get Alicia in the room. She had always been a tigress in bed and mesmerized by impressions of wealth. A balcony room at the prestigious Marriott would no doubt raise her sexual performance—yearning to please her man. He wanted to see the look on her face when he opened the door to the room.

When the leaves of his cube offered access into the lobby, Isaiah stayed in the revolving door and made the full circle, exiting out the other side.

"What in the name of the ark is he still doing here?" he mumbled to himself.

Alicia followed him outside. They stood on the sidewalk in front of the hotel. "What's up?" she asked.

He ushered her away from the door and further down the sidewalk at a brisk pace. "A former student of mine is at the front desk. He knows me—and my wife. He was supposed to be off at six o'clock." He cast his head toward the heavens. "For the love of Malcolm X," he cursed.

Alicia craned her neck to take a look. "Who? The white kid?"

They stopped walking as Isaiah looked up and down the sidewalk. A sense of panic accompanied his darting eyes.

"Can't you sneak me in? Let's go around the back," she said.

"No, they have too many surveillance cameras, and he watches them. If that little twerp sees me with another woman he could tell my wife. I think they're Facebook friends and I'm pretty sure he has designs on her. Little pervert."

"You are talking about the white kid, right?"

"Yes, but he has some kind of black fetish."

She nodded decisively. "Good for him."

Her comment drew a sharp look of condemnation from Isaiah.

"Oh, forget him. Buy me a black scarf and I'll wear it like a hijab."

Isaiah rolled his eyes. "In the first place, you'd need a niqab. Secondly, that's all I need. 'Oh, hi, Principal Hightower, deacon of the Evangelical church, what are you doing here at the Marriott with that nice Muslim lady'?"

She stomped her foot. "Why are we talking religious talk when all I want is a really good fu—"

Isaiah tugged her hand. "There's a Savannah Sleeper motel a few blocks over. We'll go there."

Alicia didn't answer.

"Come on, baby." He nudged her. "After that show at Dark Alleys? You can't leave me now. I'll make it up to you."

"You better," she snapped.

Isaiah grinned. "The Savannah Sleeper it is."

They passed by a liquor store on the way. Isaiah popped in and picked up a champagne bouquet. Wrapped in pink and white cellophane were an ice bucket, two long-stemmed champagne flutes, and a modest, yet acceptable, bottle of bubbly. He also bought a bottle of mineral water.

They carried on walking down the street past a parade of shops. Isaiah felt a bit silly carrying a cellophane-wrapped package on his way to a sleazy motel, but it put a smile on Alicia's face.

"Will you be visiting Savannah often?" Alicia asked.

"I may be back," he replied.

"I like surprises and all, but a little heads-up would be nice." With that, Alicia grabbed his hand and pulled him into *Cell Force One* phone shop and headed for the flip phone section.

"Whattsup?" the young Hispanic clerk garbled.

Isaiah failed to conceal his eyeroll.

"We want a burner—I mean a pay-as-you-go phone," Alicia answered.

"What the dickens for?" Isaiah whispered in her ear.

She faced him and whispered back. "Because, sweetheart, you don't, or won't, be calling me on your phone. This way we can keep in touch and you can give me a little notice when you're coming to town."

Alicia glanced at the clerk and pointed to the $19.95 phone. "I'll take that one. And put twenty bucks on it."

"Alicia, you don't have to—"

"Yes I do."

When the clerk handed her the phone she put her number in it. "This is your Alicia hot-line. Keep it safe. And by the way, it wouldn't hurt to leave your other phone laying around from time to time so your wife can find it. You know, in case she wants to check up on you."

"Yvette doesn't do that. She trusts me."

"Are you sure about that?"

"Of course I am."

Alicia handed the phone back toward the clerk. "I'd like to return this phone."

"But if it makes you feel any better ..." Isaiah snatched it out of her hand. "Thanks, baby."

***

He paid cash at the motel and checked in under the name Thomas John.

They walked down the long corridor to room 135.

Alicia slipped her arm through his. He didn't push her away.

"Mmm ..." she cooed. "We're using aliases now. I like it. Am I Mrs. John?"

He shook his head. "No, that wouldn't be much fun, now would it? You just be yourself. That's much more erotic than a Missus."

Alicia smiled. "A mistress. Gotcha, Mr. John."

Inside the room bubbles flowed like expensive lava out of the bottle, splattering on the gray carpet and Alicia's strap-on stiletto heels. She giggled as Isaiah raised the bottle, gave her a wink, then poured the champagne into one of the flutes sitting next to the ice bucket. He filled the other flute with mineral water.

"It's so good to see you again, Alicia."

"You too. So tell me again, why are we here and not at the Marriott?"

"It's that kid, Josh McKinna. He's a former student of mine."

"What was that 'black fetish' thing all about?"

"He used to run with an African American group in school. He even got himself a black girlfriend, then joined the same church where Yvette and I worshiped. He was the only white face in a chapel of over two hundred."

"Wow," she cooed.

Isaiah put his hand up. "Enough about him. What about you? You look well—and hot."

"Do you mean here, or did you enjoy seeing me in the club?"

"Both. You're a beautiful sight—with or without clothes."

They raised their glasses and sipped the drinks.

"So what brings you to Savannah?" Alicia asked. "Surely you didn't come all this way *just* to see me—although I'd be flattered if you did."

He reached over and squeezed her left breast. "Of course I did. I had a little fundraiser to do on the side, but you're why I'm here, baby."

Alicia stepped in and clutched his crotch, gently massaging him. "And here's my fun-raiser. You've already seen me naked, now it's my turn. Get your clothes off, Hightower."

Isaiah set his drink down and took off his shirt. "You got it, baby."

Chapter 7

After an hour of amazing sex, Alicia lay curled in his arms. Her eyes were closed yet contentment radiated from her young face.

He studied her. Her skin was tight and unblemished. He admired the youth in her high cheekbones and tight jaw.

Three orgasms in an hour. Half your age and you still outpaced the girl. Self-satisfaction and pride transferred a smile to his lips. He often thought that Alicia helped him avert any potential mid-life crisis. She boosted his ego more than any material possession could have ever done. He always felt as if he dropped twenty-five years when he was with her. She was his fountain of youth.

Alicia came to. Her beam broadened when she looked at him, then snuggled her face into his chest. "You still got it, Principal Hightower."

"Let's not cross that line. Let's stick to Mr. John?"

"Oh, suddenly there's a line?" She circled her fingers through the hairy patch on his chest—still free from gray. "But I did seduce you, didn't I? When I was your student."

"Alicia, you carelessly threw yourself at your vice principal when you were flunking. I took pity on you and made sure you got passing grades. I saw your potential."

"You saw my assets."

"You flashed me!"

"And it worked." She giggled as she snuggled further into his chest. "C-cups for C grades. It was a fair trade."

Isaiah smiled at the distant memory. Alicia's senior year, four years ago. He summoned her to his office to discuss her failing grades at the request of her teachers. They all said she was bright but lacked focus. It was up to him to get her to buck up. As she sat across from his desk he asked the logical question, *"What are you going to do with your life without an education?"* Without hesitation, she pulled the string on the back of her halter top and revealed her breasts to him. *"I could always be a stripper."*

He was speechless. To his embarrassment, he grew hard as he ogled her. Luckily he had the large oak desk in front of him. He did his best to remain professional and commanded her to get dressed and leave immediately. As irony would have it, that hard-on bred a soft spot for her. He had a word with her teachers and pleaded for her leniency. He had to concede some lab equipment and updated history books, but they obliged.

Making love to Yvette that night was like watching the same movie for the ten-thousandth time but with foreign subtitles. New images flashing vividly on the screen while his mind offered a new perspective to an old favorite. Things cannot be unseen, thankfully. Alicia's breasts was not an image he wanted to erase. Then when he saw her living up to her sub-standard potential at Dark Alleys those memories came flooding back—except now he

57

could act on those impulses without getting thrown out of the education system.

Five years later, here he was. Banging a former-student-turned-stripper. But now he was determined to help her to better herself. Once and for all. To God be the glory.

Isaiah stroked her hair. "I stuck my neck out for you back at Savannah High, you know. You have your diploma because of me. Maybe it's time to raise your game. Make something of your life."

She propped herself up on her elbow and looked him in the eyes. "But I did make you hard in your office that day, didn't I?"

"Alicia," Isaiah snapped. "We must never speak of that."

"But I'm not your student anymore—"

"No, but you are an employee of the Dark Alleys gentlemen's club. We never speak of our brethren or dancers, or what they've been involved in—past, present, or future."

"Well, I can never forget that day—"

"Yes, it was special." He hoped the concession of an exceptional experience would head her off. He needed to steer her back to reality. His lips puckered skyward as he exhaled heavily. "But isn't this more fun? The mistress and the married man?"

"I don't know. The student flashing the vice principal was pretty hot."

He reached over and held her by the face. "Never speak of that again. That could cost me my career." He delivered a stern look before releasing his grip. He lay back flat, staring up at the ceiling.

She lay back down. "What if we were married?"

A proposal of marriage? As absurd as it was, he also found it flattering. A forty-nine-year-old man with a twenty-two-year-old big-boobed-bombshell? Yes, he would be the envy of every man in South Carolina and beyond—he would also be a divorced man out of a job. "That's crazy talk."

She pressed it. "No it's not. You could leave your wife and start over with me?"

"Come on, Alicia. I can't do that."

"Why not? What is she now? Sixty?"

He sighed. "Forty-one."

"Well, I'm practically half her age. She's not going to be bearing you any fruit at her time of life. You need someone to carry on your legacy. You need offspring to continue the respected Hightower name. Let me be the mother of your children. The mother of your legend."

"The time's not right. Besides being up for the COTS award, Yvette and I are heavily involved in the church in Hilton Head and we're working on some Ebony Evolution projects. We need to portray a united front."

"In case you haven't noticed, I have the qualifications to promote black causes. And I sing one hell of a Kumbaya."

Isaiah remained solemn. "I'm sure you do, and you shouldn't say hell out of context. But let's leave things like they are at the moment."

Alicia nestled back into his arm. "Okay, but in the meantime, I'll have to keep taking my clothes off to turn a buck. Is that what you want your girlfriend—or mistress—or whatever I am, to do?"

"You could get a different job."

"What? Working at McDonald's?" Alicia gave a negative shudder of her head. "No, the hours getting naked suit my schedule and the tips are fantastic—especially with my new boobs. There's a new member there. Man is he a good tipper. I think for the right lap dance I could get him to buy me a car."

"What?" He shot upright. "That's prostitution! You are not a prostitute, Alicia, and you must never accept gifts from men. That's—"

"Immoral?" Her hand slipped under the sheet. "Lighten up, Daddy. I'm just saying, I could get more than just money out of these guys if I wanted to."

She rubbed her breasts against his side as she massaged his hardening manhood. "And there's another guy—I think he's a weatherman—he said he might be able to help out with some booty shots. You know, some filler to give me a more rounded butt. That should add to the tips and I could start a little nest egg."

"Your buttocks are fine, Alicia. Besides, stripping isn't your lifelong career, now is it?"

"I know, but—"

"But nothing."

Alicia exhaled a heavy breath. "But without the butt, you're telling me you're happy to let Reverend Theis continue to masturbate to me?"

"You know about that?"

"Sometimes he does it right under the table."

Isaiah grimaced. He was surprised to be hit by a tinge of possessiveness. "What if there was another way? What if I could help you with some donations toward your efforts? Then you could spend less time at Dark Alleys, maybe even quit, go to college, get a degree, and stop accepting gifts from weirdos."

"Weirdos?" She laughed. "Well, if I was subsidized, maybe I wouldn't have to be so nice to the *weirdos*."

"Okay, leave it with me. In the meantime, stop identifying brethren—even if just by occupation." He gave her a comforting pat. "Do you know why it's called Dark Alleys?"

She shook her head.

"If a member tells on a brother, he will be found in a dark alley in an unexplained and unsolvable way. I'm surprised no one ever mentioned that to you."

"All they told me when they hired me was that if I ever breathed a word about anyone I saw inside they'd kill me."

He nodded. "Good, we're on the same page."

Isaiah's phone rang from the bedside table. "Who's that calling at this hour?"

He picked up the phone. Yvette's name was displayed on the screen. "Something must be wrong." He pushed Alicia to one side and put his finger to his lips in a pre-emptive gesture for her to be quiet.

He pressed the talk button. "Yvette? What's wrong? Is everything okay?"

"Where are you?" she asked.

"I'm at the hotel. I was sleeping until you rang. What's wrong?"

"Which hotel?"

"The Marriott."

"On the riverfront?"

"Yes. Yvette! What's wrong?"

"Oh ..." Her end of the phone went quiet for several moments. "Well, it was just that it was after midnight and you never called to say goodnight. You usually do when you're away. I was worried."

"Is that it?"

A sniffle came through the line. "Yeah ... that's it."

"Well, there's nothing to worry about. The meeting ran late and I was really tired when I got back to the room. I forgot."

"Well, as long as you're okay."

"Yes, I'm fine."

"Okay ... I guess I'll see you tomorrow."

He looked over at Alicia. She was playing with herself sexually.

"I might have another meeting tomorrow. I might not make it back until Sunday. You'll be okay, won't you?"

"Oh?"

"Yvette? Are you okay?"

"Yes, I'm fine. Okay, see you whenever you're done doing what you have to do." She hung up before he could respond.

He briefly stared at the dead phone.

Alicia was bringing herself to a climax. He joined in and finished her off.

***

Yvette stepped out of the elevator—cursing her stupid shoes as they clip-clopped across the stupid floor of the stupid Marriott hotel, wheeling her stupid stewardess-type mini-suitcase behind her. All because she was stupid enough to try to surprise her husband. Something wasn't right. She had never known Isaiah to lie, but even O.J. Simpson would have a job talking his way out of this one.

"Mrs. Hightower," a voice called out from behind the reception desk.

She stopped in her tracks but didn't turn around. Instead, she stood still, looking toward the

62

ceiling and God above, taking deep breaths to collect herself.

Josh McKinna stood beside her. "Going somewhere? I can hail you a taxi if you need one."

"No, I'm going back to Hilton Head. Mr. Hightower is too busy to see me—" She stopped herself. Why should she tell a hotel clerk what her husband is up to?

"Is he not here? I thought I saw him come back."

She turned and faced him. "You couldn't have possibly seen him come back. I've been in the room the whole time. I told you—he's working."

"Aren't you going to wait for him? He should be back soon, shouldn't he?"

"Mr. Hightower is very busy on this visit. He has a lot to do and I don't want to be a distraction."

Josh's bobbing head showed agreement. "I can see where you're coming from, Mrs. Hightower. A woman as beautiful as you, well, you'd be a distraction just being in the same room."

She forced a smile. "That's very sweet of you to say, Josh. Thank you."

"Will you be okay getting back? It's—" He glanced at his watch. "One o'clock in the morning."

"I'll wait at the airport and get the next shuttle to the island."

"I know it's none of my business, Mrs. Hightower, but—"

She began walking away as soon as she heard the but. "You're right, Josh, it's none of your business."

He stood, watching as she walked away. He raised his hand in a limp attempt at a wave. "See you on Facebook."

The journey to get home turned out to be a long one for Yvette. If she had stuck around for Josh's "but" perhaps he was going to tell her there was a shuttle leaving from in front of the Marriott Riverfront Hotel that would eventually connect with the shuttle to Hilton Head Island. Instead, she got a taxi to the Savannah airport and waited for the connecting shuttle to Hilton Head. Then grabbed another taxi for the twenty-five-minute journey to her house. She didn't drive down in her car thinking her and Isaiah would be driving back together.

If she and Isaiah had traveled together in the Voyager the whole trip would have taken about forty-five minutes instead of the six-hour pain in the ass she had to endure. Once she deciphered the timeline her ire grew.

She climbed in the shower and decided to get together with Gloria Huntington. She could use a friendly face to talk to. However, Gloria never rose before 8:30 a.m. and even that could take an act of God or a house fire.

At 8:31, she called. After Gloria quizzed her if her house was actually on fire, they agreed to meet at The Southern Ranch for lunch.

Yvette arrived at twelve o'clock sharp and was shown to a table by the window overlooking a green pasture. It provided an image of serenity away from the touristy hot spots. She sipped tap water while she waited for Gloria who arrived twenty minutes later. No surprises there.

The waiter spread linen napkins across the laps of his beautiful and well-dressed guests, returning a few moments later with two glasses of Chardonnay as they requested. With the presentation of the wine, they each ordered a salad as their main courses—Yvette going for the strawberry and poppy seed salad while Gloria opted for salmon with baby shrimp.

Bright pink lipstick marked Gloria's glass when she set it down after her first sip. She dabbed the corner of her mouth with the napkin. "Why are you back early? I thought you and Isaiah were doing what happily married couples do when they're—shall we say—having a good time."

Yvette rubbed her finger around the edge of her glass. "You know Isaiah. All work, that man. He's doing some research for some boy who got shot. He got tied up in a meeting and was working late. He would've been tired when he got back, so there wasn't much point in me sticking around."

"Who was the boy? Another young black life gunned down by police?"

"No, this was actually a white kid shot by African Americans."

Gloria jilted backward. "Whoa? That's a little out of his ordinary, isn't it?"

"The kid was a student at Hilton Head last year. He wasn't even Isaiah's student, but the police chief of Savannah started bawling about gang crime and Isaiah had to go running down there to stick a pacifier in his mouth. The big baby."

The salads arrived and Yvette took a hearty stab at the greenery, shoveling in her first bite.

"Really?" Gloria chuckled.

"Well, something like that." Yvette set her fork down and leaned in. "To tell you the truth, I'm worried, Gloria. Isaiah should have been back at the hotel, but he wasn't. I think he might be—"

"Working too hard," Gloria finished for her. "Just as you said. I know and I agree. The man has limitless energy in helping *all* mankind. Black, white, whatever the color, Isaiah Hightower is there to champion all causes."

Yvette shook her head. "No, he wasn't at the hotel when I called. But he said he was. He lied to me. Why would a man lie to his wife?"

Gloria reached over and touched Yvette's hand. "Don't even go there. I'm sure there's a simple explanation. I cannot tell you how much respect and admiration I have for the man. After all he's done for Ebony Evolution. He is not only a man of his people, for his people, but a man for *all* of God's people. He's not an activist, he's a humanitarian. And that's why he's going to get that COTS award. You must be the proudest woman in all of the South. And the luckiest."

Yvette forced a smile. "Yes, his image is unstained, isn't it?" She stared into her bowl, poking at her salad, but her appetite had already disappeared.

"What's wrong, Yvette. You look flushed."

She looked at her friend. "Something's not right. Isaiah … he …" She couldn't bring herself to admit what she thought. She hoped by presenting the suspicion Gloria would have announced the unthinkable. But she didn't. She confirmed Isaiah's saintliness.

"He's working too hard, my dear, that's what's wrong. You said it yourself."

Moisture formed in the corner of Yvette's eyes. She didn't want to cry. She wouldn't. She was a woman of steel and velvet. Isaiah got the velvet— the rest of the world got the steel.

"Why don't you go on vacation with him?" Gloria suggested. "Just the two of you. No work. No crusades. No saving the world. Couples need alone time."

Yvette's face scrunched. "I don't know. He always has something going on."

"Girl, Isaiah is the most caring man I ever met, and I know that caring extends to his wife. If you say the word, he'll be whisking you off without a second thought."

Yvette looked at her friend from under long lashes. "What's the word?"

"Hawaii."

Chapter 8

Isaiah stayed with Alicia in the motel until just past noon. After another session of intimacy, he gave his sex kitten cab fare to get home before he headed back to the Marriott to get cleaned up and changed.

On his way walk back to the hotel, Chief Webster called and they agreed to meet at a local coffee shop.

Isaiah sat in the back of the room at Stoneridge Coffee House waiting for his friend. He stood up when he saw Webster's large frame sidestepping around other customers on his way toward him. He extended his hand as Lionel approached. "Chief Webster, always a pleasure."

Webster took Isaiah's hand and returned a firm shake. "Chief, not Lionel? How'd you know this was business?"

"You have a certain look on your face. A business look. Maybe God had me guide you to a coffee house, not a bar, to keep your thoughts sober."

"Hey, man, I've had a rough day. I thought I was meeting a friend and I could really use a drink."

"I am your friend and the espresso here is pretty potent. You have your confidant and caffeine—what more do you want?" He delivered his gorgeous smile.

The chief's eyes briefly closed as he shook his head. "Okay, Isaiah, you win. When we're finished here, you go visit the Book of John and I'll go visit the bottle of Jack."

Hightower chuckled. "Of course. We all need friends, be it paper or glass." He extended his hand to the chair opposite him and the men sat down.

"I'll drink to that—when we're done here, that is."

The waiter came around and the men placed their order. Lionel ordered a double espresso. The waiter left to get the power punch of coffee and Isaiah's skinny latte.

Isaiah grinned at the chief. "You took my suggestion. I always thought you were a black, two sugars guy."

Lionel cocked his head to one side. "That worries me. You remember how I take my coffee? Does Yvette know?"

"What she doesn't know won't hurt her." The corners of his mouth turned up.

The chief's brows furrowed. "Now I am worried."

Isaiah waved a dismissive hand. "Lighten up, this is business. So what's up?"

The waiter returned with the drinks.

Webster produced a handkerchief and patted his forehead. "It appears the media isn't done with this David Marsh thing yet. They want to know what we're going to do about it."

"What's there to do?"

"Exactly. We have two suspects in custody charged with murder, but they're asking why a white guy was killed while walking with a person of color. Is anyone safe in Savannah?"

Isaiah sipped his latte, leaving a thin white mustache clinging to his upper lip. He pondered for a moment while his mind drifted to Alicia. He couldn't keep funding her want for a better life out of his own pocket—let alone coming to Savannah every other week without Yvette by his side without her getting suspicious. He needed money from an unknown source. Alicia needed money from a known source—him. And Chief Webster needed a smokescreen. "I have an idea. To keep his death from being in vain, we set up a kind of trust. The David Marsh Foundation to carry on his enthusiasm for equality and his vision for justice."

"And how do we do that?"

"What if I set up a charity to raise money to give assistance to a kid to go to college, paid for by the David Marsh Foundation."

Webster wagged his finger. "That's good. I like it. But all that trouble for one kid? That's a little limited, is it not?"

"Hey, if a kid needs help he'll take what he can get. I can't guarantee an amount."

"So this trust pays a couple of grand towards college tuition for an underprivileged person who wants to better himself?"

Isaiah nodded. "Yes."

Webster bobbed his head. "Well, it's not a bad idea. Do you have anyone in mind?"

"As a matter of fact, yes. Yes, I do. A young girl who wants to get a degree to better herself, but she needs help. She is exactly the type of person I want to help with the foundation."

"What's her name?"

"Alicia Saunders."

"What's her background?"

"Early twenties. African American. Divorced parents."

"Is she working now?"

Isaiah adjusted the knot on his tie. "Odd jobs."

The chief stared at his hands, rotating his coffee cup for several moments. "Sounds like you put some thought into this."

"Is there a problem?"

"I don't know. It's risky putting this in the limelight. We need to be careful."

Isaiah pushed himself forward in his chair. "Think about it, Lionel. A young man gets killed, yet as a result, another youngster gets a college degree, all with help from the David Marsh Foundation. We need someone to follow in David's footsteps."

"What does she want to study?"

Isaiah didn't know. She joked around when he asked her that question. It could be dog grooming for all he knew. "I'm not sure."

Chief Webster's face hardened. "David's area of study was criminology. Get me someone interested in law enforcement."

Isaiah nodded. "Okay, I think she might be."

The chief leaned in. "But, I think we need a white person."

"What! Since when do you take preference for white people to get an education over underprivileged African Americans?"

"Since the kid who got shot was white. Then the chief crusader for Ebony Evolution comes riding into town and gives a scholarship to a black girl in the name of the dead white boy. That's when."

Isaiah leaned back, retreating into his own thoughts. The chief had a point, but he either had to

71

give Alicia an education or new buttocks. He steepled his fingers, resting his chin on the tips. "But the Saunders girl needs help."

"Fine. Then give it to her—along with a white kid. In fact ..." Webster's face lit up as he clicked his fingers. "That's it! We send a white boy and a black girl to college following in the footsteps of David Marsh. We'll show this city we have no fear and present them with the exact same scenario that David Marsh died for. Yes!" The chief gave a little fist pump.

"That's a big ask."

"Then hold on to your hat, cowboy, because I'm about to ask for more. It should be more than a contribution. I want two kids to get a degree with zero costs to them. Full tuition and books paid for. And let's send them to David's alma mater, Chatham College."

Isaiah chuckled. "Why don't you throw in room and board while you're at it?"

"Good idea. Let's go the whole damn hog." The chief folded his arms, looking smug.

"You can't be serious." Isaiah pulled out his smartphone. His fingers went to work on the keypad. "You're talking over fifteen-grand per student per year. Maybe more. And you want to send another white kid to Chatham College?"

The chief smiled. "No fear, my brother. We'll show these punks."

Isaiah shook his head. "I don't know, Chief."

"What's thirty-grand to a fundraiser such as yourself? And if you enlist Yvette you'll probably rake in forty K."

"So you want me to kick the program off with a black *and* a white candidate? Savannah tearing down the barriers between racial divides. Is that the angle?"

Webster nodded approvingly. "You can spin it any way you want. If you can raise enough money in the foundation to award two candidates scholarships at the same time, fine. If not, get me a white one or forget it."

Isaiah leaned in. "Lionel, I might have a problem getting my core supporters to donate that much money to white causes."

Chief Webster closed the gap between them, meeting Isaiah halfway across the table. "Then we *will* have a problem with this foundation."

"Then I guess I'll have to do some serious fundraising. You might be seeing a lot more of me." If God needed him in Savannah, he would come. Isaiah smiled at that prospect.

The chief aimed his finger at him. "Next time bring that lovely wife of yours. How is she by the way?"

"Yvette? She's good. My rock."

"Yes, I know."

Isaiah sipped his coffee, wishing the conversation hadn't gone there.

Chief Webster stood up. "You got any ideas for the white candidate?"

"Not yet. I'll go back to the hotel and give it some thought."

"You do that." Webster extended his hand and they shook. "Okay, I need a drink. Keep me posted on your progress."

Isaiah stayed seated as Webster walked toward the exit. He pulled out his burner phone and dialed Alicia.

She answered on the second ring.

"Hi, baby. I'm leaving tomorrow. Why don't you come to the Marriott tonight so I can give you the treatment you deserve? Don't stop at reception, just come straight up to my room, five-twenty-six. I'll be waiting for you."

"I can't wait," Alicia said.

"Me either. And bring your handcuffs."

***

Isaiah left the coffee house and headed back to the hotel. He pressed the button to summon the elevator and waited.

Josh McKinna popped out from behind the reception desk and walked over. "Hello, Mr. Hightower."

Isaiah shuddered his head in disbelief. "Don't you ever stop working?"

"Overtime. Can't beat it."

"I suppose not."

The elevator dinged and the doors opened. Isaiah stepped in. He wasn't in the mood for chit-chat so he was happy when the doors began to close, leaving Josh behind.

"It was so nice to see Mrs. Hightower yesterday. Too bad you missed her," Josh called out.

Isaiah punched his fist through the opening before the doors fully closed. The thick metal doors retracted. Isaiah stepped out of the elevator. "What are you talking about?"

The young man took a step back. "Mrs. Hightower. She was here, last night. Didn't she tell you?"

"No, she wasn't. She was at home. I know, she called me."

"Oh … perhaps I got it wrong. Maybe it wasn't Mrs. Hightower. Perhaps it was—"

Isaiah closed in until they were chest-to-chest. He kept marching until he had Josh pinned up against the wall. Their faces not more than an inch apart.

"What happened, Josh?"

"Mrs. Hightower came in just after eight last night. She was dressed up really nice. She said she wanted to surprise you, so I let her in your room so she could wait for you."

Rage induced spittle sprayed as Isaiah hissed. Josh was pinned between the principal's chest and the wall. "You let her into my room? Whatever happened to guest privacy?"

Josh's eyes widened and filled with fear. There was a tremble in his voice. "She insisted ... but then she left."

"When? When did she leave?"

"About one a.m."

Isaiah opened his arms wide, looking towards the heavens. "Let the rapture take me now."

A sharply dressed man in his early forties approached Josh and Isaiah and stood beside the pair.

"Is there a problem here?" His Southern drawl spoke with authority.

Isaiah's eyes narrowed. "Who wants to know?"

"I'm the manager of the hotel and it appears you have a member of my staff pinned against the wall, shouting at him."

"It's okay, Mr. Conrad," Josh offered. "This is Mr. Hightower. I know him. He's my former vice-principal."

Isaiah glowered at Josh then turned his attention to the manager. "No, it's not okay." He jerked his head toward Josh. "This member of your staff let a non-paying guest stay in my room without my consent."

Josh's pitch was frantic. "It was his wife, Mr. Conrad. I thought it would be okay."

"That's irrelevant," Isaiah snapped. "As it happens, it's our anniversary coming up and I bought her a special present and had it in the room." He delivered a vicious stare at the young clerk. "It was unwrapped."

Mr. Conrad's lips spread straight and narrow across his tanned face. Not quite a grimace, but the look where tough decisions come from. "You know the hotel has a policy against letting a non-paying guest in the room without consent, Josh."

"Yes, s-s-sir, Mr. Conrad. But Mrs. Hightower was here to surprise him. I thought it was a wonderful idea."

The manager looked at Isaiah. "Don't worry, Mr. Hightower. I'll deal with this and I offer you the hotel's most sincere apology. You won't be charged for your stay."

Mr. Conrad motioned for Josh to follow him.

"Just one thing, Josh," Isaiah called out as they walked away. "Did Mrs. Hightower say anything when she left?"

Josh turned around. "Just that you were the hardest working man she ever met and she didn't want to be a distraction."

Isaiah stood in the same spot, his gut-churning as the two figures disappeared through a door behind the reception desk.

***

Isaiah sat on the bed with the "Daddy's Home" bear waiting for Alicia. Yvette was going to be a whole other problem, but he decided to focus his attention on Alicia for the time being. He'd have the drive home to figure out how to handle Yvette. There wasn't much point in letting that obstacle interrupt his current mission.

He had to tell Alicia she'd be going to college on a grant. God had bestowed many responsibilities on him for his time on planet Earth, and helping others better themselves was one of those duties he took seriously. He gained a great deal of satisfaction knowing he assisted others to grow and realize their full potential as human beings. And converting a striptease artist into an officer of the law would earn him a special place in paradise. He would live on a cloud not far from God. He earned it.

He stepped back into his current reality. Somewhere between God and Yvette was Alicia. He'd have to get some extra cash on the side for her expenses, then she would be well and truly indebted to him. And Dark Alleys would be gaining a friend in the police force. He took a moment to recognize David Marsh's sacrifice. Isaiah had to ensure it wasn't in vain.

A knock on the door at around eight o'clock aroused him. A quick peek through the spyhole confirmed it was Alicia, although he wasn't entirely sure at first with her dark sunglasses and trench coat. She swanned in when he opened the door.

He assessed the full-length tan raincoat. "Let me guess. You're in your birthday suit under that."

She removed the glasses and gave a gentle tug to the belt, freeing the garment. She stood before him in a police uniform. "Surprise."

His jaw dropped. "What the—"

She produced a pair of handcuffs from a leather pouch hanging from her thick black belt. "You wanted me to bring these, so I figured someone needed to be read their rights—but then again, we may skip the legalities and go straight to police brutality."

Isaiah chuckled. "I like it. But before we get down to business, officer, I have some news for you."

"Good news, I hope."

"You have no idea how fitting your outfit is." He couldn't contain his smile any longer. "I'm going to get you into college. All expenses paid!"

"Really? When?"

"Next semester. Chatham College. Room, board, tuition, books ... everything. And I should be able to get you some extra money for expenses too. That's great news, isn't it?"

Her eyes darted around the room. "Umm ... yeah, sure, that's great. Chatham College. Wow. Okay, but I didn't know they offered cosmetology courses."

He fluttered his lips. "Pbbt, you're not going to be a make-up artist, you're going to be a crime solver."

She leaned in. "Say what?"

"I have you lined up for a criminology degree. Just like David Marsh. It will be his charity that's paying for your education. You won't have to strip anymore."

She opened her arms, looking down at her uniform. "Is that what this is all about? I thought we were playing a game."

"We'll play a game later, baby, but we're talking about your future."

Her pretty face crinkled. "My future is being a cop?"

He nodded. "Isn't that great?"

"I don't know what to say ... A cop, like, doing good deeds?"

"Yes, isn't that exciting? Your friend Tanya will be so proud of you showing support for her boyfriend. And here's the best part." He collected the bear off the bed. "I'll be spending more time in Savannah raising money." He handed her the bear. "Daddy's home, baby. Now lock me up!"

She looked away. "Lock us both up," she mumbled.

Chapter 9

Isaiah parked the minivan in front of the garage, grabbed the bouquet of pink carnations neatly wrapped in waxed green paper off the passenger seat, and headed for the front door.

He stepped into the entranceway of the wood-framed house and was immediately hit with a blast of sunshine beaming through the skylight in the vaulted ceiling. He looked around and yet again marveled how Yvette always kept the place so immaculately clean and tidy—never a cushion or plant leaf out of place. The woman would have held an exorcism if a dust ball ever managed to gather itself under her furniture.

"Yvette," he bellowed, as he made his way to the open plan kitchen. "Yvette!"

He laid the flowers on the island in the middle of the kitchen and flipped the switch on to the electric kettle.

Yvette walked into the room wearing a pink tracksuit. She never had to do anything with her short-cropped hair, it was always in a wash-and-wear ready-to-go state. She wore large hoop gold earrings, which meant it wasn't a housework day. She wore studs when she intended to scrub.

"Hello, Isaiah," she greeted him.

He flung his arms open. "What? No hug? No kiss?"

She walked up to him and gave a peck on the cheek. "How was your trip?" she asked, as she kept moving on her way to the fridge—pulling out a container of raspberry yogurt.

"Umm, yeah … fine. Are you okay?"

"Why wouldn't I be?"

He shrugged. "I don't know. You just seem a bit strange."

"Strange?" She faced him, slamming the container of yogurt on the counter before firmly planting her hands on her hips. "You want to know what's strange?"

Isaiah picked up the flowers and attempted to disarm her with his smile. "I got flowers for the woman I love. That's not strange."

One brow peaked above narrowing eyes. "How very thoughtful of you. Did you buy them from the gift shop at the Marriott? I would have preferred a 'Daddy's Home' teddy bear."

"I—"

"Where were you?" she demanded. "Because you certainly weren't at the Marriott."

He laid the flowers down. "Look, darling, I can explain. I had to move hotels. When you called, I was in my hotel. I just forgot which one I was in. I was groggy. I wasn't thinking straight."

"What do you mean, you didn't know where you were? When did you start drinking?"

"There was a mix-up."

"Did Josh McKinna have anything to do with the mix-up?"

Isaiah nodded decisively "Yes, yes he did. How'd you guess?"

"Is that why he got fired?"

"Fired? What do you mean—fired?

"He's not very happy about working for a multi-billion dollar company that is willing to brush him aside because of a guest's whim."

"How do you know this?"

"He posted a rant on Facebook."

Isaiah stepped in. "What did he say?"

"The posting was pretty vague, but he mentioned that he could go to jail if he disclosed too much due to a confidentiality agreement in his contract. I guess the Marriott has an interest in protecting its guests against any adverse or inadvertent disclosures." Yvette's large eyes studied her husband.

Isaiah turned his back on her as he swallowed hard, grabbing a cup from the cupboard and making himself a cup of tea. "Did he say anything else?"

"No, so I PM'ed him."

Isaiah turned around. "You sent him a private message?"

She affirmed with a nod. "You know what he did?"

He shook his head.

"He defriended me."

"What?"

"I sent him a message, and when I checked to see if he replied half an hour later, he's not on my friend list anymore—and he blocked me."

"Kids are like that these days." Isaiah focused on stirring his tea. "You don't have to *do* anything, they just—"

Yvette looked her husband dead in the eye. "I don't believe you."

"What do you mean you don't believe me?" His nostrils flared. "What did that little squirt say?"

"He didn't say anything, Isaiah. I was there. I was at the Marriott Friday night hoping to surprise you. Josh let me into your room and all your stuff was there. When I called you after midnight, I was in your fucking room! You lied to me. You said you were there, but you weren't. I even looked under the bed, but no, no Isaiah."

"That's probably why he got fired. He let you into my room, but it wasn't *my* room. I think the boy's on drugs."

"Bullshit. Your clothes were there."

"Quit cussing!" He reached in his pocket and pulled out his wallet. "Okay, you want to look like a fool?" He handed her a slip of paper. "You see that? It's a refund from the Marriott Riverfront hotel. After I unpacked my clothes, they told me they had overbooked and I had to move hotels, but I had a meeting to go to. They were supposed to move my belongings while I was at my meeting for David Marsh, God rest his soul. On top of that, they booked me into a motel called The Savannah Sleeper. Do you know how disgusting that place is? And no, I don't have a receipt for the fleapit motel because the Marriott picked up the tab. After all, it was their screw-up that put me there in the first place. That's why he got fired and that's probably why he defriended you. The boy's embarrassed— and ashamed. And so he should be." He thumbed himself in the chest. "And they did it to your husband. Not to mention, I didn't have my toiletries and had to wear the same clothes the next day because that idiot didn't bring my belongings over."

"But he called your room for me like he thought you were still there. And he gave me a key so I could wait for you in the room. He obviously thought you were still staying at the hotel."

"Maybe the drugs kicked in and he was high as a kite. I don't know. All I do know was Josh was supposed to fix it, but he didn't. He let you into someone else's room. No wonder he got fired." He shook his head in disbelief. "I'm telling you, Yvette, the boy's on drugs. The hard stuff." He wagged his finger at the credit note in his wife's hand. "Look at that. There's the proof. Why would the Marriott give me a refund if I had stayed there?"

Yvette studied the refund receipt, then lowered her head, pressing her fingertips to her forehead. "Oh my God. I don't know what to say."

"You can say you're sorry." He stepped closer. "And since when did you start using the 'F' word and mammal dung expletives? And what's with this teddy bear?"

"There was a stuffed animal on the bed. It must have been the new guests'. I know you don't go in for stuff like that. I should have realized something wasn't right." She looked up, draping her hands over her husband's shoulders. "Isaiah, I'm sorry. I should have known there was a logical explanation. Let me make it up to you."

"There's nothing to make up for. Just believe me in the future." He held her by the shoulders and looked into her eyes. "Let's forget the whole thing."

She wiped away her tears. "No, I'm going to make it up to you. Let's go to Hawaii as soon as you get some time off."

"Hawaii? I can't see that happening. I have to set up the David Marsh Foundation. I have to find a couple of beneficiaries the foundation can give to and I'm going to need a lot more money to keep Chief Webster out of hot water."

"Chief Webster needs money?"

"That's not what I meant. It's complicated."

Yvette's eyes went soft, and her voice pleading. "Please, Isaiah. We need some time alone together." Her lips curled into a naughty smile. "How would you like to be the beneficiary of my affections?" Her hands gracefully glided down the sides of his Jaeger suit as she lowered herself to her knees. "This is for Hawaii." She looked up at him and smiled as her hands moved to his zipper.

"That won't be necessary. I can't see us going to Hawaii."

She ignored him and pulled down his zipper. "A girl can still try." She reached inside his pants.

Isaiah sighed. "Yvette ..."

"And I want you to go back to Savannah and get Josh McKinna his job back ..."

Then she began the bribery in earnest.

Chapter 10

Isaiah found Josh McKinna working at Bubba Suds car wash on the outskirts of Savannah, just as Mr. Conrad said he would. During a lengthy discussion over the phone, Conrad stated that he hated to fire Josh as he was a top-notch worker—one of the best in the hotel—but he could not allow members of staff to pick and choose which rules to obey. Letting non-paying members of the public into a guest's room without prior consent was one of the top sins an employee could commit. Automatic dismissal was non-negotiable.

Nevertheless, the decision to terminate Josh was a painful one and accompanied by the unease of where the young man could turn to gain employment instead of ending up on welfare. Part of the process to help alleviate Mr. Conrad's guilt was to call his cousin who owned Bubba Suds hand car wash and secure Josh a job—which he did.

Isaiah was motioned into one of the open bays. Josh stepped forward in blue coveralls sporting the Bubba Suds logo and knee-high black rubber boots. The young man looked over the nearly spotless Chrysler.

He focused his gaze on Isaiah. "It doesn't look like you're here for a car wash."

Isaiah hopped out. "Sure I am." He pointed to the slightly soiled hubcaps. "Look at that. It's disgraceful."

"If you insist. As I have recently found out, the customer is always right."

"Look, Josh, about that—"

"Don't worry about it. My mother always said I was too kind for my own good." Josh aimed the nozzle of a large plastic spray canister at the car's wheels, giving them a good soaking of degreasing soap.

"Why did you defriend Mrs. Hightower?"

Josh stopped spraying. "With all due respect, Mr. Hightower, did you really come all the way down here to discuss my Facebook friends?"

Isaiah shook his head. "No, of course not. But she was upset."

Josh resumed spraying. "If you must know, I was embarrassed. I tried to do something nice for a friend and I wound up losing my job for it. It wasn't even in a heroic way. I looked like a total idiot."

Isaiah didn't move as the kid walked toward him, still spraying. "So what about your future? Have you thought about your career path?"

Josh stopped spraying and squared off with his former vice principal. "I had a good career path going. I was training for a security post at the hotel. Mr. Conrad told me in a few years I could probably make it as head of security. But now, because I was fired for breaching security, I'll never get a job protecting people and property."

"Is that what you would like?"

The lad nodded. "If you'll excuse me, sir, I need to keep washing. I already got fired once talking to you."

Isaiah offered a sympathetic smile. "I apologize, Josh.

"Thanks."

"Are you interested in law enforcement?" Isaiah asked.

"I would be, but I have a conviction for grand theft auto. I stole a police car as it happens, so that's not going to happen. A job in security was about the best I could have hoped for, but now that's gone down the drain."

Isaiah cocked an eyebrow. "A police car?"

"I did it on a dare." Josh dropped his gaze toward the ground. "I won the dare, but lost out on a career."

Isaiah positioned his head to look up at Josh's fallen eyes. "What if I could get you into a program to train you as a police officer?"

"I'd like that, but I can't see how."

"Would you be willing to go to college?"

"Mr. Hightower, I can't afford tuition—or the time it takes. Thanks but no thanks. I'm destined for a life at Bubba Suds. All I can ask of you is for a tip—if I do a good job, of course."

"Don't give up just yet. Let me see if I can work some magic for you. You deserve it."

Josh shrugged. "I'm not going anywhere, Mr. Hightower. If you find some magic, bring it on back. I'll be here. Now if you'll excuse me, I really need to get back to work. Bubba doesn't put up with slackers."

***

Isaiah made his way to the Savannah police station in his shining Voyager. Mr. Conrad was right. Josh was a top-notch worker. His minivan never looked so good.

He was shown into Chief Webster's office and a few minutes later Webster's secretary returned with two coffees.

"Do you have someone for me?" The chief asked.

Isaiah folded his arms, then rested his chin in his hand. "I got some serious spin for you, Lionel."

Chief Webster rolled his eyes. "I don't like the sound of that."

"You're going to love this—so will the mayor." He paused to sip his coffee, whetting his whistle for the big pitch. "I want to nominate two students to complete a degree in criminology at Chatham College, all expenses paid, courtesy of the David Marsh Foundation."

Webster folded his arms. "Those were my terms, not your suggestion."

"Nonetheless, I think you'll be pleased."

"Okay, who are the candidates?"

"Alicia Saunders, as you know. Ambitious, hard-working, African American, and poor."

"She fits half the bill. Who do you have to represent the white population?"

"Josh McKinna. Josh has always had an interest in a position in security, but never thought he could become a police officer."

"Why not?"

"He has a criminal record."

"What's the rap?"

"Grand theft auto. A police car."

Chief Webster laughed. "You have got to be kidding me. And you want to give him a scholarship?"

"Think about it. A white criminal, but the black girl's clean. The white guy has a shady past! How's that for role reversal? We can pitch it that all criminals aren't black, and you're giving him a second chance."

89

"People might say he's only getting a second chance because he is white."

"He stole a police car. How forgiving is that?"

The chief rubbed his bald head. "I don't know, Isaiah … but I must admit, it does have some merit."

"It's an opportunity, Lionel. The dead white kid helps a black girl and one of his own kind. It's diverse and it's perfect. It's an opportunity for the Savannah Police Department to turn a tragedy into an inspiring story of help and hope."

Chief Webster smirked. "And a leading activist for Ebony Evolution is seen helping both white and black."

Isaiah raised his cup of coffee in a cheers gesture. "And so is the chief of police."

"So you found the thirty K to send both kids to school?"

Isaiah sipped his coffee. "I'm working on it."

"Did you ask Yvette to help? If anyone can raise money, it's that woman."

Hightower momentarily tightened his lips to one side. "Perhaps. We'll see how this plays out."

"Bring me two kids—excited kids—and thirty grand, and we got a deal."

Isaiah nodded. "I'm going to talk to one of the candidates right now."

***

It wasn't so much the candidate Isaiah was interested in seeing before he returned to Hilton Head, but his candidate's place of business. He promised Alicia he'd lead her to a better life. To do that, he needed cash—lots of it.

Much of his fundraising came in the form of cash donations. He needed to get the David Marsh

Foundation up and running and create a surplus for *Alicia-dentals*. He had $500 in cash to get the ball rolling, but if he was ever going to raise $30,000 he needed a faster way than bake sales and speeches. He came to Dark Alleys to invest it—not throw it away on titty-dances.

He ignored the big-bosomed blonde covered with tattoos making love to the brass pole on stage as he walked past—almost—and went straight to the back of the club. He passed through a thick red curtain and looked at the three doors. The one on the right was where the girls could take clients for a private dance. The middle door led members to poker tables and a roulette wheel. To the left was the betting lounge. Isaiah turned left.

TVs hung on three of the walls. They were all tuned to the introduction of a boxing match.

Behind the counter stood an older gentleman with very dark skin and cotton white hair. He greeted Isaiah. "Hello, Brother. What can I do for you on this fine Georgia evening?"

Isaiah nodded. "Brother." He pointed to one of the TVs. "What's with the boxing? It's only five o'clock. Is this a repeat?"

The clerk shook his head. "No. it's coming from London, England. They're five hours ahead. It's ten p.m. there."

"Oh. Where's the dog racing? I need to place a bet and win some cash."

"Which dog are you betting on?"

"I don't know. I need to see who's running."

The old man handed him a racing form and a betting slip. "Fill it out and bring it on back."

Isaiah moved to one of the leather couches and sat next to a young guy—early thirties—who he hadn't seen before. He must have been a newer member. But the club's membership was 80% white, so he was pleased to see another black member in their midst.

He looked over Isaiah's shoulder. "You're into the dogs, huh?"

"I have to be into something. I need some serious cash."

The young guy pointed to the pre-match analysis on the TV. "What about boxing? At least your odds of winning are fifty-fifty."

"Hmm …" Isaiah stroked his chin and studied the screen. "I know less about boxing than I do about the dogs, and I don't know much about dogs. Who's fighting?"

"Tyrell Lewis and Cory Logan."

"You might have a point. The black guy looks pretty big."

The guy raised his eyebrows. "Yeah, that's Lewis—an Englishman."

"Is he any good?"

"Oh, yeah, he's good, but Cory Logan is better."

Isaiah's face creased. "Really? Since when do white guys win boxing matches?"

"Victory knows no color. Besides, he's the favorite, and with a win tonight he'll be on his way to a shot at the title. He's hungry. Lewis is trying to prove he's still got it, but he doesn't. Logan is trying to prove he has what it takes, and he does."

"I don't know. It just goes against the grain."

"What grain?"

"White grain."

The young guy laughed. "Well, he's a neighbor."

"How's that?"

"He's from South Carolina. Hilton Head."

Isaiah smiled. "You don't say. Thanks, ... ?"

"William."

They shook hands.

"Thanks, William. I'll be right back."

Isaiah walked to the betting window and pulled out an envelope containing cash. He placed it on the counter in front of the betting clerk. "Five-hundred on the white guy."

"No dogs?" the older guy asked.

"I'm hoping the white guy is a pit bull."

The clerk nodded and handed Isaiah his betting slip.

Isaiah returned and sat next to William. He was surprised at how far he sunk into the black leather. Comfort from the couch came quickly, but he was slightly uncomfortable betting on white over black. In the end, he rationalized it to backing the American over the Brit. That felt less guilty.

They stared at the fifty-two-inch screen. The opening bell brought shouts from other members standing by the TVs and from those who found comfort on the other sofas in the lounge.

William was right. Cory Logan packed one mean punch. Tyrell Lewis was in trouble from the beginning. Logan turned up the heat with each round. Isaiah soon found himself enjoying the fight. Or perhaps he enjoyed seeing himself winning.

Seventeen minutes later, Isaiah walked to the betting window to collect his $900 winnings after Logan knocked out his opponent in the fourth round. It wasn't enough to pay for two student's tuition, but it was a start. He thought he best use some of it to take Yvette to dinner and enlist her help for some fundraising. Chief Webster was right.

She certainly had a talent for raising money. If he was going to raise thirty grand—no, he'd better make it forty to cover *Alicia-dentals*—he needed to pull out all the stops.

Chapter 11

Isaiah stood to one side and opened the heavy wooden door to the restaurant.

Yvette tucked her envelope purse under her arm as she passed through the doorway. "Oh, Isaiah, you know how I love this restaurant," she remarked. "This is a nice surprise."

"Well, darling, I may not be able to give you Hawaii, but I can certainly give you a nice steak dinner. And may I say how radiant you look tonight."

Traces of crimson etched her ebony skin. "You did mention it at home, but I never get tired of hearing it."

Isaiah stepped to the podium and gave the hostess his name. A few moments later they were shown to a booth next to a window. The setting sun left an array of purples and pinks glimmering off the rolling waves of the Atlantic Ocean.

The Hightowers barely glanced at the menus before they both ordered well-done sirloin steaks—his with onion rings, hers with fries.

"You were in an awfully good mood when you came in last night," Yvette said. "I take it you had a good outing in Savannah. By the way, I forgot to ask, did you get Josh his job back?"

"Better than that. And the trip went well. It went very well—or I should say, it has the potential to go very well."

"That sounds like something you'd say about one of your below average students. 'He has potential.'"

"Well, Josh McKinna does."

"Josh McKinna and potential? I thought the Marriott was his plateau. He hasn't turned to crime since you got—I mean, since he got fired, has he?"

Isaiah's hand balled up into a fist. "I didn't get him fir—" He stopped, took a deep breath, and let his gorgeous smile surface. He reached over and stroked her hand. "Mr. Conrad at the Marriott fired him, darling, not me. And Conrad won't take him back. But that doesn't matter. I'm helping the boy."

"Helping him how?"

Isaiah's smile turned into a smug grin. "What do I do?"

Yvette tipped her head to one side. "I'm going to say you help people. But with that, you help the black community. Josh McKinna is about as white as they come. What's your angle?"

He lightly shook his head. "No angle, and true, I do help people, but that wasn't the answer I was looking for." He placed his hand on his chest. "I'm an educator, and Josh McKinna is in for the best education of his life. And how is that possible? Because yours truly has set up a charity for young people of America to become police officers."

"Really!" Her excitement was undeniable. "That will help with your nomination for Citizen of the South."

He grinned. "Perhaps."

Yvette squeezed his hand and smiled. "That's great, and I'm so very proud of you. And, I like Josh and everything, but ..."

Isaiah's eyebrows peaked. "But what?"

"It's just ... I wish you'd stay focused on the black community."

"I am. My first candidate is a young, African American woman. She's bright, but doesn't have much money. She's perfect. I told Chief Webster she was the one I wanted to send to Chatham College to study law enforcement, paid for by the David Marsh Foundation."

"Now that's more like it. So, what does this have to do with Josh McKinna?"

"The chief says I have to send a white person."

Her eyebrows knitted together. "What? That's outrageous. That's what's wrong with this country. Everything's stacked against us in favor of white—"

The waitress interrupted when she brought their steaks. "Can I get you folks anything else?"

"Yeah, a vodka," Yvette demanded.

Isaiah leaned in, eyeballing his wife. "Since when do you drink hard liquor?"

"Since Chief Webster started wronging his people. What kind of person has he become? A Chardonnay just isn't going to get it on when we have people like him stabbing people like us in the back."

He leaned forward and spoke in a low growl. "You will not be drinking hard liquor in public or badmouthing the Chief of Police—our friend as it happens." He briefly turned his attention to the waitress, who stood there slack-jawed. "Cancel the vodka."

She threw a glance to Yvette who curtseyed a nod of agreement. The waitress left without saying a word about the dinner she just delivered.

Yvette leaned over the table toward her husband. "Look, Isaiah, just because you swore off booze because your father got killed by a drunk driver does not give you the right to embarrass me in public. And I'm not driving." She retreated to her upright position.

Isaiah softened his tone. "Let's enjoy the dinner and I'll proceed with my story." He stopped to say grace, which included asking God to pardon his wife for wanting to wander into the playground of alcoholism, and that a special blessing be thrown Chief Webster's way for all the help he was giving to the David Marsh Foundation to find the right students for the program. Amen.

He took a bite of steak and let out a quiet moan of approval before continuing. "I told Webster not having an African American in the program was a deal-breaker. So we agreed that in the best interest of the foundation, we will enroll a black and a white student. Building bridges between racial divides in the name of law and order. That kind of thing."

"Good for you for holding your ground. Since you did that, I'm glad Josh will get a shot at an educational opportunity that he can put to good use. I'm pleased it was him and not some random token white."

"On the downside, because of Chief Webster's demands, we need a whole lot of money. Obviously, the foundation will build up funds over time with donations and fundraising, but Lionel wants to put both kids in at the same time for the ..." He air-quoted, "... grand opening."

"He has put the pressure on you, hasn't he?"

He bobbed his head. "Yes, he most certainly has. We have a little less than five months, which brings me to my next question. How would you like an opportunity to excel?"

"I already keep the cleanest house in South Carolina. What more can I do?"

"Fundraising."

Her eyes widened. "Really? You want me to raise the money?"

"I most certainly do. You're the best money raiser I know. We need about forty thousand."

"Oh, Isaiah, I don't know what to say. I'd love to. You know how much I enjoy this type of work. I'd be honored. But forty thousand? That's a bit steep, isn't it?"

"It's not just tuition. Webster wants the charity to pay for room and board as well, and I'll need a little extra for my travel expenses."

"Then I'll have to up my game." She threw her arms in the air. "I'm so excited. Maybe Gloria will help me."

"Whatever you need to do, darling." He leaned forward. "You do realize you'll have to raise money for Josh too. We need to appeal to the white community as well as the African American side."

She dabbed her lips with the napkin. "I see."

"I'll be spending time in Savannah overseeing certain aspects of the program."

Her face lit up. "Does that mean I'll be accompanying you to Savannah when you have to go?"

"We'll see, but it may be best if we split up our resources. You should focus your efforts here in the

Hilton Head area. There's a lot of money around here."

"And a lot of white people."

"Is that a problem?"

Yvette's head dropped and she stared at the tabletop. "No, not really." She raised her gaze to meet Isaiah's eyes. "But it is easier to stir black people into actions against injustices than it is to get white people to support a cause that benefits African Americans."

"Fair point, but Josh should be good for some Washingtons. Don't forget about him."

"No, you're right." She held a hopeful glint in her eye. "I can do it. Still … I'll come with you sometimes to Savannah, won't I?"

"We'll see."

She rubbed her foot against his leg under the table. "In any event, I'll be glad to be doing something I love. Thank you for asking me and putting your faith in me."

"You're welcome." He pointed at her steak with his fork. "Now eat your dinner."

***

Yvette met Gloria Huntington at Mac's Crab Shack, a quaint little—umm … shack—that specialized in fully dressed Dungeness crab. The outlook over the ocean was far-reaching. On a flat sea, it's thirteen miles to where the sky meets the water. Yvette always felt the horizon was only ten miles from Mac's Shack. If the sky touching the ocean was the entrance to heaven then she felt a little closer to paradise sitting in the crab shack.

Mac's was the first place she and Isaiah ate at when they arrived at Hilton Head. It was the oldest restaurant on the island and she liked the juxtaposition of the rustic timber-framed building that looked like it might topple over with the next strong wind, while the waiting staff wore red vests over their crisp white shirts, black bow ties, and long black aprons. Formal attire within the confines of decaying wood. She loved it.

The waiter served the ladies their crab and shrimp salad, grating a generous portion of parmesan cheese on each. His name tag read "Romeo." He was gorgeous with his chiseled jaw, high cheekbones, and dark curly locks—but Yvette was sure he was gay. There was that fantasy out the window—not that she would ever cheat on Isaiah—just grab an escape from reality now and then—but probably not with Romeo.

"Well? You sounded pretty excited on the phone," Gloria said. "What's going on in your world?" She speared a shrimp and crouton with her fork and popped them her mouth.

Yvette's glow was undeniable. "Isaiah wants me to help with some fundraising. He's putting me in charge of the Hilton Head operation."

Gloria's eyebrows peaked. "Operation? What are you raising money for? A Barak Obama superhighway going from sea to shining sea?"

"Not quite, but I might put that on my list." She paused to take a sip of her Chardonnay. "We need to raise money for his foundation that will pay for underprivileged kids to get an education in law enforcement. Detective school or something ... I think. Isn't that exciting?"

"Cops and guns. My favorite themes." A mini-eye roll followed.

"I was wondering if you might want to help me."

Gloria smiled and lightly nodded. "I'm not much good at fundraising, but of course I'll help. Your Isaiah is amazing. Putting black youths on the police force. I applaud him one-hundred percent."

Yvette used her fork to shift the lettuce leaves around the bowl. "It's not exclusively for African Americans. There might be a white guy getting some benefit from it." She raised her head to meet her friend's eyes. "But it's okay, we know him. It's one of Isaiah's former students."

"So the beneficiaries have already been selected?"

Yvette nodded.

"How many are there?"

"Two. One white, one black. Boy and a girl."

"How much money does he need to raise?"

"Forty thousand."

"So it's a four-year degree?"

"No, just a year."

"What? Are you insane? Where is he sending them? Harvard?"

"Don't be ridiculous. It's an HBCU college in Savannah." Yvette wondered if she made a mistake asking Gloria for help. Besides providing another pair of hands, Gloria was very wealthy and might be willing to make a donation of her own—thanks to Isaiah's help and a payout from the state of South Carolina. When her husband had been executed by the state for a triple murder, Gloria, with Isaiah's help, successfully proved it was a case of mistaken identities—and then Isaiah made sure the entire country knew about it. Their tenacity cleared her husband's name and earned her a $3.5 million settlement.

Gloria leaned in and spoke softly. "Yvette, dear, small colleges do not charge twenty-some-odd-thousand dollars a year to educate kids on how to arrest people."

Yvette's eyes flickered, holding back emotions of disappointment. "I don't know all the ins and outs of the arrangement. All I know is the kids are supposed to get room, board, and an education for twenty-some-odd-thousand each. My husband has asked for my help and I intend to give him my full support. As my friend, you can help me or not. I don't really care. I was only asking. If you have something better to do, then by all means, don't let me stop you."

Gloria reached across the table, patting Yvette's hand. "Oh, honey ... I'm sorry. I didn't mean to upset you." She shrugged. "I don't know, maybe colleges are that expensive these days. I might be out of touch, it just sounds pretty pricey. I'm not doubting you—or Isaiah." She reached into her purse and pulled out a checkbook. "Look, I may not be able to help with a physical presence, but at least let me give you a donation."

"You don't have to do that." But that was exactly what Yvette wanted her to do. A little boost to get her started, but she wanted to play it cool—even though it was difficult to hide her excitement.

"I insist," Gloria demanded. "Now, who do I make it out to?"

Yvette reached in her purse and read from a piece of paper. "The David Marsh Foundation."

With surgeon-like precision, Gloria finished her signature by crossing the 't' and putting the tittles on the 'i's. She pulled the check from the book and handed it to Yvette.

Her hand shook as she reached for the donation. She hadn't even begun the fundraising campaign yet and she already had a check for ...

"One hundred dollars?"

Gloria smiled. "You're such a good fundraiser you probably don't need my money, but I feel it's my Christian duty to help."

"Yes ... well ... umm ... that's... that's unbelievable. Umm ... thank you."

"Not at all, my dear. It's the least I can do."

That's true. You certainly couldn't do much less.

Chapter 12

Yvette sat in bed in a turquoise nightgown with her face in full frown. Her arms were folded across her chest, pulling the silk fabric tight, highlighting the smallness of her breasts. She liked her barely B-cups. They complimented her slenderness and Isaiah always insisted he was a leg man—and she had plenty of leg propping up her five-foot-nine height.

Isaiah lay next to her, reading the Bible. The clock on his nightstand showed 10:36 p.m.

Yvette released a soft, yet angry, sigh. "It was unbelievable. Can you imagine? A hundred dollars. One hundred stinking dollars. She spends more on getting Fluffy clipped at the dog groomers, and she gives me a lousy hundred bucks to educate kids. The nerve of the woman."

Isaiah didn't look up. "At least she helped," he remarked, not taking his nose out of the good book. "I'm a little surprised she gave anything at all to tell you the truth. Did she know it was for a white kid?"

"And an African American. I told her about the black girl you fought to get in. And what does she do? She leaves me thirty-nine thousand, nine hundred bucks short."

"Surely you didn't expect her to stump up the whole cost of tuition for two students. You know she's always been a little tight."

Yvette looked at her husband, her eyebrows arched high. "A little tight! She's downright stingy. Mean, she is. That woman is mean. And stingy."

"Did she give it joyously?"

"I don't know. I guess so."

"Then there you go." He turned to Yvette. "You know God is watching us, right?"

She tried to disguise her eye roll but failed. "Yes, of course."

He returned his attention to the Bible and stabbed at the page with his finger. "This is a miracle that I'm reading this passage while we're having this conversation. Now pay attention." He cleared his throat. "Each of you should give what you have decided in your heart to give, not reluctantly or under compulsion, for God loves a cheerful giver. Second Corinthians nine, seven."

"Am I supposed to find comfort in that?"

"Yes, yes you are." He closed the book, leaned over, and gave her a peck on the cheek before rolling over and going to sleep.

"Well, God doesn't love the mean and stingy woman who won't help her friend in a time of need," she mumbled.

She turned her light out and closed her eyes. Her mind raced on how to raise money without Gloria Huntington, keeping sleep at bay.

***

Yvette loved it when she was in a fundraising mode. She was up at five-thirty, jumped in the shower, and had her face on in under half-an-hour. It was just as well Gloria refused her invitation for hands-on help. Gloria would spend a half-hour merely rolling out of bed and another hour and a half applying her make up. Despite her foundation

106

being thick enough to ski on, Yvette could still see the blemishes of her teenage acne hiding underneath. However, she did concede, even with her not-so-perfect skin, Gloria was a stunningly attractive woman. But her good looks conflicted with punctuality. She would never be on time for important events. Attractive or not—naturally or artificially—below the skin lay a mean and stingy person.

Yvette stood in front of the halogen top stove cooking bacon and eggs.

Isaiah came into the kitchen taking exaggerated sniffs. "Something smells good."

"You've missed some time at work lately, so I thought you should have a hearty breakfast to help deal with everything you might have to put right today."

"Becker is a good vice principal, and he hasn't called me, so I'm sure everything is okay."

"That's what would worry me—him not calling."

Isaiah sat down as she served his breakfast. It was a ridiculously large table considering there were only the two of them in the household. There was a breakfast bar in the kitchen, but Isaiah hated sitting on stools. All meals were served in the dining room. On the occasions when they had guests, the table would seat ten comfortably—and formally—with high-back chairs padded for extra coziness for those long after-dinner conversations and debates.

Yvette sat opposite him with a cup of coffee and a piece of toast.

Isaiah looked across the table. "Leggings and stud earrings. Is it a housework day?"

"No, it's a fundraising day."

"Are you washing people's cars? I'd get a couple of teenagers to do that if I were you."

"Nope. It's sale day at U-Lock-It."

He took in a mouthful of scrambled eggs. "Oh, yeah. That's where you bid on storage units people leave behind, isn't it?"

"Yep, six months unpaid rent and it goes out to the public for auction. They have five units up for bid. You never know what you might find."

"Wait a minute. You're buying stuff to sell? Is this for the foundation? You should be collecting donations for that. Donations ... that means free, in case you forgot. There's a lot more money in selling things you pick up for free."

"I'll only pay a couple of hundred bucks if a unit looks promising, and who knows? I might find a gem. I'll have an auction myself next week to start raising money for the foundation. In the meantime, I'll canvas friends and neighbors for donations." She rested her forearms on the table and leaned in toward her husband. "Did you know the quarterback for the Atlanta Falcons has a house on the island? I'm going to stop by there. Maybe he'll donate a signed football or something."

He chuckled. "You're going to walk up to a multi-millionaire's house, unannounced, and ask him for a football?" Isaiah shook his head. "People like that don't want to be bothered. That's why he has a house on the island. To get away from the public. Don't go bothering the man. Let him have his peace and just stick with your storage stuff and knick-knacks from the neighbors."

"Are you kidding me? A football signed by a Super Bowl-winning quarterback? That has to be worth hundreds, don't you think?"

"Don't do it, Yvette. The man likes his privacy."

"How do you know? He's probably an egomaniac who thrives on recognition and celebrity status." She took a bite of toast.

"No, he doesn't."

"You talk like you know him."

"Okay, I've met him."

"You know him? Where'd you met him?"

He picked up the silver pepper shaker and splashed an abundance of the black flakes on his eggs. "At a fundraiser."

"Really? That's good to know. That gives me ammo. If he's into raising money for good causes then he'd probably want to help. I'll do a little Isaiah Hightower name-dropping, flash him a Yvette Hightower smoothie smile, and he'll be eating out of my hand. I'm getting that football." Her words of determination hung on the walls like freshly glued wallpaper.

Isaiah's attention left his peppered eggs and focused on Yvette. "Don't. Name-dropping is so vulgar."

Yvette brushed her foot against her husband's leg. "Well, maybe if you kind of bumped into him, and said, 'Hey, Troy, got any autographed footballs going?' And he'd say, 'Sure, Isaiah, anything for you.' Then you wouldn't have to name-drop because you two would already know each other's names." She beamed at her logic.

He sighed. "Okay, I'll talk to him. I'll see if I can get you a Troy Dugan signed football, you just promise to leave him alone. Okay?"

"Really?"

He nodded.

Yvette stood up with a big smile splashed across her face. "In that case, see if you can get me a jersey too. Wahoo!" She leaned over and kissed her husband. "You're going to be so proud of me, baby. I'm going to get you all the money you need. And with what's left over, we're going to Hawaii!"

She bounded out of the room with a distinctive spring in her step.

***

Betty greeted Isaiah when he walked into the office with a piping hot cup of coffee. He eyed a cinnamon roll on a paper plate sitting on the edge of her desk. If she uttered the words "This is for you, Principal Hightower," he would have a serious look at getting her a raise.

"Mornin', Principal Hightower. I hope you've been using your time down yonder real smart."

He ignored the grammar stammer as best he could. "Yes, I have, Betty. Thank you." He glanced at the cinnamon roll. *Shoot.* He took the coffee and stepped toward his office.

"Oh." She picked up the cinnamon roll. "I got ya this. It'll be good with your caffeinated bean juice."

Isaiah smiled. "Bless you. You will reap rewards for your kindness."

"Just seeing those pearly whites gives me heaps of joy."

His grin widened as he marched on. "And I like giving you 'heaps of joy.'"

He sat in his leather button-back chair and pulled out a napkin from the top drawer. He took a bite of the roll and let out a moan of pleasure. A deep moan—one of the ones that enhance the flavor. He hoped it was loud enough that Betty would hear it and know she hit the mark—and do it again. After a sip of coffee to wash it down, he wasted no time in drafting an email to the superintendent with regard to offering Betty a raise. An extra fifty-cents an hour should put a smile on her face and another cinnamon roll in his belly.

Betty ran the office like the captain of a warship. Isaiah recognized from day one that the students were more afraid of her than of any principal that may take the throne. She claimed her two hundred and fifty pounds were due to big bones—not Big Macs.

In the time it took him to catch up with the vice principal and dotted some i's on backlogged paperwork, lunchtime arrived.

Betty knocked on the door and poked her head in. "I'm just going to lunch, Mr. H. Can I get ya anything?"

Isaiah leaned back in his chair. "I did have an errand—" He waved his hand around. "No, never mind. I shouldn't bother you with personal runs."

She stepped inside the room. "No trouble. I'd be plumb happy to help."

"If you're sure it's not an imposition …"

"Nada problem. What can I do for ya?"

He pulled out his wallet and took out several bills. "If you wouldn't mind, could you stop by Wally's World of Sport and pick me up a regulation NFL football and an authentic Atlanta Falcons jersey. Number one, and make sure it has Dugan's name on the back."

The secretary placed a hand on her large hip and solemnized her face. "Principal Hightower, I know youse come from Georgia, and you was probably brought up on the Falcons … but you in

111

the Carolinas now. I think it's about time you got yourself a Panthers jersey." She erupted in a belly laugh.

Isaiah chuckled along with her. "Next season, I promise."

She wagged her finger at him. "I'm gonna hold ya to that." She walked across the room and took the cash. "I'll be back in an hour or so."

"Take your time," Isaiah said. "Oh, and get me a black magic marker too."

"Sure thing, Mr. H."

Isaiah opened up his email draft to the superintendent. *Make that a dollar.*

Chapter 13

"Isaiah! Isaiah!" Yvette bounded into the house like a schoolgirl who just got her first kiss from the most gorgeous high school football star and then couldn't wait to brag to her best friend about it. Yet her happiness exceeded the standard teenage happiness—this was real life.

Isaiah stepped out of his office looking perplexed by the frantic shouting. "What is it, darling?"

"I did it! I did it! And all thanks to you." She rushed her husband and delivered a full-on kiss to the lips. Then the cheek. Then the other cheek. Then a return kiss to his dazzling lips. "Thank you, baby. Thank you so much."

"You're most welcome. Now, would it be too much to ask what I did?"

She pulled checks and cash out of her purse. "Nine thousand smackers." She kissed him again.

"What? From your auction? What the heck was in that storage unit? What did you sell?"

"The storage unit? Junk, mostly, but there were a few nice pieces, and the quantity of stuff netted a thousand."

"And they gave you another eight grand just for being gorgeous?"

"Don't be silly." She pointed to the big smile on her face. "I would have gotten more than that for this."

He sighed. "Got, not gotten."

"Sure," she said indifferently. "But seven thousand two hundred dollars is what you get when two rich women with a crush on the hottest football player in the NFL start bidding for his jersey to sleep in. It must bring the fantasy closer to the skin."

His brows furrowed as he tried to untangle her words. "Have you been drinking?"

"Your Troy Dugan stuff!" She fanned herself and took a deep breath. "Okay ... these two women started bidding on the autographed football, but some dad trumped them and bought it for his kid's birthday present. He paid eight hundred bucks for it. Then the jersey came up—and these two women about orgasmed."

"Yvette! For crying out loud, this was a charity event, not some smut show. Do you mind?"

"Sorry, but their excitement was obvious. It was like the *Hilton Head Housewives* reality show. A couple of rich bitches—"

"Yvette!"

"Sorry. Anyway, these two women obviously had a crush on Troy Dugan. They went back and forth until the heir to the Victory Vodka distillery empire beat out the Sugar Empress with a bid of seven thousand two hundred dollars." She wrapped her arms around his neck. "All because my hubby knows Troy Dugan and got him to sign his jersey. You're the best." She delivered another kiss.

"Wow ..." Isaiah rubbed his chin, taking in the magnitude of his gift. "That's great. I had no idea it would net so much."

Yvette did a little shoulder shimmy. "That's what happens when you get two horny bit—when you get two sophisticated socialites chasing a fantasy. It was great." She thrust her arms over her head. "Nine grand, baby. Nine grand."

"You did well. Still, a long way to go to get to the goal, but you're off to a good start. I know you'll get results." He gave her a peck on the cheek. "I'm proud of you."

"Thank you. Yes, I'm thrilled with the result and I will get the job done. I'm so pleased. I want to take you to dinner. My treat."

"Your treat? Big Macs all around then?" He smirked.

"Just bring your appetite and your business brain. I have some more ideas I want to share with you. Be prepared to be impressed."

"I'll look forward to it. And it's really not McDonald's?"

"Get your glad rags on, Papa, we're going downtown." She patted his cheek and walked off.

***

Luciano's was busy. When Yvette called to make a reservation she was told they were fully booked. Then she dropped the Hightower name and a table suddenly became available. Upon arrival, the maître d' greeted Isaiah enthusiastically. Yvette thought she detected some kind of secret handshake, but that would be silly. Isaiah wasn't a Mason.

William, the maître d', showed them to the best table in the restaurant: a semi-circle booth in the corner which sat on a raised platform overlooking the entire dining area. Yvette was excited and disappointed. She loved people watching and the table was perfect for her to indulge in her favorite pastime. You had to be *somebody* to be seated there.

She wasn't sure if it was Isaiah's principalship, his deaconhood, or his activist status that got them seated there—and she couldn't have cared less. They were the royal couple of Luciano's for the evening and that was all that mattered.

She was also disappointed. She had to stay focused on her business plan and convince her husband she was the best person—the only person—who could raise the money and that he made the right decision putting her in charge. That meant she would have to miss observing the other diners to keep Isaiah's undivided attention. Isaiah wasn't much of a people watcher but more dedicated to making sure he was the person being seen and acknowledged as an important member of the community. That would be a distraction from Yvette's efforts if other diners stopped by to say hello or profess their admiration to the most important man in the restaurant.

After they ordered Yvette went to work.

She reached into her oversized purse and pulled out a pad of paper and a black easy-glide fine point pen. "I have several ideas. If you don't like one we can move on. I'd also like to implement more than one. After all, none of these is a forty-thousand dollar idea in and by itself—well, thirty-one thousand now—but we need to get a few things going to raise that kind of money."

"Of course. Good idea." Isaiah splayed his hand and wiggled his fingers in a casual wave to a gentleman who acknowledged him from the other side of the room.

Yvette tapped her pen against the pad regaining his attention. "I have an idea for a Meat and Eat. Teams of four will have thirty minutes to barbeque and eat as many hamburgers as they can. The team that cooks and eats the most wins. I called Panda foods and they'll donate the ground beef for the burgers, and they're also going to put up ten pounds of beef as a prize."

"That's great, darling. That sounds wonderful." Isaiah continued to scour the room, followed by another wave to a couple in the back.

Yvette cleared her throat and carried on. "Now I'm really excited about this one. I think we can get some good money for entry fees. I've spoken to Rolling Hills Golf Club. They're going to let us use their golf course from five p.m. to dark free of charge, in exchange for promoting them as the premier golf club on the island. What do you think about speed golf!"

Isaiah shook his head disbelievingly. "Speed what?"

"Speed golf. Teams play as many holes as they can from five o'clock until they can't see anymore. We'll have to limit the number of teams, but we'll make them pay a premium." She rapped her pen on the pad as she gave it some more thought. "I still have to work out some of the finer details, but the golf club said they'll help me set it up."

"Yeah. Good. That sounds fine."

"And then there's a treasure hunt. But what I intend to do with this is add a twist. Instead of—"

Without a word, Isaiah scooted out of the booth and walked across the restaurant.

Yvette could do nothing but watch as her husband left in the middle of her pitch and strutted to the other side of the dining area where he struck up a conversation with a young couple—in their early thirties, she guessed. They looked too young to be parents of any of his students, so she assumed it must have had something to do with the shooting and the David Marsh Foundation. Why else would he be talking to a white couple? Yes, that was Isaiah. A caring man. He was more colorblind than she was when it came to doing good deeds and spreading compassion.

After a manly handshake with the dark-haired guy and a polite nod to the blonde, a rather lengthy conversation followed. The guy nodded in agreement with whatever Isaiah was saying and the blonde did a lot of laughing and touching Isaiah's arm like she was an Armani quality control inspector. Yvette watched as Isaiah extended his arm toward their table. The guy, along with his companion, followed him and headed toward Yvette and the *power* table.

Isaiah opened his palm toward his wife. "Cory, this is my wife, Yvette Hightower. Yvette, this is Cory Logan and his friend … ?" He leaned in toward the buxom blonde.

"I'm his manager, Charlie Gillettie," she said with a pleasant British accent lining her reply.

Yvette remained stone-faced. "Manager of what?"

Isaiah pointed to the seat. "Please," he interrupted as he slid in next to Yvette.

The young couple sat as instructed.

"I hope you don't mind, darling, but Cory and Charlie will be joining us for dinner. Can you believe it? William was going to give them a table next to the kitchen?"

"That was my fault," Charlie confessed. "I forgot to book a table and we would have been eating in the scrubs—" she threw Cory an admiring

118

glance, "until I dropped his name, and suddenly they had a table for Cory 'Incorrigible' Logan—albeit not the best seat in the house by any means. Nonetheless, it was very kind of Mr. Luciano to squeeze us in, and even more kind to be invited to your table, Mr. Hightower. And generous." She nodded to Yvette. "And to you, Mrs. Hightower. Thank you."

Yvette whispered to Isaiah. "Yes, very generous. What about our meeting?"

Isaiah ignored her comment. "Darling, we are dining with the next heavyweight champion of the world and his delightful manageress."

"Heavyweight of what?" Yvette asked.

"Boxing, what else?"

"Since when did you start following boxing?"

Isaiah smiled as any enthusiastic fan would. "I've always been a fan. A *huge* fan. Especially since young Cory here came on the scene."

Cory made a weak clearing of the throat. "Actually, I'm a middleweight, and I have been around a while."

Isaiah flicked a dismissive hand. "But you're still a champion."

"No, not yet. Charlie wants me to have another warm-up fight before I take a shot at the title."

Isaiah summoned the waiter and handed the newcomers menus.

Charlie looked the menus over, sighing with indecision. "Everything looks so yummy." She peeked over the top of the menu. "Can you recommend anything, Mr. Hightower?"

"Please, call me Isaiah." He held his smile until he gathered her attention. "The steaks are delightful, of course, but they may be a bit pedestrian for

119

someone with a sophisticated palate. If you like earthy food, the Portobello mushrooms are divine."

Charlie slammed the menu closed. "You got me pegged in one go. Mushrooms it is." She smiled.

Isaiah smiled.

Yvette rolled her eyes as Charlie and Isaiah shared a magic mushroom moment.

The boxer ordered Angel-haired pasta with shrimp and everyone was happy as they waited for the food to be delivered—except for Yvette. Her time and platform had been compromised.

"So, you like this fighting thing, do you, Cory?" Yvette asked.

He bobbed his head in the affirmative. "Love it. In many ways, I'm the underdog."

"Underdog?" Isaiah remarked. "How's that? I saw you fight. You're a master in the ring."

Yvette leaned sideways, cocking her head toward Isaiah. "You saw him fight?"

He ignored her question. "Go on, Cory."

Cory smiled. "As boxers go, I don't fit the profile. First of all, I'm white."

Yvette's eyes narrowed. "And you consider that a handicap?"

"No, but there aren't that many white boxers. Not good ones anyway. And I was brought up in a two-parent family right here on the island. I am anything but a typical boxer."

Yvette crossed her arms across her chest. "So, what is a typical boxer like, Mr. Logan? Go ahead, feel free to stereotype."

Cory shifted uncomfortably in his seat. "Well, Mrs. Hightower, statistically speaking, I fight a lot more black guys than I do white guys."

Yvette spoke in a matter-of-fact manner. "Are you suggesting that the ghetto is a better training ground for fighting than your membership at a state-of-the-art gym?"

Cory's face creased. "No—

Her tone sharpened. "Or is it that blacks are more prone to violence, hence making them better fighters? Is it naturally in their blood? That is the stereotype, is it not?"

Isaiah reached over and grasped her hand. "Now, now, darling. I'm sure Cory's not suggesting there's any correlation between blacks and a natural-born thirst for violence."

Cory's gaze darted between the Hightowers. "Not at all. I have the greatest respect for all my opponents, especially black boxers. I'm sure their road to the ring was much tougher than mine."

"How's that?" Isaiah asked, almost sounding sympathetic.

"I got into a fight in school. It changed my life."

"Yes," Yvette acknowledged. "School fights change a lot of lives."

Isaiah gave his wife a sideways glance, hoping that would shut her up. "Oh," he said, returning his attention to Cory. "You got kicked out? Uneducated. Down and out? Then turned to boxing to avoid a life of crime?"

"Not exactly. But sad to say, that's how many of my counterparts entered the sport. Mine was a different road. For one thing, I loved my first school fight and kicked ass. It felt good—no, it felt great. Empowering." He smiled and gave a nod to his manager.

Charlie smiled back. "Whatever it takes, mate. I'm just glad you got in the game."

"Sounds like you're a regular Rocky Marciano," Yvette quipped. "Or a playground bully."

"I'm neither, Mrs. Hightower. I'm simply saying it was my choice to enter the ring. Some people don't have the options that I did."

Yvette cupped her hand behind her ear. "Excuse me? Are you suggesting that the black boxers had two choices in life? Fighting or crime? Of which both choices are barbaric and uncivilized."

"I wouldn't limit it to blacks, no. Underprivileged people of any color will have fewer choices in life."

Isaiah patted his wife's leg. "It's okay, darling. I'm sure Cory isn't interested in opening up a debate on the subject."

It was Yvette's turn to ignore him. "Was your first fight with an African American?" she asked.

Charlie's cute dimples flattened. "Does that matter?"

She shrugged. "I guess not. We all bleed red, right? Except for royalty. I believe their blood is blue—is that correct?"

It was Charlie's turn to shrug. "Don't know. I'm an Essex girl, and I bleed bloody red."

Cory patted Charlie's hand while he looked at Yvette. "Yes, it was with a black guy, but he accused me of cheating on an exam to get me kicked off the football team. I was the starting wide receiver and he was my backup. He wanted me off the squad so he could have the starting gig. So I kicked his ass. It was nothing to do with race. Not on my end anyway."

"Yes, superiority is an aphrodisiac, I suppose." Yvette remained solemn. "What is it now? The crushing of the bones? The blood splattered around the rink?"

"Yvette," Isaiah patted her hand. "Cory and Charlie are our guests. This is no time to pontificate pacifist views with a future world champion." He gave his attention to Cory. "You'll have to forgive my wife. She doesn't understand boxing as a sport." He turned back to Yvette. "And it's a ring, not a rink."

Yvette sat back in her seat, arms folded even tighter across her chest, and wearing a scowl any diva whose dressing room was too small would have been proud of.

The waiter returned placing Cory and Charlie's dinner in front of them.

Charlie took a deep breath of appreciative acknowledgement as she eyed the stuffed Portobello mushrooms topped with marinara, sautéed spinach, and crispy panko-crusted goat cheese.

Isaiah leaned forward. "Your mushrooms look delectable, Charlie."

She agreed. "This looks scrummy. Great recommendation, Isaiah."

An uncomfortable atmosphere hung over the table as Yvette continued to sulk. Isaiah ignored her and attempted to keep things on an even keel.

"So, you're a local boy, Cory," Isaiah said.

"Correct. Born and bred on the island."

"You must have a pretty big fan base here."

He nodded. "I get pretty good support throughout all of South Carolina, but yeah, Hilton Head, in particular, has been very good to me."

"Did you graduate from Hilton Head High School?"

Cory raised his fist in cheer. "Go Seahawks."

Isaiah smiled. "Good. That's good. Have you heard of David Marsh?"

"Can't say that I have."

Yvette leaned over and whispered to her husband. "Where are you going with this?"

"Shush," he whispered from the side of his mouth. "David was also a local boy and a student at Hilton Head, like you. He got a scholarship to a nearly all-black college in Savannah. He was chasing his dream, studying criminology, and playing football. He had a promising future. But sadly he got killed in a drive-by before any of his dreams could be realized. Tragic, it was."

"Sounds like it," Cory agreed.

"I'm setting up a charity in his name. The aim of the foundation is to give scholarships to underprivileged kids to train in law enforcement. We're trying to raise money."

Charlie raised an attention-getting finger. "I hope you didn't ask us to join you just so you can get a donation from Cory," she said. "With all due respect, Mr. Hightower, people try to tap him for cash all the time. In his profession, his income is public knowledge with each fight, and then the scammers come out of the woodwork with their begging bowls for good causes. I trust you respect my concern and understand my policy of not donating to Tom or Harry because they usually turn out to be Dicks."

Isaiah cocked his head to one side. "That's not what I was after." He smiled. "And please, call me Isaiah."

"What *do* you want ... Isaiah?" she asked.

"Yes, Isaiah," Yvette echoed, "What *do* you want?"

Isaiah patted his wife's leg under the table to quiet her. "Many of the kids still remember David with great fondness. He was a boy following his dreams. I wonder if you would consider talking to the kids at school. Hearing a success story such as yours may encourage them to follow their dreams. And hey ... let's be honest—what kid wouldn't want to meet a world champion?"

"I'm flattered," Cory said.

Charlie clicked her fingers. "Wait a minute ... Hightower ... the principal of Hilton Head High?"

"Yes, that would be me," Isaiah confirmed.

Charlie pushed forward, her large breasts hovering over her plate of food. "Aren't you the guy that got the Bare Trap closed down?"

Isaiah glanced at her ... Portobello mushrooms "Yes, that would also be me."

Yvette noticed her husband's roaming eyes over Charlie's assets. "Don't tell me that put you out of a job," she mumbled.

Charlie eyed Yvette. "Excuse me?"

"I said he did a good job."

Charlie blinked a few times trying to shake off Yvette's hostility. "Why don't we go one better?"

Isaiah leaned in. "I'm listening."

"What if Cory gave a speech at the Civic Center. You could sell tickets to the event to raise money for the foundation."

"What!" Yvette screeched.

Cory and Charlie's heads jerked toward Yvette's squeal.

"Perhaps not," Cory said.

Charlie put her hand on his shoulder. "Think about it, Cory. Not only will it raise money for a worthy cause, but it'll also raise your profile."

"I don't know. It doesn't feel unanimous." He cast his eyes toward Yvette. "What do you think, Mrs. Hightower?"

"As the chief fundraiser for this cause, I disagree with your girlfriend. I think you should just make a modest donation and call it a day. Making a speech would detract from your rigorous training schedule, would it not?"

"Umm … I'm his manager," Charlie said. "Nothing more, and this is our way of offering your husband a token of our gratitude." She scowled at Cory. "The Bare Trap was Cory's weakness and a major distraction to his training. Thanks to Mr. Hightower, he's more focused than ever before and has never trained harder."

Cory sunk a little lower in his seat.

Yvette rolled her eyes. "Great. Violent and perverted," she mumbled.

Isaiah held Yvette's arm. "Can I talk to you for a moment, darling? In private." He pushed Yvette along the booth. "If you two will excuse us a moment."

They nodded their consent.

Isaiah escorted her to a quiet corner of the restaurant, next to the bathrooms. "What are you doing? Why are you trying to sabotage my efforts to raise money?"

"Your efforts? It was that British hussy's idea to get her punch-drunk perverted Romeo involved. I don't need his help, Isaiah. You put me in charge of raising the money. Don't go pulling the rug out from under me without asking me if I need help from a blonde bimbo and her bonehead boxer boyfriend—which I don't, as it happens."

"This is an opportunity. Let's seize the moment of their generosity. He's the ideal person to raise money in Hilton Head."

"Why? Because he's white?"

"It doesn't hurt, given the cause, and he's a celebrity."

"You haven't even listened to my ideas yet."

"You've done a wonderful job, darling, but a little more help won't hurt. One Cory Logan speech has to be worth a lot of holes of speed golf. You can still do your events, but let Cory help us raise some big money."

She ran her finger under the lapel of his jacket. "How do you know *I* won't be the big money bringer-inner? I want to help you and prove I can do this. Just listen to my ideas."

"I will, but let's see what Logan can bring in. Then you make up the shortfall. Just support me on this."

She drew a deep breath. "You know I don't like boxing. And why."

"That has nothing to do with this." Isaiah stepped closer. "Remember that time we were in New York. And you really wanted to see Elton John." He took on a Biblical tone. "A person I view as nothing more than a piece of commercial fiction—but it was important to you. So I went. It's called support, Yvette."

Her eyes left him in favor of the floor. She was mad. All she wanted was a night with her husband. She wanted him to be impressed with her ideas. Maybe he'd even say she was smart. But Isaiah wanted her to yield to some rich white guy with an appetite for violence. She took an immediate dislike to Cory Logan and his bimbo girlfriend just for destroying the intimacy of the night with her husband, if for nothing else. Although there was something else. But now wasn't the time. She was duty-bound to support her husband. She had to do it for Isaiah—and for this Daniel, Doug, David guy—or whatever the hell his name was. Bringing up the Elton John concert was a low-blow—he must have been desperate. Guilt pricked her conscience. She looked him in the eyes. "You're my husband, of course I'll support you."

Isaiah gave a game-winning grin. "That's my girl."

"Just promise you'll listen to my ideas after you get this Cory thing settled," she appealed.

"You got it."

Isaiah turned to leave.

Yvette grabbed him by the arm. "One more thing ..." She gave him a meaningful glare. "Keep your eyes off her Portobello mushrooms."

His glistening white smile widened. "What mushrooms?" He kissed her on the cheek. "Let's get back to that table. Smile, and tell Logan how much you'd like him to help us raise money."

"That's what I do, support my husband."

The Hightowers returned, Isaiah sliding in first leaving Yvette on the outside—which was how she felt—metaphorically and literally.

Yvette ran her finger along the edge of her plate. "I apologize, Mr. Logan, if I've offended you in any way or if I've come across as unappreciative—either for your professional achievements or for any help you might give us for the Daniel Marsh foundation."

Isaiah bumped her leg. "David," he whispered from the side of his mouth.

"David," she repeated.

"Please, call me Cory, and there's no need to apologize if you're not a fight fan. My mom's not too thrilled about my chosen profession either."

Yvette remained serious. "Of course not. No mother would want to see their son become a vegetable by choice."

"Yvette," Isaiah whispered. "Don't demean the boy's profession."

She shrugged innocently. "I was joking."

Cory laughed. "It's okay, Mr. Hightower. I can see your wife is passionate about her beliefs." He looked at Yvette. "It's an admirable quality."

Isaiah threw his wife a quieting glare. "Silence is also an admirable quality."

After a short break in conversation following the reprimand, Isaiah picked it back up again. He looked at Charlie. "I think it's a terrific idea. You're quite the girl. World-class manager and a great promotional mind. I'm impressed."

Charlie addressed Yvette. "Just for the record, I'm not his girlfriend. I'm his manager and the person in charge of looking after his professional and financial affairs. I get him top dollar for his fights and then make sure he keeps it. That's it." She looked across to Isaiah. "As for the speech, you're welcome. My dad was a Bobby back in England and got stabbed in the line of duty. So when it comes to raising money for law enforcement causes, I'm in."

Isaiah frowned. "I'm sorry to hear that but grateful you have elected to help our cause. I'll look into booking a venue and getting some tickets sold."

He turned toward his wife. "You'll help me with that, won't you, Yvette?"

"Of course." She shot Charlie a look. "I support my husband in all he does."

"Good for you."

The table fell quiet again.

Yvette pointed in Charlie's direction with her fork. "Those sure are some large mushrooms. I wonder if they're organic."

"I hope so. I detest anything genetically modified."

Isaiah put his arm around her shoulder, squeezing her tight. "She's the best, this woman."

"You're a lucky man, Mr. Hightower," Cory commented.

"Yes, yes I am," he acknowledged. "And please, call me Isaiah."

Cory spun his fork into his food collecting a sizable mouthful of pasta.

The pasta twirling around the tines unlocked the aroma for Yvette. She got a vestige of parmesan and garlic. She looked at her plate of cod and French fries and wished she had ordered what he had.

"When's your next fight?" Isaiah asked.

"We're sneaking one in," Charlie said. "Since Cory didn't exert too much energy on Tyrell Lewis in London he has one next week before he goes for the title next month."

"Interesting," Isaiah hummed. "Will that be enough time before the title fight? I mean, what if your next opponent gives you a rough ride. Will you have enough time to recover?"

Cory laughed. "The promoters want to raise my profile before I fight Alexander Eubanks for the championship. So they're throwing Ricky Rodriguez my way. That kid is so lame I can pick the round I'll knock him out in."

Charlie patted his hand. "Don't get too cocky. You know what happens to those who get overconfident."

"I also know what's going to happen to Rolly-Poly Rodriguez." The boxer balled up his fist and shook it at Isaiah. "Go ahead, Isaiah. Name a round."

"The third."

Cory grinned. "It'll be hard to keep the kid in the fight that long, but I'll carry him—just for you. Put some money on it."

Yvette leaned over her plate. "My husband doesn't bet."

"Too bad. He could have bought you a new purse, and shoes to go with it."

"He doesn't gamble, and if he did, I wouldn't wear blood money on my feet anyway."

Charlie nudged Cory. "Looks like we're dining with principals, mate. One headlines at the school, the other one wears them on her sleeve." She laughed, then winked at Isaiah.

Yvette's brows furrowed. "Is there something wrong with—"

"Where's the fight going to be?" Isaiah interrupted.

"Atlanta. We're using one of the fight venues from the '96 Olympics." Cory synchronized his air-punching and declared, "The good ole red, white, and blue."

Isaiah backed him up with a "Halleluiah!"

Yvette stood up. "If you'll excuse me, I'm going to the ladies' room before you two break out in a rendition of "God Bless America.""

Yvette was out of sight when Cory pulled out his oversized wallet, opened it up, and produced two tickets, holding them out. "Here's two tickets to the fight. Somehow I don't think your Missus is too keen on a ringside seat to see me beat someone up, but they're yours if you want them."

"Hmm ... I don't know. I'd like to, but ..."

"Go on, Isaiah," Charlie urged. "Have a night out with one of your mates. The fight is sold out. Whoever you take will owe you big time. May as well get a favor out of it if nothing else."

Isaiah took the tickets. "Since you put it like that." He leaned in. "But I'd appreciate it if you didn't mention it to Yvette. She is a pacifist of epic proportions. She doesn't understand man sports."

"Neither does my mom." Cory raised his glass for a toast. "To men being men ... scholars being scholastic ... and Ricky Rodriguez laying on his ass in round three."

Chapter 14

Isaiah walked into the kitchen and flipped on the switch for the electric kettle. "Would you like a cup of tea?" he asked Yvette.

"No thank you. I think I'll go up to bed. I have the auction tomorrow."

"You were quiet on the way home," he commented.

"I was trying that 'Silence is golden' routine you suggested."

"Don't be upset, darling. You know as well as I do that Cory Logan is a solid bet for raising a substantial amount of cash for the foundation. I'm not undermining you. I'm championing the David Marsh Foundation."

She put her hands on her hips. "Since when is nine thousand dollars chump change? I haven't even got going yet and you're shelving my ideas in favor of some bonehead boxer who may be brain-damaged. Are you sure he can even read and write?"

"He doesn't have to. All he has to do is speak."

Yvette looked down at the slate tiles. Her voice was just above a whisper. "I wanted to do this, Isaiah. I want to help, to support you. You're a good man, Isaiah Hightower." She stepped in and touched his hand. "Let me champion your vision along with you. We're a good team. I'm here for you—in any way you need."

"I know you are." He kissed her forehead. "Logan happened to come into the restaurant and I seized the moment. When God opens the door of opportunity, I'm going to answer it."

"That's fine. Just don't use me as your doormat."

"I'm not, baby. Accept the help I'm giving you."

"I don't want help, I want support."

"And that's all I want. Support."

"Good. I'm glad we're both looking for the same thing. Good night, Isaiah." She turned and walked out of the room, heading to bed.

He stayed in the kitchen and poured himself a cup of tea. Once Yvette's footsteps made it up the steps and the bedroom door closed he went into his office and got his burner phone out from behind the filing cabinet. He texted Alicia.

I will be in Atlanta next week. Let's meet.

Two minutes later a reply came back.

Hilton or Marriott??

Isaiah smiled. *Ur choice!*

***

Cory walked into the private function room of The Horseshoe Inn. About thirty people milled around, carrying on conversations that filled the air with a rambling buzz. Another ten people had already taken their seats waiting for the event to begin.

Cory found Yvette Hightower standing next to the stage studying some index cards she held.

"Hello, Mrs. Hightower. How are you on this fine Carolina afternoon?"

She glanced at him and managed to suppress her surprise to see him there. She returned her focus to the cards she held. "Oh, hello, Gary."

"Umm ... It's Cory."

"Of course. What can I do for you?"

"Actually, I was hoping I could do something for you."

She lifted her gaze from the index cards to him. "Oh?"

"I know your husband put you in charge of fundraising, and I heard about this auction, so I came straight to the chief. I'd like to help."

"I thought you were giving a speech that was going to raise millions."

Cory's dimples showed as he smiled. "I don't think a boxer can draw that kind of revenue from just speaking. Throwing punches maybe—"

Yvette shut him up with arching eyebrows.

"Never mind. No, I want to help, here and now."

"You do know this is a charity auction, right? People are donating their unpaid services for bids that will go directly to the foundation." She looked at an index card. "Doris Johnson is offering to walk your dog for a month." She shuffled the cards. "Tom Lazoff will perform six hours of handyman work. I reckon some widow will pay a few hundred for that." She moved another card to the top. "Amy Eichar is offering a therapeutic massage." She shuffled the cards. "So tell me, Cory, what's your specialty skill?"

"Training. I'd like to offer a week's training with me. It would be a serious workout and something the person could learn from to construct their own routine."

"So, you're not really sacrificing anything?"

135

He leaned forward. "Pardon me? You don't call training with a professional boxer a service worth paying for?"

"You're going to be training yourself anyway, aren't you? So it sounds to me like you're getting a workout partner for free. Maybe you need the motivation. You're not giving up your time, Mr. Logan. You're getting company for something you'd be doing anyway."

"Have I done something to offend you? I mean, I want to help you raise money for your cause—a good cause—and you basically accuse me of being lazy."

"I never accused you of being lazy."

"Lazy, lack of motivation—is there a difference?"

"I wouldn't know. I've never suffered from either. I've had to work damned hard for everything I've ever obtained. Harder than most. Something people like you would never understand."

Cory stepped closer. "And what kind of person would that be?"

"Privileged."

"You sure you don't mean white?"

"Don't be ridiculous. I have some white Facebook friends. Poor, hard-working, and decent."

"Let me tell you something, Mrs. Hightower. I chose a profession where I am a minority. I have to work harder to prove myself to be an equal in this sport, probably much like you think you have to work harder to prove yourself as an equal to your Hilton Head peers. But I do not cast aspersions about others in my sport because of race, color, or creed, yet you seem to think the color of my skin gives me a sense of entitlement and eliminates any hardships I may have to endure. I can assure you, it does not."

"How dare you compare your struggles to mine."

Cory held his hand up. "Never mind. Forget it. I can see our mindsets don't match and you obviously have trouble accepting help from someone you deem as 'privileged.' I withdraw my offer to provide services. And I suggest to you…" He pointed to her stack of index cards. "If there's a pledge in there for psychiatric help, take it. And if you need help paying for it …" He pulled out a hundred dollar bill. "Here. Donate that." He slapped it in her hand and walked away.

Yvette stood slack-jawed. She watched him exit the room. "Bastard," she mumbled.

Chapter 15

Isaiah and Alicia trekked up the steps of the noisy arena, making their way almost to the top row. Seeing the squared circle some light-years away was a strain, but Isaiah liked the idea of sitting in the gods. He was much less visible. He wasn't a well-known figure around Atlanta, but he was aware that his reputation proceeded him wherever he may travel. Being caught ringside on a TV camera would be an embarrassingly stupid move. The father bringing his fifteen-year-old son to the fight couldn't believe his luck when Isaiah offered him a trade—two ringside seats for two tickets in row 218. Straight swap.

Being new to boxing, and a relative novice to gambling, he wanted a taste of the spattered spit first hand and you couldn't get that from a TV screen. Dark Alleys only allowed a maximum bet of $1,000. Isaiah agreed with that policy. Dark Alleys' primary function was a club of lust. Betting was a side game and there was no point in sending the club into bankruptcy for fast dogs or blindingly quick knockout punches. He had borrowed $3,000 out of the David Marsh Foundation account. Charlie gave him the name of a Vegas bookie and he placed it all on a Logan KO in the third round which got him good odds. He could do a lot with the money he was set to win.

Alicia wiggled into her seat and fiddled with her sunglasses—lowering them, then pushing them up again. "Can I take these off now? I can't see a thing?"

"Yes," Isaiah whispered, "but be ready to put them back on if anybody comes up to me."

She draped herself on his arm. "This is so cool of you, Isaiah. Bringing me out in public like you're not ashamed of me. You don't know how good that makes me feel. Can we go away some time? There must be someplace we could go and act like a normal couple."

"We'll see."

He glanced around his surroundings. Although he didn't recognize anyone, he moved Alicia's arm to rest on his knee out of open view—yet still allowing for public touching of some description. Isaiah had brought Alicia as an aphrodisiac. Although it made him nervous, it also excited him. She loved public displays of anything: lust, affection, nudity. She had made that clear in past conversations. The risks he took now would transition into heightened sexual chemistry in the bedroom later. As Charlie pointed out, she would owe him big time.

If he did get recognized, he'd simply introduce her as a representative of the David Marsh Foundation, but he wanted to avoid encounters of that ilk if possible. That's why he insisted she wear a big floppy hat and sunglasses the size of small swimming pools. She may not be identified as his mistress, but there was little doubt that she was not Yvette. Anyone who knew him would know that.

"This is kind of funny," Alicia commented. "Our first outing as a couple and you bring me to a boxing match."

"Well, it is for the foundation." He winked.

"And here I thought you were bringing me to see alpha males in action to get me horny—as if I needed any extra stimulation. Being with you is enough to get me—"

He raced his finger to her lips. "You don't need to tell me." He pointed to the ring. "Look, it's about to start. Shh …"

"Ladies and gentlemen …" The ring announcer made the introductions followed by the referee giving the fighters instruction.

With the ringing of the opening bell, Isaiah suddenly felt like Pavlov's dog—having a bloodthirst for the first time in his life. Ten seconds into the fight and Cory delivered a right hand that sent a loud pop echoing through the arena. Deafening cheers rocked the place. Rodriguez wobbled and put his glove over his jaw. Cory brought a left uppercut into Ricky's gut that Isaiah felt in row 218. The boxer staggered into the ropes, struggling to stay upright.

Isaiah jumped to his feet. "No!" He shouted. "Stay up, you son-of-a-barbequer."

Alicia grabbed his arm and tugged him back into his seat. "I thought you wanted the white guy to win."

"I do, but not yet."

"What? That doesn't make any sense. Do you want to see the Mexican take a brutal beating first? I don't know about you, Isaiah. I thought you were a compassionate man for *all* human beings."

"Will you shut up? You don't understand."

"Shut up?" She stood up, glowering at Isaiah. "Did you just tell me to shut up?"

"Hey! Sit down, will ya?" the man behind her yelled.

She re-sat herself, arms folded firmly across her chest.

"He's got to make it to round three." He patted her knee. "Just be quiet."

"Shut up?" She mumbled. "Maybe you should try leading by example."

The rest of the first round went by with Logan doing more dancing than punching. Perhaps he was making good on his promise for Isaiah's sake. If Cory really could take Rodriguez whenever he wanted, Isaiah was impressed. Next time he'd bet more.

When the bell to start round two sounded, Cory came out of his corner with more resemblance to a ballerina than a prizefighter. He floated around the ring offering light jabs that the pudgy Mexican easily dodged. In turn, he avoided Rodriguez's punches with ease. The crowd turned ugly. Boos echoed within the arena with mixed cries of "wimp" and "pansy."

Alicia didn't seem bothered one way or the other. "You know what … I've been thinking about getting a car—"

Isaiah's face crinkled. "A car? This is no time for trivial conversations." He punched his fist into his hand in anticipation of some more action. "Pay attention to the fight."

Alicia looked toward the ring and offered her assessment. "I think I'd bet on the Mexican. That Logan guy doesn't look so good if you ask me."

"Well, no one's asking you," Isaiah grumbled. "We need Logan to flatten this guy in the next round or were leaving."

"But if Logan flattens him in this round, we'll be leaving anyway, right?"

Sometimes Isaiah hated the female sense of logic. It was so … obvious—lacking any sense of depth. He took a breath, then whispered in her ear. "If Logan knocks this guy out in round three, I'll get you a car. If he doesn't, I may need to borrow some cash from your tip stash." He looked at his investment—both of them. She said it herself that she was getting better tips since he enhanced her. Her breasts were plan B—or D, as it were—if Logan did happen to lose, but he still hoped he wouldn't have to go there.

Alicia shot to her feet. "You better knock that son-of-a-bitch out, Logan, or I'm coming after you myself," she shouted at the top of her voice.

Heads turned in her direction.

Isaiah ducked, shielding his face with his hands. Just what he needed. Attention being drawn to them. Yes, Alicia's logic was totally transparent. He'd need to take that into account next time he appealed to her "logical" side.

Boos continued to fill the arena as round two ended with next to no action whatsoever.

After their thirty-second break, the boxers came out of their corners to start round three.

Rodriguez opened with a right jab to Logan's jaw that staggered him. A crisp left followed, backing him onto the ropes. That brought Charlie Gillettie out of her seat, slapping her open palm on the canvas and shouting angrily.

"Mother of Jerusalem," Isaiah cried out.

Cory responded. With machine gun rapidity and sniper accuracy, Logan picked Rodriguez apart. Punch after punch landed on Ricky's face and body. Six right jabs to the abdomen followed by a left hook square on the jaw staggered him. Then a monster right cross connected flush on his face and Rodriguez went to the canvas—hard.

A fountain of red spray shot upwards from the impact. Blood soiled the white canvas from Rodriguez's face.

"One," the ref counted, standing over Rodriguez's body. "Two ..."

Cory moved away from the fallen body. He held his fists over his head victoriously, bouncing on his toes as he danced around the ring.

"Eight ... nine ... ten!" The referee waved his arms over his head frantically.

It was official. A Cory Logan knockout in the third round over Ricky Rodriguez.

Isaiah sprung to his feet. He turned and grabbed Alicia. Both of them jumping up and down in unison in each other arms. Smiling and shouting.

He did it. The white guy did it. Just like he said he would.

Isaiah liked him. Cory Logan was a man of his word. Isaiah was now a richer man and Alicia would no doubt show her gratitude in the most pleasing ways for the car he pledged to give her. Yes ... life was good.

Chapter 16

Isaiah drove the brand new Volvo SUV into the circular drive of his Vista Oaks home. He stepped out of the vehicle, pulled a handkerchief from his pocket, and buffed a fingerprint off the chrome door handle. He took a step back and admired his new acquisition.

He strolled into the house and made a cup of tea. Yvette sauntered in the kitchen giving her husband a warm smile and a kiss on the cheek.

"How was Atlanta and the conference?"

"The conference was good. Atlanta was bad."

"How's that?"

"You first. Everything okay here?"

"Yes, good. Remember that boxer who said he was fighting in Atlanta?"

Isaiah searched the ceiling for a moment. "I vaguely recall him mentioning it, yes. You didn't watch it, did you?"

"Don't be silly. Guess what? He knocked the other guy out in the third round, just like he told you he would. I saw it on the news."

"Did he really?"

"Talk about clairvoyant, or blind confidence—I'm not sure what it would be classed as, but imagine being able to predict when you can take an opponent out. Maybe you should have put some money on him. That would have been worth a pretty penny."

"I'm sure it would have been." A sly grin spread across his lips. "Wait a minute. Is my wife suggesting I take up gambling?"

"No." Her head drooped conveying her shame at the immoral submission. "It's just that I keep thinking about going to Hawaii ..." She raised her head. "And how a nice little windfall might be the ticket—" She stopped and pointed out the window. "What in blue blazes is that?"

Isaiah looked at the new Volvo. "Oh ... Surprise! I was going to tell you—"

"What? You did not buy a new car."

"I have good news and bad news."

She pointed at the car. "Is that the good news or bad?"

"Both. I didn't want to worry you, but the Voyager got stolen in Atlanta."

"Stolen? You can't be serious. What the—? Why didn't you tell me?"

He stepped in and put his arms around her. "Because there wasn't anything anyone could do. I filed a police report, got in contact with the insurance company, and got it sorted out."

"You bought a car without me?"

He took Yvette by the hand. "How else was I going to get home?"

"But why didn't you—"

He tugged her toward the door. "Come on. Let's take it for a spin."

Once on the driveway, Yvette folded her arms across her chest as she dug in her resistance—physically as well as emotionally. "I cannot believe you bought a car without me."

"But it's a Volvo. That's what you always wanted, right?"

She glanced at the car from the sides of her eyes, not wanting him to notice her looking at it. She wanted to look pissed, not pleased. "But I didn't even get a say in the color."

He swept his arm toward the car. "Blue, your favorite color."

A smile briefly pushed its way past her anger. He was right. She did want a blue Volvo, but it was still a shock. She liked the Voyager, but it was more a suburban white guy's car. A Volvo was better suited for his principal image. She forced her lips to flat-line, not wanting him to think he'd get off the hook that easy. "Where'd you get the money? Don't tell me you put the down payment on the credit card. Do you know how much interest they charge?"

He wrapped his arms around her. "I told you. I organized it with the insurance company."

"That quick? Don't they have to try to find the stolen car first?"

"They were supposed to give us a rental car for a month, but I persuaded them to skip that step because it would just cost them more money in the end."

Yvette looked puzzled. "But don't they have to—"

Isaiah rolled his eyes, getting bored with the inquisition. "Look, I used the Hightower charm. We've been with them for years and I sweet-talked Ramona. She was happy to help."

She wagged her finger at him. "I knew Ramona had a thing for you. I guess I shouldn't be surprised you managed to charm her." She stepped forward and poked him in the chest. "Just make sure insurance is the only thing you and Ramona talk about."

"Of course. I'll stick to the boring stuff with her." He hugged her. "So you want to go for a ride while it still has that new car smell?"

Deep down she was happy. Isaiah took a bad situation and turned it around to please his wife. Her husband was something else. "Why not? I guess we better stop somewhere and pick up an ABBA tape." She grinned.

"Sure." They hopped in the car and buckled up. "You just wait. This car will make you feel Bjorn again."

***

"Boys and girls ..." Isaiah stood in front of the packed auditorium. Except for a few football jocks flirting with the cheerleaders, he had the school's undivided attention. "We have a special guest today. We have a future world boxing champion to speak to you about life choices. Cory 'Incorrigible' Logan is going to offer insight into career selection. Not only do I want you to listen, I also want you to tell your parents that he will be speaking at the Hilton Head Civic Center this Friday night. Tickets are still available. He's helping us to raise money for your former classmate David Marsh's foundation to help other youngsters. Not only is he raising money for a good cause, but it's also your chance to get your parents out of the house on Friday night." His pitch sent a ripple of murmurs among the students. He knew if there was one thing teenagers wanted on a Friday night it was their parents out of the way. What a way to sell tickets. "Here he is, Cory Logan."

Principal Hightower led the applause.

Cory stepped up to the mic. "Hello, future alumni."

"Hello," the students barked back.

147

"My career path was looking like an arranged marriage. My dad is a surgeon, my mom is a dentist, so it seemed only natural that I entered a profession that helped people. Instead, I beat the crap out of guys for millions of dollars ..."

The gymnasium erupted with cheers, whoops, laughter, and deafening feet stomping on the bleachers.

Isaiah sat back and listened—amused, mostly. Cory connected with the kids. It wasn't the kind of message the principal himself would have advocated, but it was a message about being true to oneself and following your dream—your own dream, not a perception that has been bestowed upon you by society, parents, or expectations. He could respect that. Judging by the way Cory held the youngsters' attention there was little doubt Friday would be a sellout. Isaiah could imagine dinner table conversations all over the island tonight. *Mom, Dad, you* have *to go listen to this guy!*

Cory finished his talk just over a half an hour after he started, at Isaiah's pre-speech request. It was okay for Mom and Dad to listen to an hour speech, but students needed to get back to learning. This was a teaser for them, and to *sell those tickets*.

After the speech, Isaiah led Cory through the halls back to his office. Betty brought Isaiah his coffee and Cory a bottle of sparkling mineral water along with a glass of ice and a slice of lemon.

"Great speech, Cory. I can tell you're an educated man. I hope the kids got that as well."

"As opposed to a boxer on the edge of mental vegetable-ism." He grinned. "It was my pleasure."

Isaiah tipped his head to one side. "Your parents are both professional people? That's unusual for a fighter, isn't it?"

"Yes, that's what I tried to tell Mrs. Hightower. I'm not your typical boxer, but she didn't seem that interested."

Isaiah waved his hand around. "Once she discovered you were a white guy that beats up black people it was game over."

Cory laughed. "At least you have a sense of humor about it."

"It's no joke. It stirs up—"

Cory put his hand up. "No need to explain. I get it. But I am puzzled why she doesn't want me to help."

Isaiah suppressed the urge to elucidate. The past was the past and it has nothing to do with Cory Logan. "She had a little luck raising some money and now she thinks she's Rockefeller."

"So why wouldn't she let me help with her auction?"

"Say what?"

"I think this David Marsh Foundation is a great idea. I wanted to do more. So I offered Mrs. Hightower my training services to auction off, and she accused me of looking for a free training partner. She said that I would be the one getting the benefit."

Isaiah's nostrils flared. "She did what? She never said anything to me about that."

"She basically told me to take a hike. It just hit me as strange that someone trying to raise money would turn down an offer to train with a professional boxer." He shrugged. "In future, I'll

149

approach you instead of Mrs. Hightower. I think she wants to be left to do things her way."

Isaiah still had a face of confusion. "She turned away your help?"

Cory confirmed with a dip of the head. "Don't say anything to Charlie, I haven't told her. Besides getting shunned, she'd be mad if she thought I was giving away my time and getting distracted from my training. Charlie thinks you are an awesome man doing an incredible thing, but she doesn't like me getting out of my training cycle or doing freebies."

Isaiah nodded modestly. "Thank you, and I understand her concerns."

The men sipped their drinks and enjoyed a moment of silence. Men could do that. Enjoy each other's company without having to fill the air with words. Personalities can flourish in stillness. Sometimes Isaiah liked to pick up on people's vibes, not words. Cory had a calmness and confidence in him. He didn't have to say it—it was just present.

"Do you have your speech ready for Friday night?"

Cory nodded. "Charlie wrote most of it. She doesn't like it when I say I get paid millions to beat people up. She softened it up to make it more parent-friendly. A little less aggression is probably a good thing."

"Charlie seems to have her head screwed on pretty straight."

Cory offered a crooked smile. "She's a bulldog. You don't want to tangle with her. Do you know why she goes by Charlie?"

Isaiah shrugged. "Charlene? Charlotte?"

"Gladys."

Isaiah scrunched his face. "Say what?"

"Her mom was a big Gladys Knight and the Pips fan. She always hated that name, and as a young girl growing up she was picked on all the time. Kind of like me, she took to fighting and liked it. But rather than fight for free, she would arrange fights and make the kids pay to watch. Can you imagine a twelve-year-old girl promoting her own fights and making money at it? She was a genius."

Isaiah laughed. "I'd say so. Geez. I've been in education for over twenty-five years and never produced a boxing promoter—and she did it herself. Impressive. Please don't tell that story to any of my students. That's all I need—pay-per-view fights at the Hilton Head High School gymnasium."

"No worries. It'll be our secret. Anyway … she liked the promoting side so much she took it up as a profession, but there were two problems. No fighter, myself included, would want a manager/promoter named Gladys. And the other promoters would not respond to or talk to a woman trying to promote a fight, let alone a woman named Gladys. So she legally changed her name to Charlie. When promoters starting seeing Charlie on papers, they just assumed it was a man and she started getting fights. Now she's established herself as a top promoter."

"That's an amazing story. And you two never, you know …"

"Nope. Strictly professional, but mind you, she sometimes does act like a wife. 'Do this, don't do that,'" he mocked. "And by the way, Charlie might be happy with you, but I'm pretty pissed off."

"I'll talk to Yvette. That was wrong what—"

"Forget the auction. Man, the Bare Trap? That was my outlet and you had it closed down. Why?"

A brief smile appeared before Isaiah returned to solemnness. "Have you heard of Rodney Harris?"

Cory looked puzzled for a moment and then nodded, albeit un-assuredly. "That name sounds familiar."

"He was a nineteen-year-old African American who was shot and killed by police. Okay, the kid was committing a robbery, but he was unarmed. Rodney's father wanted me to raise awareness and bring the police tactics into question. But before I could ..." Isaiah leaned forward. "Rodney's sister was a stripper at the Bare Trap. The father didn't want that getting out. He was afraid, and I agreed, that the police may try to divert attention from their actions by bringing the entire family into disrepute. One doesn't get as much sympathy if the whole family looks like degenerates."

"So you just put your Billy Graham hat on, and voilà. The closed sign goes up."

"Not quite. I played the race card."

The boxer smirked. "Don't tell me they wouldn't let you in because of your color."

Isaiah smiled. "No, but there were only two minorities dancing out of twenty-three. If you ever want to force a government agency into action, accuse an establishment of discrimination."

Cory stroked his jaw. "I do remember a black girl there."

"That would have been her."

"And no one ever found out about Rodney's sister?"

"I gave the council an out. Instead of crying discrimination, I suggested some of my students cited their life ambition as being dancers there, so we could say it was to save the students of my nearby school from being influenced by its immorality. There would be less digging that way. Otherwise, the media would want to find out who the minority dancer was."

"So my pleasure is being deprived because of color imbalance?"

Isaiah grinned. "Leave it with me. I think I can hook you up. Do you like Savannah?"

"It's okay."

"Good. I'll fill you in later, and we won't tell Charlie."

Cory rubbed his hands together. "I like the sound of that."

"Do thank her for putting you forward to help raise money for my foundation. I can't thank you enough. Both of you. And I'll have a word with Yvette."

"No worries. I'm looking forward to Friday. I hope I can raise a bundle for you."

"Me too, champ. Me too."

Chapter 17

"I think Isaiah gave me my bargaining chip," Yvette concluded. "Whether he likes it or not, Hawaii is getting closer." She took a solid nip of her Chardonnay.

Gloria Huntington agreed. "I can't argue with you there. I'd even say that Isaiah let you have that chip on purpose. What man would buy a new car without consulting his wife and not expect consequences?"

"He even let me buy a lottery ticket, which he had always put on the same plateau as gambling. You know, throwing away a small sum of money in hopes of a big payout, but the odds are stacked ninety-nine percent against you."

Gloria cocked an eyebrow. "Really? Where's the sin in that? I would assume if you won he would insist on giving ten percent to the church."

Yvette let out a satisfying sigh. "But in the end, he did get the car and the color I wanted. I keep telling him he should convert to Catholicism and run for Pope."

Romeo set her Cobb salad sprinkled with sesame seeds in front of her. "Will there be anything else, Mrs. Hightower?"

"Not at the moment, thanks, Romeo."

He turned his attention to Gloria. "And for you, Mrs. Huntington?"

"I'm fine, gorgeous. Thank you."

The waiter dipped his head, smiled, and walked off.

Yvette leaned over the table. "You can't call him 'Gorgeous,' Gloria. That's insulting."

"Why's that? A fire-breathing, alpha, female can't tell a homosexual man he's gorgeous? Give me strength. What's the world coming to?"

Yvette smiled. Not out of agreement, but amusement. Gloria would never change. Romeo was lucky he was gay or she'd eat him for breakfast.

"You mentioned this Cory Logan guy on the phone earlier." Gloria sprinkled some salt on her soup. "What's got you all worked up about him?"

"He's an arrogant, ignorant, asshole, bastard."

"Yvette Hightower! Using language like that. And you the wife of a deacon. Shame on you."

She hung her head in mock shame. But Cory Logan was a bastard and she wasn't going to let a little shame, real or not, get in the way of her rant. "He thinks he has more obstacles than black boxers. How dare he? Has he ever even been to the Hood where you fight for survival and street cred?"

Gloria didn't even look up from her salmon bisque. "Have you?"

Yvette slapped her hand on the table. "Of course not. Do I look like a ghetto queen? But I've done research and I've spent time with people from the Hood. I know what it's like."

Gloria raised a spoonful of deliciousness to her mouth. "Have you spent much time with white people?" She sucked the soup off her spoon. "White people who might not be racist?"

"Of course. My dad was a courier for FedEx. He knew lots of white people."

Gloria focused on Yvette—eye to eye—with total intensity. "That wasn't my question. I'll ask you again. Do you have disdain for white people?"

Yvette grabbed her napkin off her lap and dabbed the sides of her mouth. "You know me better than that. I'm not a racist."

"Then why do you hate this guy so much?"

She poked at her salad, her eyes focused on a crouton. "I never told you I had a brother?"

Gloria leaned in. "No, you haven't. Gay?"

"No." With a deep breath, she raised her head to engage Gloria's intrigued expression. "You didn't know me before I married Isaiah, but my maiden name is Tyson. And my dad *loved* boxing. So much so that he named my little brother Michael."

Gloria bobbed her head. "Okaaay ..."

"Michael? Mike? Mike Tyson? Not surprisingly, Mike Tyson became a target. When he was in fifth grade, there was a sixth-grader named Robert Marciano. Unsurprisingly, his nickname was Rocky. It was decided by the Berwyn Elementary School bullies that a fight between 'Rocky' Marciano and Mike Tyson would be a classic." Yvette stopped to dab her welled-up eyes with a napkin.

Gloria extended a comforting hand for Yvette to take should she need it.

Yvette stared at her friend with tears running down her cheeks. "Rocky won. Michael was taken to the hospital with brain contusions and hemorrhaging, but the damage was too severe. He died three days later." She straightened her back and wiped away falling tears with a shaking hand. "Michael didn't even like fighting," she said defiantly.

Gloria covered her open jaw-dropped mouth with her hand. "Oh my God …"

Yvette regained her composure with a quick sniffle.

Gloria stroked Yvette's arm. "I'm so sorry. I had no idea."

"It's not something I like to talk about, but now you know."

"I'm guessing Rocky was white to boot."

Yvette nodded. "With a rich white dad whose rich white lawyer claimed it was a playground scrap that Michael instigated. Of course, it's always the black kid who starts the fight."

"So this Rocky kid … he didn't get charged?"

"Ha," Yvette huffed sarcastically. "Since Michael's beating was so bad the judge ordered Robert to attend anger management classes. Of course, that was to show the Tyson family that the judge felt our pain and it would give young Marciano a chance to reform—although none of this was his fault—and he would denounce any and all violence in the future." Yvette folded her arms across her thin frame, jerking her head to one side and staring out the window. "I hope that little shit rots in hell, escorted by his hotshot lawyer."

Gloria put her hand to her chest, feeling her friend's pain. "Yvette, that's tragic … I'm so sorry, but that was one screwed up kid. You can't blame a whole race—"

Yvette held her hand up. "I don't want to talk about it."

The rhythm of a British accent broke the moment. "Hello, Mrs. Hightower." Charlie Gillettie stood at the end of the table. "I wanted to say hi and thank you again for inviting me and Cory to join you and your delightful husband for dinner at Luciano's. That was very kind of you. Ta."

Yvette turned, and after split-second eye contact, she nodded. "You're welcome. Enjoy your lunch." Yvette picked up her fork and stabbed her Cobb salad—spearing a chunk of chicken and popping it in her mouth.

Gloria's gaze shifted between her friend and the pretty blonde. Her eyes finally landed on Yvette. "Aren't you going to introduce me?"

Yvette drew a deep breath. She flicked a hand toward Charlie. "Charlie, this is Gloria." She reversed the gesture. "Gloria, this is Charlie." She took another stab at her salad. "I can recommend the Cobb salad, Charlie. Well, we don't want to hold you up. Enjoy." The lettuce leaves found her mouth quickly after the introduction, ending the conversation—or so she hoped.

Gloria's finger swished the air between the women, trying to connect them. "How do you two know each other?"

"We met at dinner the other week," Charlie said. "Mrs. Hightower and Isaiah were kind enough to invite us to join them at their table."

Gloria poked her fork in Charlie's direction. "I've dined out a lot with Yvette and she doesn't make a habit of inviting random people to join her at her table. And who's us?"

Charlie shifted on her feet, prompting Gloria to pat the chair next to her.

"Please, sit," she invited Charlie.

Charlie looked at Yvette, who rolled her eyes.

"If that's okay," Charlie said, looking at Yvette.

"Free country," Yvette quipped before another lettuce leaf was soon between her jaws.

"Any friend of Yvette's is a friend of mine," Gloria insisted.

"I never said she was a friend," Yvette muttered.

As soon as Charlie sat down Romeo appeared. "Shall I bring you the amenities for dining at this table, madam?"

Charlie sought Gloria's attention. "Am I joining you for lunch or just here for a chinwag?"

"A what?"

"A chat. Am I eating or talking?"

"Let's try doing both."

Gloria and Charlie laughed. Yvette plunged the tines of her fork with dagger force into her salad.

"Can I have a cheeseburger and a beer? Blue Moon, if you have it."

"Of course, madam," Romeo confirmed before promptly disappearing.

Gloria leaned back and eyed her up and down. "Girl? How do you stay so thin eating junk like that?"

"She eats a lot of mushrooms," Yvette muttered.

Gloria and Charlie gave her an odd look, then ignored it.

"I skip rope with my client," Charlie answered.

Gloria put her hand on Charlie's shoulder. "Let's back up. Square one. Shoot."

Yvette slammed her fork on the table. "Charlie is the manager, or concubine, for that bonehead boxer. They came into Luciano's and Isaiah felt sorry for them because the multi-millionaire bone-crusher had to sit next to the kitchen. So he extended them an invitation to sit with us."

Gloria rolled her head toward heaven then back again. "Oh, I see ..." She touched Charlie's leg, lowering her voice as she leaned in. "You weren't at the table in the corner that overlooked everything, were you?"

"No," Yvette snapped. "We were. Isaiah and me. Then Isaiah went chasing money for this trust, but he didn't have to chase very hard because Miss Charlie here offered herself—" she stopped and took a sip of wine creating a suggestive pause," ... and her boyfriend's services."

The table fell quiet for a moment.

Charlie stared at a stone-faced Yvette but didn't return fire.

Gloria broke the awkwardness. "Oh? How come you didn't tell me about this?" she asked Yvette, then turned to Charlie. "That's very generous of you. And who's your boyfriend?"

Charlie pried her glare from Yvette and addressed Gloria. "I think this foundation Isaiah set up is a marvelous idea. Cory Logan's a professional boxer, and I'm his manager. We wanted to help, and he's not my boyfriend. Just a title-contending client."

Yvette stared until Charlie engaged eyes with her. "I'm sure my husband values your opinion very highly. I'll be sure to tell him you approve of his work."

Romeo returned and placed Charlie's cheeseburger in front of her. "Would you care for any—"

Charlie shooed him away. She leaned forward over the freshly delivered burger. "Have I done something to offend you, Mrs. Hightower? Because if I have, I apologize. But all I know is your husband

160

invited me and Cory to dine with you. And we did. When your husband asked Cory to deliver the speech to the students, I thought that was very admirable, but that wasn't going to raise any money, now was it? I wanted to help. I was doing you and your husband a favor. This is the second time someone from your table has invited me to join you, yet you spit venom my way every time. What's your game?"

"My game, Miss Gillettie, is to make my husband happy. I do that in various ways—and besides the obvious, one of those ways is through fundraising. Now you and your over-privileged boyfriend come waltzing in, hijacking my efforts, all so you can get some free publicity and a free training partner."

"Excuse me, Hightower, I don't know what the hell you're talking about. I get eighteen percent of all of Cory's earnings. I threw you a freebie. That's eighteen percent of nothing. I didn't realize it was important *who* raised the money. Well, good luck, lady." Charlie stood up. "Just for the record, Cory is not my boyfriend, but I keep him on a tight lead. I'll be sure to keep him well away from you and your husband, and your efforts." She nudged her cheeseburger toward Yvette. "Enjoy the burger. Don't forget to tip the waiter."

Charlie stormed out of the restaurant.

Gloria sat wide-eyed. "Wow. What got into you? She seemed like a nice girl."

"You mean besides stealing my thunder? And she was eyeing Isaiah up all through dinner. Giving him that British accent and hanging those jugs over her Portobello mushrooms. The man couldn't help but look. I couldn't either! It was a sad display. Sad."

161

Gloria pulled back, frowning. "What are you even talking about? The girl was trying to help you and Isaiah and you're worried about her mushrooms? Whatever the heck that means."

Yvette swatted the air. "Never mind. But I don't like big-boobed, blonde, British, bimbos sniffing around my husband. Good causes or not."

"I think you need to dial down on that angry knob. She seemed genuine to me. Take the help while it's there if you really care about this David kid." Gloria took a sip of her wine, pinkie extended, ending the lecture.

***

Isaiah sat in his comfy leather chair waiting for Yvette to come home. He had been having a good day—a very good day until he heard about Yvette's auction—then he got that phone call. The glass of ice-cold lemonade sitting on the mahogany side table could quench his thirst but it could not cool his anger. But he was a rational man. He'd hear her explanation before he unleashed his wrath. A woman scorned had nothing on Isaiah irritated.

The front door opened and the synchronized rhythm of the heels and toes of stilettos announced Yvette's entrance. She walked into the living room and sat on the brown velour couch opposite Isaiah.

A quick upturn of the corners of her mouth was her subtle hello. "How was your day?"

"Good, very good," Isaiah responded. "Cory Logan gave his speech at school today. The kids loved it."

"That's nice."

"Then ... he told me you declined to let him help at your auction."

She remained indifferent. "I didn't need his help."

Isaiah scooted forward, perching on the edge of his chair. "Then, after we laid all the groundwork to sell bundles of tickets for his fundraising speech, I got a phone call."

"Oh?"

"Yes. From Charlie Gillettie."

"Still sniffing, was she?"

"What? Oh, never mind. She said Cory wasn't able to give the fundraising speech and if I had any questions as to why I should ask my wife. So, I'm asking."

Her face steeled. "Okay, I don't like that boxer and I don't like her. She barged in on me and Gloria having lunch, bragging about how she manages this Logan guy, so I knocked her down a peg or two. And I don't like her trying to get her meat hooks into you. So there." She folded her arms across her chest. "Besides, we don't need them. I can raise the money. Hand me back the reins and I'll get you all the money you need."

"So this is about you?"

"No, it's not about me, it's about Dan—"

"You don't even know the boy's name!"

"Whatever the boy's name is—it's about him—but it should be about me. You gave me a challenge so let me answer the call without self-promoting celebrities climbing aboard for causes they know nothing about." She stood up, looking down on him. "I love you, Isaiah Hightower, and would do anything in the world for you. I've always supported you in everything you've done and will continue to do so. But this is my gig, so let me gig it my way— and without that English tramp trying to butter your muffin." She turned and walked out, much to Isaiah's disbelief.

"We need forty thousand dollars and I have to refund Logan's ticket sales," he called out behind her. "You're not going to get that kind of money with speed golf!" He studied the wood floor. "Where in Shakespeare's name did that come from?" he mumbled. "What does that even mean, butter my muffin?"

He sat stunned for several moments before pulling out his phone and scrolling through the numbers.

"Hello? ... Cory? Isaiah Hightower. I wonder if we can meet up. Maybe we can make a deal ..."

Chapter 18

Isaiah sat at the back of Ace Arabica's coffeehouse waiting for Cory. The last booth on the left offered a small amount of privacy in the busy shop, away from the hustle and bustle of the customers lined up waiting to give their order at the counter. He watched with amusement as a cute redhead ordered her skinny latte or whatever it was while simultaneously texting what must have been seventy-five words a minute. He was impressed.

Cory skirted sideways through the crowd, briefly stopping to pick out a bottle of sparkling mineral water from the open cooler on his way through.

He slipped in the booth opposite. "Hello, Isaiah."

"Hello, Cory. Thanks for meeting me."

"That's okay." A small *shiff* escaped as he twisted the cap of his mineral water followed by a refreshing *ahh* from his gulp that followed. "I feel bad pulling out of the speech at the civic center, but boy was Charlie pissed. And when Charlie's pissed, I duck. She is one person you don't want to cross swords with."

Isaiah cocked his head to one side. "Yes, so you've said. What's her side of the story? What got her so angry, exactly?"

"In a word, Mrs. Hightower. Your wife is mightily upset with me and Charlie for upstaging her. We thought we were doing you a favor, but apparently, your wife feels we insulted her ability to raise money. At least that's how Charlie read the situation. She didn't realize it was a competition."

"It's not, or shouldn't be. Yvette needs to learn she doesn't have to do everything herself. Anyway …" He waved his hand around. "She's never going to raise the money we need by August on her own, so I was wondering if you could help."

"I would've been happy to help, but we tried that remember? You know I said I don't want to upset Charlie? Well, I don't want to upset Mrs. Hightower either. She seems to be a formidable force herself. And Charlie doesn't allow me to make donations. 'It'll only open up the floodgates' she says."

"I get that," Isaiah said, "and she's right. Don't worry about Yvette. She doesn't need to know about this. I need a favor."

"Doesn't need to know about what? I didn't give a speech, my time was rejected, and I'm not giving a donation. What else can I do? And if I did do anything, it would be hard to keep it quiet. Dammit, I miss my privacy. Charlie was willing for me to give a speech to help you, of course, but she also wanted it for my own publicity. She has a good business brain and she won't be happy if there's not some self-promotion in it for me. In fact, she'd be livid."

"Did you say something about privacy? Or lack of it?"

"Yes, the lack of it."

"What if I can get you some privacy?"

Cory sighed. "I'd do anything for a little of my own space. It's a pain in the ass living your life in the limelight. Sometimes I'd like to just be an average Joe that no one recognizes. I miss that."

"What if I can get you that? A place where you're anonymous. A place where you can indulge in pleasures away from the public eye."

"This isn't some funny religion or cult, is it?"

Isaiah laughed. "Far from it. It's a gentlemen's club and all members have to be invited by another member in good standing with the club. We all sign non-disclosure agreements—enforceable by an old-fashioned system greater than the law."

"Sounds interesting. What's the catch?"

"There's no catch. We're all respectable members of the community, many high profile, who want to keep our reputations intact. Confidentiality is our highest priority." He leaned forward and whispered, "And it will help replace the absence of the Bare Trap. Interested?"

Cory moved closer. "Does a bear shit in the woods?"

Isaiah smiled. "There's a joining fee."

"How much?"

"Ten grand."

"And it's sworn secrecy?"

"Guaranteed."

"What are we swearing secrecy to?"

"Girls, gambling, betting, drinking … the usual fabric of manly pleasures. But no drugs."

"Sounds like fun. Is this in Hilton Head?"

Isaiah shook his head. "No, Savannah."

He wagged his finger. "Ah, yes, is this what you mentioned earlier?

Isaiah nodded.

"Sounds great! Can I get a tour?"

"If I get you in, can you do something for me?"

"Depends what it is."

"I need a prediction."

Cory closed his eyes and placed his first two fingers against each temple. "I predict Charlie nor Mrs. Hightower would like what we're talking about."

"Okay, I'll give you a point for your clairvoyance. Now give me a point for your ability to predict."

Cory squinted. "Predict what?"

"That was a great fight against Rodriguez. Can you always name the round you're going to knock an opponent out it?"

Cory leaned in and spoke softly. "Umm ... *you* named the round, remember?" A knowing smile crossed his lips.

Isaiah smiled back. "Yes, yes I did. Could you do it again? If I picked a round?"

Cory grinned as he shook his head. "So you did have a bet on me."

The principal nodded.

"I thought Mrs. Hightower said you didn't gamble."

"I don't usually, but you sounded too convincing to ignore. And Mrs. Hightower doesn't know *everything* I do. I like my privacy too." He grinned. "Besides, I put the money I won toward a good cause."

The boxer chuckled. "To tell you the truth, I did carry him to round three just in case you had a bet."

"Thanks. So can you?" Isaiah asked again.

Cory shook his head. "No, not really. Rodriguez was a journeyman, and yeah, I was confident I could take him when I wanted to.

Eubanks is different. He's a world champion. I may need to adapt my strategy as the fight develops. Sorry, Isaiah, I'm a boxer, not a bookie."

"But you're confident of a win over the next guy, right?"

"Eubanks? If I wasn't one hundred plus percent confident before every fight, I'd have no business in the ring. No fighter is there to pussyfoot around. I'm the best fighter in the business, and I'd bet you my Ferrari that any boxer you asked would say the same thing."

"So this Eubanks guy … when do you think you'll take him? Early, middle or end."

Cory smiled. "You're determined to place a bet, aren't you?"

"It's kind of fun."

"And risky. Let me ask you this, what would you do with the winnings?"

"Put it toward good causes, of course."

"Then why enlist me to help with fundraising at all? I mean, why not just gamble to raise money."

"I said I was going to put it toward good causes, not donate it to charity."

"Oh, I see …" Cory leaned back. "Would Mrs. Hightower be considered a good cause?"

"She might be."

Cory nodded. "What's her pleasure? Jewelry? Clothes? Pampering?"

Isaiah laughed. "All of the above. But right now she's going on about a trip to Hawaii."

Cory scooted forward in his seat. "Then you know what? Forget all this betting crap. That's high risk asking me to deliver a preset round knockout. What I can do for you—I have a little oceanfront house in Kauai. If you want to borrow it sometime, let me know. It's very private. She'd love it."

"No! I mean, no thank you. She'd want some posh hotel in the heart of Waikiki." He placed his fingertips on his chest. "Me personally, I would love some time away in seclusion, but I can't see that happening."

"Well, if you change your mind, let me know. If you want it for a week or two I'll get you the keys."

Isaiah gave a single nod. "Thanks, I'll bear that in mind. Now, what round do you think you'll take Eubanks out?"

Cory laughed. "I gotta hand it to you. You don't give up."

"There's a lot at stake. I have to keep Mrs. H. happy, of course, but I also need money for the David Marsh Foundation. God love her, but Yvette can't raise that kind of money on her own. Perhaps I can top up her efforts with a knockout in round …" Isaiah edged forward in his seat. His eyes begging for a prediction. Anything. A hope. A prayer. *An ever-loving prediction! Please!*

Cory conceded a nod. "Okay. I'll try, but keep it light. No more than five hundred, okay?"

Isaiah nodded feverishly while he salivated. "What round, champ?"

"I've studied Eubanks. If he doesn't get an early knockout he flags in the middle rounds. Let's go for seven."

"And you think you can do that?" Isaiah asked, searching for reassurance.

The force of Cory's nods increased. "Sure, why not. As you said, it's fun."

Isaiah nestled back into the booth, grinning broadly. "Seven. God's holy number. I like it. Good call."

"If you have connections with the man upstairs, let's use it. Halleluiah."

Isaiah gave a fist pump. "Halleluiah, brother!"

Chapter 19

"Hickory dickory dock, the mouse is on the block."

The oak door creaked open allowing Isaiah and Cory to slip inside.

Cory's heart raced as he looked ahead to the dark velvet curtain separating the inner sanctum. He had some explaining to do to Charlie as to why he had withdrawn $10,000 in cash. Although she always had his best interest at heart, it was his money. If he wanted to pay cash for his mom's tummy tuck for her birthday gift he should be able to. That's the kind of gift that demands the respect of silence—and Charlie duly vowed to never question Mrs. Logan about her birthday present. Cory didn't like lying to Charlie, but he reckoned it was a good one and congratulated himself for being inventive.

He smiled as Madonna singing "Like a Virgin" drifted through the air. *Not likely.* If it was, he'd demand his money back. He never considered himself a degenerate, but when his career was beginning to take off, he was caught on someone's cell phone coming out of a liquor store at 9 a.m. The tabloids had a field day portraying the promising young boxer as a raging alcoholic.

Then, when his best friend's bachelor party ended up in a brothel, stories circulated that Cory Logan was not only a drunk, but a man-whore as well. That escapade ended a lucrative endorsement contract with an underwear company, and Charlie lowered the boom, tightening her grip on his personal life. Their relationship was always strictly business, but she would not tolerate her biggest client imploding on lack of morality issues when his earning life would probably end around the age of thirty-five—and he was fast approaching his best before date. It wouldn't be long before he could do what the hell he wanted. In the meantime, she wanted to make sure he made plenty of money for retirement while he still had the drawing power to make big money.

Cory couldn't argue with any of her decisions. She had been right every time about everything and made him a ton of cash. But he missed the fun.

Isaiah pulled the curtain to one side. *It's Cory time.*

The boxer stepped through and was not disappointed. A Korean girl massaged her breasts on the stage, licking her lips as she scoured the darkened room. Her prominence was highlighted by her space being the only area in the room lit up except for a few dim fake candles on the tables where patrons drooled in darkness. Cory liked that. Although he had signed the confidentiality agreement swearing to never divulge any of the happenings at Dark Alleys or ever reveal the identity of any other member, the darkness added to the security that he would not be recognized if he merely took a seat and quietly enjoyed the show.

Isaiah nudged him and pointed to a vacant table in the middle of the room. "Have a seat. A waitress will be around in a minute to take your order. I'll be back in a little while."

"Can I get you anything?"

Isaiah was gone before Cory finished the question.

True to Isaiah's forecast, a waitress had promptly showed up and returned moments later with his beer—another one of life's little pleasures Charlie disapproved of while he was in training.

A third of the way into his beer, the Korean girl left the stage, replaced by an attractive black girl.

The dark girl slinked onto the stage with a pink terrycloth towel in hand. After swishing the towel around her head, she wiped the pole with it. He was impressed. A stripper concerned with pole hygiene. He liked that.

She looked to be in her early twenties with round, fully developed breasts. He preferred thinking of them as developed instead of artificially enhanced but they were causing loin growth no matter which words he applied. She removed her skimpy bikini top, which was three cups too small anyway. He was transfixed by this beautiful girl willing to take her clothes off to earn a buck. And he was willing to give her that buck to watch.

He ignored his beer as the girl danced, wrapping herself around the brass pole in the middle of the stage with elastic ninja-type movements. When she arched her back, pushing her breasts toward the crowd, a barrage of dollar bills floated through the air and found their way to the edge of the stage. It was a rousing show of approval for her athleticism—and her nakedness.

Cory adjusted his trousers and enjoyed the girl's performance to the end. He waited until she left the stage before taking a swig a beer, lest he might have missed a second of her nudity while his head was in reverse tilt.

174

As a new dancer arrived on stage, Cory looked around the room wondering where Isaiah had gone. Not that he was overly concerned. The beer was cold and the girls were hot. A vow of secrecy shrouded the entertainment. What more could a red-blooded, recognizable man want?

As he digested his extreme good fortune in being introduced to the club, the cute black dancer who had just left the stage sat in the chair next to him—fully clothed—albeit scantily clad.

"Did you enjoy the show?" she asked.

"Damn straight I did. You're quite the talent."

"Thanks. You know, a girl works up quite a thirst doing that. Any chance you might—"

Cory held up his hand, cutting her off. "Say no more." A gesture to the waitress summoned her over where she took the dancer's order for a glass of wine. When she returned the waitress asked Cory for twenty dollars to cover the tab. He didn't question the outrageous price and threw in a couple of extra bucks for the waitress's trouble.

The dancer raised her glass, thanked him, and took a sip.

"I'm guessing that's not the house wine," he commented.

The girl smiled. "You must be new here."

Cory nodded.

She leaned forward. "If you buy any of us girls a drink in here, it's twenty bucks. Beer, wine, soda—it doesn't matter. We ... " she placed her hand on her chest, "get a cut. So when you buy us a drink, you're saying 'Thank you, please sit with me a little while. I'd like to enjoy your company.'"

"Oh, I see. Fair enough. Thanks for cluing me in. I appreciate it."

"You're welcome."

He extended his hand. "I'm Cory."

"Decided to use your real name, huh?"

"You know me?"

"I've seen you fight, but don't worry, no one is going to say anything. Still, you would not believe the number of John Smiths I've met in here."

"So what's your name?"

She grinned. "Jane."

Isaiah charged across the room and stood next to Cory and the dancer's table. "Alicia! What are you doing here?"

"That's kind of a stupid question," she replied.

Cory pushed back from the table. "Should I leave you two alone?"

"Yes," Isaiah said. "Please excuse us." He grabbed Alicia by the arm and marched her to one of the private rooms in the back. He firmly sat her down on the massage table.

"I didn't mean what are you doing here?" He opened his arms to indicate he didn't mean Dark Alleys as a whole. "I meant, what were you doing there?" He pointed toward the room outside. "Talking to Cory Logan?"

She offered a half-assed shrug. "He looks like a good tipper."

Isaiah shook his head. "I told you I was coming tonight. I don't like you talking to other men when I'm here."

"Sorry, but I need the money."

He threw his arms open. "I told you I'll help you financially. I gave you a thousand dollars and a new car for crying out loud!"

"Umm, thanks for the grand, and the car is used. And a motor vehicle doesn't equate to food—or rent."

He rubbed his forehead. "I'm trying to help you out, Alicia. Can't you find another job until you get into college?"

She folded her arms. Her demeanor grew frosty. "McDonald's has a hiring freeze at the moment."

He thrust his finger under her nose. "Don't be ungrateful, Alicia. I'm taking a lot of risks for you."

"And I'm wasting a lot of time waiting for you to dump your wife," Alicia stated. "How long do you expect a girl to wait?"

He caressed her shoulders. "I told you this would take a little time. We've had a little setback. Cory didn't deliver the speech as I had hoped, which would have given us the cash flow I needed. Now I've had to soften him up with a membership here to get some inside boxing tips. But I want you to stay away from him. I don't want him buttering your muffin."

"What the hell does that mean?"

Isaiah shook his head. "I'm not sure. Something someone said. But stay away from him."

"Why? If you're trying to get money out of him, shouldn't I be trying to help you by being nice to him?"

"Alicia … I'm trying to get you a better life. You're a student—an inaugural student—of the David Marsh Foundation. I need you to be above reproach."

"Oh, yeah, the cop school thing. I almost forgot."

"I will get you some money, but you need to quit working at Dark Alleys. And stay away from Cory Logan."

"What's the big deal? None of these guys are going to say anything about me stripping."

He took a deep breath. "I don't like guys ogling you."

"You can't go changing the rules just because you don't like guys being nice to me," Alicia complained. "And speech or no speech, I need money now, and that Cory guy is rich. Did you see his watch?"

Isaiah stepped in. "I placed a bet on Logan. When that comes good I'll have loads of money. In the meantime ..." He reached into his back pocket, pulled out his wallet, and handed her $150. "Here. This should tide you over for a while."

She took the cash and waved it around. "Isaiah, I can make this much in four or five hours. More if I—"

He handed her another hundred. "Give me some time, baby. Remember, you're going to be a cop one day. It might help to start practicing living a respectable life."

She took the bill and sighed heavily. "What am I supposed to do in the meantime? I need something to do. Or something to look forward to."

Isaiah looked at her wrist—or more specifically, the bracelet on her wrist. He lifted her hand into his, taking a closer look at her copper bracelet with a large turquoise stone set in the middle of it. "That's an unusual piece?"

Alicia glanced down, smiling. "I told you the weatherman likes me. It's not really my style, but I try to wear it when he's in the audience. He got it in

Arizona. He'd said he'd take me there this summer to pick out matching earrings for it."

"You can't do that!"

Alicia looked at her bare fingers. "I'm a free agent. I thought maybe I should do some traveling this summer."

He placed his hand on her knee. "Is that it? You want to take a trip?"

Alicia cocked her head and lowered her eyes, looking coy. "Principal Hightower, are you offering me LSD?"

His face contorted between disgust and rage. "No! Don't be stupid!"

Alicia giggled.

He lightened up and forced a smile. "Okay, you got me. So it's a vacation you're after?"

"Maybe."

"How would you like a vacation with yours truly? Someplace where we don't have to sneak around."

She clasped her hands and mocked excitement. "Oh my gosh. You wouldn't consider taking me all the way to North Carolina, would you?"

Isaiah grinned sarcastically. "No. But if you'd rather, I could always cancel Hawaii."

"Hawaii!" she squealed.

"A private villa on the ocean in Kauai. Interested?"

"Mister, you just bought yourself the best blowjob in town." She lowered herself to her knees and undid his trousers …

Chapter 20

"Hickory dickory dock, the mouse is on the block."

The oak door opened and Cory stepped inside Dark Alleys. He pulled back the curtain that hid the sin within from the outside world. After Isaiah cut out on him the week before, leaving him to drink on his own until after midnight before reappearing, Cory decided to make the visit by himself this time. He was still unsure of the ropes, but he'd figure it out. If he was lucky, perhaps he'd get some help from that cute black stripper he met last week. He was drawn to her face of purity—an angelic look that hid the actions of a bad girl. Her debauchery was shrouded under a cover of innocence. He found the contrast an incredible turn on.

He ordered a mineral water when the waitress came around. Not that he didn't want a drink, but he was driving. After his title fight, he would be downing a magnum of champagne in the backseat of a chauffeur-driven limousine.

He finished his first drink and had still not seen the girl he came to see.

The waitress stopped back, tracing her finger along his muscular forearm. "Care for another drink?"

"Yes, I will. The same, please. Can you tell me if—I'm not sure of her name—but I think it's Jane or Alicia? Is she working tonight?"

"We don't have a Jane, but Alicia should be out in about five minutes. Should I tell her who's asking?"

Cory held his palm up. "That won't be necessary. She may not even remember me. It was a pretty brief encounter."

The waitress leaned down and whispered in his ear. "If it's a brief encounter you want, I get off around midnight."

He smiled. "Kind offer, but no thanks. I'll see how it goes with Alicia."

"Sure thing. I'll be back in a minute with your drink."

Shortly after the waitress returned with his drink, Alicia appeared as the center of attention. It was a Thursday night and not very busy. Cory moved up to a seat as close to the catwalk as he could get.

The dancer sauntered around the stage, casting Cory a glowing smile as she strutted past him, playfully flicking the terrycloth towel toward his face. She grabbed the pole using the towel and wiped it from top to bottom. Then she concentrated on the middle of the pole, rubbing with slow steady strokes, gradually increasing the speed. She rapidly stroked the pole until she had every tongue in the joint wagging. She flung the towel across the stage and pulled the string on her tiny bikini top in one fluid movement releasing Isaiah's gift for the world to see. Dollar bills drifted onto the stage from the few guys around. Cory put down five bucks as he got what he came for, but hoped to expand their encounter.

Cory soaked up every ounce of energy Alicia put on the stage. She eyed the five-dollar bill he

181

placed in front of him. Her ass wiggled as she strolled over to him in her transparent high-heel platform shoes. Looking down on him, she smiled.

Cory took an extended look up those long legs to her G-string, which covered nothing except perhaps a few pubic hairs that may have been missed while shaving. He reached around his erection and pulled out a ten-dollar bill from his front pocket and slapped it on the stage.

Alicia's smile broadened. She began a slow descent. Gliding on her platform shoes, her legs stretching farther and farther in each direction, opening herself up as she slid into the splits. Once she was fully down on the floor, she pulled her pubic guard to one side giving Cory full exposure to her pudendum.

Nope, she didn't miss anything shaving.

He forced himself to engage her eyes. "You look incredible."

"Thanks," she whispered.

"Can I buy you a drink when you're done?"

"Of course you can. You want some advice?"

"Sure."

"When I'm down there, I'll have my clothes on, and you won't have anything to look at except my eyes. So while I'm up here …" She held his head by the sides and redirected his gaze to her boobs. "You may as well get an eyeful."

He put another ten bucks on the stage.

She smiled and picked up the money, tucking it into her black and gold garter belt. With legs spread wide, she did a backward somersault and sprung to her feet showing her flexibility along with everything else. After winking at Cory, she sauntered around the stage giving others a good look at her fitness, which earned her another fifty-six bucks before she headed backstage.

***

Alicia appeared next to Cory just as she had promised, fully clothed—if one considered being braless in a tank top and short shorts fully attired.

"Shall we move toward the back," she suggested.

Cory stood up. "Let's."

She took him by the hand and led him to the far end of the room, sitting at a table in the corner under dim lighting. He ordered a twenty-dollar beer for her and another four dollar mineral water for him.

"I missed you last week," he said. "We were about to have a nice chat, then Isaiah showed up and you two disappeared. I was hoping you would come back."

"Sorry about that. We had a few things to talk about, then I had to go. If I had known you were hanging around to see me … well …"

"What did you and Isaiah talk about?"

She let out a deep breath. "I know you're new here and everything, but we're really not supposed to discuss what happens between members, dancers, or anything. You see that curtain over there?" She pointed to the velvet drape where he entered.

He nodded.

"We call that the drape of amnesia. Once you step through it you better forget everything that just happened, or who you saw."

He glanced at the drape then refocused on her. "He was strange on the ride home after talking to you. Very quiet. It wasn't like him."

"He must have developed amnesia."

"Are you seeing him?"

Her eyes narrowed. "People with amnesia don't remember anything. They don't even know what questions to ask because they can't remember what they saw. I suggest you work very hard to develop your sense of forgetfulness. If you can't hone those particular skills, try minding your own business."

He clutched her hand. "Okay, sorry. You're right. I'm new here and I don't have a full appreciation of the level of secrecy yet. Forgive me. I won't ask about it again. Can we talk about you?"

"Depends. What do you want to know? You're probably going to start with why I take my clothes off. Well, McDonald's would only pay me nine bucks an hour and there was some contractual clause that I had to keep my clothes on. I found out I can make a lot more money taking them off. You just proved that. Move on. Next question."

Cory sniggered. "You sound like a girl who knows what she wants. So what do you want?"

"In what sense. I have different wants and desires."

"Are you going to stay working here until you retire?"

Alicia smiled. "You're funny. Dancers have a limited shelf life. When I'm sixty-five maybe I will be working at McDonald's and I'll *want* to keep my clothes on."

"And that's your lifelong ambition?" He looked down. "When your boobs start sagging you start flipping burgers?"

She placed her finger under his chin and lifted his gaze from her chest to her eyes. "I warned you about that. They're not sagging yet, are they?"

"Brown. You have lovely brown eyes, and no … they're not sagging."

She smiled. "Good. Maybe not. Flipping burgers with floppy tits probably violates some health and safety rule, so I think I might go to college and cultivate my brainpower. Get a thinking job."

He bobbed his head. "Admirable. What would you be studying?"

"Okay, enough about me. What's your life story and ambition?"

"That's it? You're done? A totally hot chick with brains. That's your story?"

"Tits and wits. That's me. What about you?"

Cory laughed. "Okay, but I'm not done with you yet. As for me … since you know I'm a fighter, you probably won't be surprised to hear me say my ambition is to be the middleweight champion of the world."

"And when might that happen?"

"Next week. I'm fighting Alexander Eubanks for the title."

"Next week. Wow. What happens if you win?"

"Please … when. *When* I win."

"Of course. Where is it? Vegas?"

"No. My manager actually got it arranged right here in South Carolina—Charleston. I'll be the hometown boy. That should be good for the home-field advantage."

"Great. So what are you going to do after you win?"

"I think I might take a little trip to Kauai. I have a villa there."

Alicia choked on her drink. "Kauai! Seriously?"

185

"Yep. Maybe you'd like to come with me." His eyes were hopeful—like a kid wanting a puppy.

"Besides a whole array of excuses I could throw your way, I barely know you. In fact, we don't know each other at all. Why on earth would you invite me to your oceanfront property in Hawaii?"

"I never said it was on the ocean."

"Oh ..." Alicia's eyes wondered a moment. "Well, it's an island ... I just assumed ..."

"As it happens, you're right. It is on the ocean. Anyway, what do you think? You look like a fun girl, and I'm a fun guy. We'd get to know each other walking on the beach, sipping Mai Tai's, sucking coconuts—"

"Sorry, I'm going to have to pass."

Cory lowered his head, his disappointment obvious. She was right. He didn't know her. Seeing someone naked didn't necessarily equate to a formula for good times. But he had a sense about her. He'd have to play the long game. "Okay, forget about rushing you off to a tropical paradise, would you consider a date?"

Alicia shook her head. "No, I don't think so. I better not."

"Better not? What kind of excuse is that? Do you have a boyfriend?"

"No."

"Then what's the problem?"

"I don't think it's a good idea."

"Is it because I'm white?"

"What? No. Of course not."

"Then what is it?"

Alicia stood up. "I'm leaving now. I hope your amnesia kicks in very soon. Goodbye."

She left the table and disappeared through the drape of amnesia. But there was no way Cory could forget her. He'd just have to try harder to win her over.

Chapter 21

"Charleston? Why on earth do you have to go to Charleston?"

Isaiah clutched his wife's hand. "I told you, darling, the Deacons Shining the Beacon program is going to help with some fundraising."

"You know I did pull in another two thousand dollars over the last week."

He patted her hand. "Yes, I know, and you're doing a terrific job. We just need a little more help."

"I should come with you?"

Isaiah shook his head. "You'd be bored, darling. I'll be in meetings all day, then the fundraiser at night ... besides, it's only for one night."

She stepped in, running her fingers down his chest. "Wouldn't it be nice to come back to the hotel room after a hard day to some ..." She reached down and grabbed his crotch, "Fun."

He grabbed her hand and held it. "Look, baby, if I know you're back in the room waiting for me I won't be able to focus."

She stepped back. "C'mon, Isaiah, we're married. Let's do some of the things married people do. And one of those things is going away together."

He swayed from side-to-side. "Baby, this is business."

"And I'm part of this business. I'm partly responsible for raising money for David Mon— this David kid, so let me help. Then, when all the business responsibilities are finished, we can have a little married fun."

"You don't want to mingle with deacons and such. They're stuffy."

"Why not? I'm married to one. Why shouldn't I meet your peers?"

"Okay, I'm not supposed to know, but I think some of the deacons are on the COTS board. I was going to work the judges, you know, give them some Hightower charm to win their vote."

"Well, that's different." She moved in and put her hands on his face. "We both know you should be the COTS hands down, but I agree, you go work those judges, baby. Why didn't you say something earlier?"

"I don't know. You're right, I want to win it on merit, but do you think it's okay? You know, mixing with men of the cloth, praying, giving praise to the Lord, all in hopes of getting their votes?"

"You do what you have to do, baby. Politics is politics and ass-kissing is vote-getting."

Isaiah hung his head. "Yvette, must you? Now I feel like I'm prostituting myself in the most vulgar manner. Ass-kissing? Really?"

"You can call it COTS-kissing if you want to, but you now have your wife's blessing to go to Charleston and suck up. But you owe me."

Isaiah clicked his fingers, his face lighting up. "Atlanta. How about I take you to Atlanta for the weekend after school gets out?"

"Atlanta? Why Atlanta? You looking to get another car stolen?"

"No. I don't know." He shrugged. "Why not Atlanta? You wanted to go there when I went there on business a while back. It'll be fun."

"I only wanted to go because you were already going to be there."

"I told you, baby. You're in charge of the Hilton Head operation. There's a lot of money here to be had. We need to spread our resources."

Yvette steeled her tone. "What about Savannah?"

"What about Savannah? Nothing happened. Why are you bringing up Savannah?"

She tilted her head as an eyebrow crept higher.

"Nothing happened—oh ..." He wagged his finger at her. "Are you still going on about that numbskull Josh McKinna getting himself fired? That wasn't my fault."

Her eyebrow raised further. "Did I accuse you?"

"Well, no, but—you were about to."

"That's your paranoia, not mine." She rested her hand on his shoulder. "No, if not Charelston, I want to go to Savannah. We can see some old friends. Have a meal down at Francesco's. Take a horse-drawn carriage ride. It'll be like old times."

"You can never recapture old times by going back. Let's go to the big city."

She shook her head. "No. I want Savannah or Charleston—or of course, Honolulu is still on the table. It's up to you."

They locked eyes.

Yvette won.

"Okay, okay, okay." He waved his hands around submissively. "We'll go to Savannah in a few weeks." He pointed at her. "But only for the weekend."

"That's all I need." She smiled, moved in, and kissed him. "For now," she said as she left the room. "Then Hawaii," she called out as she walked down the hall.

***

Isaiah walked into the Cobra Arena in downtown Charleston unaccompanied. He decided boxing was a man thing. Unless he could dangle a delicious piece of eye candy off his arm for others to envy, there wasn't much point in bringing Alicia. And Yvette wouldn't tolerate any event that involved boxing. Besides the brutality and bad memories boxing held for her, if she ever got past that she would quiz him all night about why he wanted to come and watch some braindead boxer. And if she ever found out he was gambling, even though it was for a good cause and to save her the embarrassment of failure, she would have a monumental meltdown.

He avoided seats in the rafters this time, wanting a better view of his investment. He bought himself a seat just above the middle tier for $750. Hopefully out of camera shots should they pan the audience. The bookie at Dark Alleys also served as a ticket master and hooked him up with the seat. Isaiah was pumped. He spent the afternoon in his hotel room praying. Praying for a Cory Logan seventh-round KO. To God be the glory and ten grand to the David Marsh Foundation. Another ten toward Alicia's living expenses to stop her taking her clothes off for dirty old men such as Reverend Theis. And there would still be enough left over to take Alicia to Kauai—maybe not business class, but he'd be able to swing premium economy. And he'd squeeze a little more of the winnings to take Yvette to Savannah. It was all doable. He still wasn't sure how she won that argument, but the appeasement was a minor concession when he looked at the big picture.

He had an aisle seat, for which he was grateful. He didn't want to be stuck in the middle of a row of hardened fight fans shouting obscenities, begging for blood, and bulging veins. A seventh-round knockout and a quick exit would suit him. Pre-fight murmurs around him served as chants of meditation. He closed his eyes and joined in the meditation.

Cory in seven. Cory in seven. God's round. God's round.

A man wearing a straw cowboy hat with a Confederate flag emblazoned on the front, worn as a badge of honor, worked his way up the cement steps. Huffing and puffing as he took them one by one, stopping at every other stair to take several deep breaths before conquering the next two. The man pointed at the seat next to Isaiah.

"I think that's me," the three-hundred-pound gentleman gasped.

Isaiah rose to let the bearded, bib-overall clad redneck pass to take his seat. He thought $750 would have bought him a better neighborhood, but apparently, he was still in the cheap seats. It was just as well he didn't bring Alicia. By the looks of his next seat neighbor, he would have either been drooling on her, which seemed unlikely, or he'd be asking for her address so he could burn a cross in the front yard. Cousin Timmy Tom would bring a pig for the roasting.

Isaiah shifted in his seat, hugging the aisle side of his red plastic chair giving his oversized companion the extra room he needed to spread out. Isaiah pulled out his phone and scrolled through the address book. He wasn't looking for anything. He just wanted the redneck to think he was too busy to talk.

The arena went black. Strobe lights lit it up in psychedelic fashion. The Rolling Stones rocked the domed building with the song "Start Me Up." A spotlight zoomed in on the challenger's entry to the ring. Cory Logan bounced on his feet, shadow boxing the lights as he danced his way to the ring, closely followed by Charlie Gillettie.

Alexander Eubanks bopped into the ring backed up by the Elton John song "Goodbye Yellow Brick Road." Isaiah smiled wondering if that was Eubanks' message to Cory that his road to the championship was about to end.

The presenter announced Cory's 27-5 record then Eubanks 39-0. *Uh-oh.* Maybe there was some merit in market research. Isaiah never looked into how good each boxer was, he just took Cory's word that he was the best boxer in the middleweight division. Suddenly a $5,000 stake for a Cory Logan KO in the seventh didn't look so promising. A rock-like feeling settled in the bottom of his stomach.

At the opening bell, Cory flew out of his corner delivering punch after punch with lightning speed. Isaiah jumped up and cheered. "You go, boy," he yelled, then caught himself and sat back down. He didn't want the boy to go just yet. A first-round knockout by Cory would result in the same zero return as if Eubanks knocked him out. The rock in his stomach increased in weight.

The redneck elbowed him. "You rootin' for the white boy?" He chuckled to himself. "I would've lost that bet."

Isaiah ignored the possible racial slur. After all, the guy had a point. "Who's your money on?" Isaiah asked. On second thought, it was too late for insight. What he really wanted was some reassurance from a real fight fan that Cory Logan had a chance.

The redneck pushed the brim of his hat up. "No disrespect, mister, but it's been so long since a white guy took a title I put a few hundred on Logan."

Isaiah was pleased to hear it. A few hundred didn't sound very confident, but maybe the guy had to get a new transmission for his pick-up truck and couldn't afford a bolder bet. "So, you think he'll win?"

"Naw … I probably threw my money away, but what the heck. He's one of us, right?"

Isaiah scowled. "How's that?"

"A Southerner. I mean a Southerner. He's a South Carolina boy."

The redneck broke the conversation to holler as Cory delivered a series of blows that staggered the champion.

"Not yet, Logan, not yet," Isaiah begged.

That drew a cocked-eyed glance from his neighbor.

Eubanks staggered around the ring, staying out of Cory's range through the rest of the round and made it to the end of round one—still standing.

Round two turned into a tactical battle. Isaiah got the impression Cory had gone for the first round knockout, perhaps trying to catch Eubanks off guard, but when he couldn't do that the fighter settled in a respectful sparring match. Each of them landing scoring punches, but nothing that looked of knockout proportion. Much of this information came from the redneck's commentary. He thought

Logan was trying to win it on points—or just "dicking" around as the redneck put it.

In the middle of round six, Alexander Eubanks quit dicking around. A barrage of blows was felt throughout the arena, then a right uppercut put Cory flat on his back. Isaiah prayed as the referee began the count. When the ref got to five and Cory still laid there, Isaiah prayed harder. Cory rose. Slowly and unsteadily, but he was up before the count of ten. That's all that mattered.

Cory was a walking vegetable for the rest of the round. He managed to protect himself and stay on his feet, but he was a zombie. The bell rang, giving him a thirty-second rest.

"Well that's it," the redneck growled. "Eubanks' is gonna flatten that pussy this round. You should've bet on your own kind, mister. Hell, I should've too. Why the hell did I ever bet on Logan? The white dream died with Rocky Marciano."

"Maybe the black guy made him mad the last round," Isaiah rationalized. It was also the prayer he sent to the Man upstairs.

"If Cory Logan even gets off his stool at the bell it'll be a miracle."

The bell for round seven rang, and the miracle arose. Cory was on his feet. Even from distance, Isaiah could see his face was swollen and what looked like a pretty nasty cut under his left eye.

Eubanks marched over to Cory's corner as soon as he was up and delivered a vicious punch to his cut eye, immediately drawing blood to begin round seven.

Cory staggered. Charlie Gillettie slapped her open hand on the apron of the ring, shouting at Cory. Eubanks delivered another blow, sending

Cory into the ropes. He bounced off with his arms swinging wildly. One caught the champ. He went down.

Isaiah shot to his feet. "You got him, Logan! You got him, man." He shook the redneck by the strap of his bib overalls. "He's got him, man. He's going to do it!"

Cory moved to a neutral corner while the ref counted. Eubanks got to his feet by the count of six.

Isaiah smacked his balled-up fist into his open palm. "C'mon, Cory," he muttered. "You got this, man. Finish him off."

Cory threw a punch to Eubanks' head. He missed. Eubanks countered. He connected. Eubanks danced, firing jabs at Cory's head, connecting with deadly accuracy, one shot after another.

Charlie beat her palm on the ring's edge, shouting instructions. Cory became Eubanks' punching bag, offering no resistance. His head flopped back and forth like a loosely stitched rag doll. The crowd roared at the destruction. The onslaught ended when Alexander Eubanks delivered a right uppercut. Cory's head snapped back, then his body fell to the canvas, face first.

Cory's trainer threw a towel into the center of the ring saving the ref the trouble of counting to ten.

It was over. Cory was defeated, ironically in round seven—the chosen round.

Isaiah was five thousand dollars poorer, but it wasn't just the loss of the money. He wouldn't be able to take Alicia to Hawaii. He wouldn't be able to give extra money to the David Marsh Foundation. And he wouldn't be able to take Yvette to Savannah.

On second thought, he had better come up with some way to take Yvette to Savannah. She was asking too many awkward questions. He'd have to find a nice, budget motel—and hope it was clean.

Chapter 22

Yvette pulled a long black dress out of the closet and laid it on the bed.

Isaiah walked in, glancing at the dress. "What's that?"

"Something a little sophisticated," she said smiling. "You're taking me to Francesco's for champagne and oysters. Then maybe we'll take in a show afterward."

"Sounds expensive."

"It is." She walked over to her husband and put her arms around his neck. "I'm so excited." She playfully wagged her finger at him. "I still haven't given up on Hawaii, but Savannah is a good start. Thanks for taking me."

"My pleasure, but we need to be careful with the expenses."

"What? Why? You earn good money and we haven't been away in ages—well, I haven't. I need this."

"I know, darling, but now's not a good time. I had an investment go bad."

"What investment? We have money in the bank. I'm not asking you to cash in your stocks to take me to Savannah. Let's have some fun."

"It's this foundation."

She cocked an eyebrow. "The foundation? You're not putting our money into it, are you?"

"No, but we need to make sure we can get it up and running comfortably before we go indulging in personal pleasures. We don't want people thinking we're going on expensive trips using the charity's money if it comes up short on cash in the end."

"Expensive trips? We're going to Savannah for the weekend, for crying out loud. It's hardly Monte Carlo."

"I know, but—"

"And what do you mean, 'Come up short?' Why would it come up short? I've raised over twenty thousand dollars."

"Well, you know … if the economy goes bad the first thing people do is stop giving to charity."

"Only the ones who want to burn in hell."

"I wish you wouldn't talk like that." He pulled a hankie out of his pocket and wiped his brow. "I'm just saying we don't want people's perception of what we do to assume it is one of deception."

"You're saying our enjoyment of life could be seen as deception."

"If we're seen eating caviar before we raise the necessary money for David Marsh, yes, it could be damaging. There's a nice little Mom and Pop motel on the outskirts and a cinema just down the road."

"Mom and Pop? A cinema?" She folded her arms. "What's for dinner? Kentucky Fried Chicken?"

"If you want."

Her eyes twitched. Moisture built up in the corner of one eye, but she wiped it away. "Oh … I see. Of course. We must think of the young man's memory first." She hung the dress back in the closet. "I'll pack my Salvation Army clothes."

"Are you okay with this?"

"Why ask me? I'll have to be, right?"

"C'mon, Yvette. You're getting that tone."

"The tone of submissiveness? Yes, that's mine." She patted his cheek. "It's okay. I don't mind as long as your hero-book character persona lives on. We all must make sacrifices."

Isaiah left the room while Yvette continued packing. Lord only knew what she'd throw in now. Cut-off jeans and halter-tops? Just what his image needed. Checking into a backstreet motel with some woman donning her best hillbilly attire and swearing blind that everything was fine. He had to rethink his plan. If he was going to take Alicia to Hawaii as he promised—and he always kept his word, unlike that jughead boxer—besides getting the money, he would have to compensate Yvette with a showering of indulgence and affection to keep her off the scent.

As for raising money for the David Marsh Foundation, Yvette was now his best hope. Maybe she could raise the 40k needed, plus a little extra for Isaiah's personal expenses. Time for plan 'B'—no 'C.' Logan winning was 'B' and that was a disaster. Plan 'C' required the trappings of extravagance. That was Yvette's weakness. Show the woman an expensive hotel room and a bottle of bubbly and she became oblivious to the real world. He kicked himself for trying to play it any other way.

He slipped into his office and shut the door. He pulled out his Visa card—the one Yvette didn't know about. He had the bills sent to the school address to keep it from her. He used it for secret rendezvous and emergency cash advances. And one of those cash advances had Alicia's boobs on it which topped out the modest credit limit on the

200

card. He called the number on the back for customer service. After doing the ten-step finger tango, dancing with all the buttons, he spoke to a person. A real one. After several minutes of pleading his case, they agreed to raise his credit limit.

Then he dialed the Marriott Riverside hotel in Savannah and booked a basic room. It would still be nice, just not with a river view. And at four times the price of the Savannah Sleeper, it would add an air of dignity worthy of a married retreat.

A wave of satisfaction carried him back up the stairs to the bedroom.

Yvette was in the process of closing the suitcase, with some difficulty, when he arrived.

From behind her, he placed his hands on her shoulders. "Did you manage to get your black dress in there? It will get pretty wrinkled, won't it?"

"I don't want Pop drooling on me, so I'll save it for another occasion. I brought my Bart Simpson T-shirt instead. He doesn't crease."

Isaiah laughed. "You know I was only teasing you."

"About what?"

"Mom, Pop, the movie, the Colonel ..."

She wheeled around. "Come again?"

"Darling, I don't think I can swing Hawaii this year, so I'm going to show you the best time ever in Savannah. You deserve it. I may have to be doing some traveling over the summer, so I need to give my chief fundraiser a perk while I can."

"Chief fundraiser? What about that blockhead boxer and the bimbo with the big—"

"Let's not talk business right now." He pointed to the closet. "Pick out your best finery and let's go paint the town."

"Seriously?"

"Of course."

She moved in, softly placing her hand on his chest. "You know how you said I had 'that tone' earlier? Well, what you're saying now puts me in 'that mood.'" She winked. "You getting me?"

He kissed her cheek. "More to the point, you'll be 'getting' me." He smiled, then smacked her bottom. "Let the good times roll, baby." He turned and walked out of the room, a small spring added to his step.

Yvette smiled as he left. "He's such a joker. I'm the luckiest girl in the world," she whispered.

***

Hard-soled shoes echoed off the marble floor. The echo stopped when the Hightowers reached the reception desk.

"Welcome to Savannah Marriott hotel," the young clerk greeted them. "May I have your name?"

"Yes, Isaiah Hightower."

The girl's eyes widened. "Oh, Mr. Hightower. One moment please." She picked up the phone and punched a number, then whispered. She hung up. "He'll be right with you."

"He? He who?"

"The manager."

Isaiah glanced at a board behind the clerk. *On Duty Manager: Mr. Tom Conrad.*

Isaiah didn't like the sound of that. Maybe Conrad was upset having to fire his best employee because of him. Perhaps he was coming out to tell him he was banned from ever using the Marriott again. He put his arm around Yvette and ushered her away from the desk. "They have a wonderful gift shop, darling," he said, guiding her in that direction.

"Why don't you go have a look while I get us checked in?"

Yvette's brows furrowed. "The manager? What does he want?"

He shrugged. "I don't know, but nothing for you to worry about."

He succeeded in getting Yvette moving in the right direction, away from the desk, just before Mr. Conrad appeared.

"Ah, Mr. Hightower." The black-haired man with a golden tanned face held out his hand. "I'm so pleased to see you back and giving us here at the Savannah Marriott another chance to provide you with excellent service. A place where your discretion and privacy are always assured."

"Thank you. I still feel bad about young Josh getting fired, but—"

Conrad vigorously shook his head. "Not at all, Mr. Hightower. He was wrong to do what he did, and it won't happen again. I can assure you." The manager clasped his hands in front of himself in an apparent gesture of gratitude at Isaiah's return. "The guest list says there will be two of you staying with us. Is that correct?"

Isaiah nodded.

"Very well, sir. I have upgraded you to the Presidential Suite on the top floor, no extra charge, of course, with a complimentary bottle of champagne for your past inconvenience. There is a reserved elevator to the rear." He pointed across the foyer. "Your key is the only key that can activate that elevator and it will deliver you directly into your room—unseen—you and your guest. You have my word it is completely private and no one will show up unannounced."

Yvette walked up and put her hand on Isaiah's shoulder. "You're right, darling. They have some wonderful things in there. I'll have a better look later. Is everything okay with the check-in?"

Mr. Conrad nodded to the lady. "Is this your special someone?"

"Yes, this is my wife."

"Your wife. Of course." The manager dipped his head. "It's a pleasure, madam. I trust you will enjoy your visit at the Marriott, and if there is anything I can do to make your stay more comfortable, please don't hesitate to ask."

"Thank you. That's very kind of you."

"Not at all." Mr. Conrad reached behind the desk, grabbed the Hightowers room keys, and escorted them to their private elevator. "If you would like to take your lovely wife to the room, Mr. Hightower, I will have your luggage sent up to your room via the front door. Enjoy your stay."

After flashing the key over the keypad, the elevator opened and the Hightowers stepped in. A punch of a button and they were whisked to the top floor, stepping out into the palatial Presidential Suite.

Yvette looked around the room. "Wow," she gasped. "This ain't no Mom and Pop motel, Mister. I thought you wanted to be low-key."

"I told you, I was teasing. You deserve the best. Look." Isaiah extended his arm toward the champagne bucket. "I've ordered in the Yvette Hightower 'I love you' package. This is your weekend, baby. Whatever you want."

Yvette hurried over to her husband. "You did all this for me? The suite? The champagne? Everything?"

"Of course I did. You deserve it."

"Oh, good Lord. I've died and gone to heaven." Yvette strolled over to the large picture window and gazed down at the river below. She turned back to face her husband, tears in her eyes. "Thank you, Isaiah."

"It's nothing."

He opened the bottle of champagne and poured Yvette a glass. He grabbed a bottle of mineral water out of the fridge and they raised their drinks.

"To a long and happy life with the woman I love." He kissed her, then drank.

Yvette's hand trembled as she sipped her bubbly. She was falling in love all over again with the most wonderful man in the world.

Chapter 23

By the time Yvette finished her second glass of champagne she couldn't resist her husband any longer and ripped his clothes off. She loved how receptive he was to her advances. They made passionate love and climaxed together. Her life couldn't get any better.

After a nap following their lovemaking session, they showered, and Yvette put on that black dress Isaiah insisted she bring. She was glad she did. She felt sexy with the tight fabric hugging her hips. She made it her goal to get Isaiah turned on again throughout the night so that she might experience another slice of his magical wizardry—also known as heaven minor.

They left the hotel and got into Isaiah's new Volvo. Yvette enjoyed the new car smell as they weaved their way through Savannah on the way to Francesco's. He turned onto Turner Street and headed west.

"Look!" Yvette pointed out the window. "That's our car. The Voyager. What's it doing in Savannah?"

"What?" Isaiah craned his neck, looking into the parking lot of the Player's Club. He only went down that road wanting a cheap thrill of taking his wife by his secret den of lust without her knowing.

"No, that's not ours," he dismissed. "That's black. Ours was blue."

"No," Yvette insisted. "The license plate ends in EE. Ebony Evolution. That's how I always recognized it. I'm calling the police." She pulled her phone out of her purse.

Isaiah grabbed her hand. "Do we really have to call the police?"

"What? That's our car! Somebody damn well stole it. And there it is. I'm calling the cops."

"What about the insurance?"

"What?"

He slapped the dash. "We might have to give this one back?" He pointed in the direction of the Voyager with his head. "We might have to take that one back. The question is, do we want it back? It's been driven around by some nasty gangster, stinking it up with the devil only knows what. You don't want it back now after they defiled it." He shook his head. "No, that's not going to wash with me."

Yvette turned in her chair toward her husband. "What do you suggest we do?"

"Nothing." He clutched her hand. "They must've needed it more than us if they were desperate enough to steal it. And let's face it, we got a new car out of it. The Lord let them have it to relieve their suffering and upgraded us to minimize our sorrow. Let it go."

Yvette stuffed the phone back in her purse. "You know, it's not easy living with someone as righteous as you. You have a kind and forgiving heart. God must surely smile on you. No doubt you'll have a special place in heaven." She pointed in the direction of the Voyager. "But those bastards are spending eternity in hell."

207

"Yvette!"

She covered her mouth, feigning regret. "Sorry."

"God will judge us all on our merits and our sins. For your sake, you better hope He doesn't judge us on our mouths."

Although she wanted to be the ticket puncher for the thief at the gates of hell, if she wanted more of Isaiah and his skill as a love-maker, she would have to live with it—the whole forgiveness thing. In the name of lust, she accepted his pardoning of the bandit.

They arrived at Francesco's and when Isaiah checked in with the maître d, she noticed him discretely eyeing her up. She assumed it was the dress, or perhaps it was her radiant beam from her husband treating her so regally. She was on fire. Above the surface and below the panty-line.

She hadn't noticed Isaiah give the man at the podium a tip, but they were shown to a premier table—off to the side out of the way of traffic, but central as to see everything that would be going on.

They ordered and Yvette sipped a very nice Chablis that Isaiah had requested for her while they waited for their Prosciutto-wrapped grissini breadsticks with cheese sauce to arrive to start the meal.

"Eh, Yvettie!" a man bellowed in a heavy Italian accent. "What are you doing in my place of worship?" A room-shaking belly-laugh followed. A bowling ball-shaped man approached the table. He outstretched both arms, inviting Yvette to stand.

She did and an embrace followed. Then the gray-haired man delivering a quick kiss to each of her cheeks.

"So good to see you, my dark flower. Where have you been?"

"I told you, Francesco, I moved to Hilton Head." She held her hand toward Isaiah. "This is my husband, Isaiah."

Francesco shook his hand. "Ah, yes, Isaiah Hightower. You are one lucky, lucky man. You take care of my flower. Yes?"

"Oh, I'm taking care of *your* flower, am I?" He knew Yvette had dined there often with her gal pals when they lived in Savannah, but he had no idea that she was adored by the owner of one of the finest restaurants in Savannah. But what the heck. The overweight Italian posed no threat to him. Isaiah chuckled. "Of course I will."

"Good. And I give you the very best Francesco has to offer."

Yvette felt like royalty when Francesco recognized her. Her, not her famous husband. Although short round men weren't her type, she was flattered nonetheless. Knowing another man desired her would add to her sexual appetite back in the hotel room. Correction: The Presidential Suite.

***

Cory admired the dancer as she finished her routine. He needed a little pick me up after his devastating loss, and a naked body was doing the trick. At least it took his mind off the pain—physical and emotional. He hadn't heard from Isaiah since his defeat, but he guessed he wouldn't be too happy with him and hoped he wouldn't bump into him any time soon. Perhaps time would heal Isaiah's disappointment at losing out on a windfall and hopefully his anger would subside before they crossed paths again.

The stripper made her way to Cory's table after her routine and sat down.

"Are you new here?" Cory asked.

"Are you drunk?" she replied. "Don't think you can fool me with those sunglasses."

Cory removed the shades revealing a black and swollen right eye.

"Holy crap. What happened to you?"

"The bad news is, I lost. The good news is, I developed amnesia. So, I'll ask you again. Are you new here?"

Alicia smiled. "Yes, I am. Glad to see the amnesia kicked in, but sorry you had to get your ass whipped to get it. Are you in the mood to buy the new girl a drink?"

"And anything else the girl wants. That's why I'm here."

"Really? Would you be buying a drink for any girl if I wasn't here?"

Cory shook his head. "Nope. And I have a present for you. One I wouldn't give to just any ole girl."

"Really?"

Cory reached in his pocket and pulled out a small jewelry box. He handed it to Alicia.

Her eyes went wide and her jaw dropped when she opened the lid. Sitting on padded velvet were three 18-carat gold earrings with onyx inlay and mother-of-pearl surround. "They're beautiful," she gasped.

"So are you. It took me a whole day of shopping to find something as gorgeous as you, and even then, this takes second place. I noticed you have a naval piercing, so I had the third one made to match the earrings."

"Cory, I don't know what to say. Thank you."

He nodded. "Thank you will work. You're welcome. Now tell me ... would you accept a drink from any ole guy?"

"Yep," she said, smacking her lips to annunciate the *P*. "It is part of the job description, but if the truth be told, I prefer to get drinks bought for me by good-looking, athletic, forgetful guys—preferably without a deformed face, but I'll make an exception in your case. Hopefully, it's only temporary. And I love the present." She leaned over and kissed his cheek.

Cory laughed. "With a bit of luck we can keep sharing moments long enough that you will see me after the swelling has gone down."

"Are you suggesting more than a one night stand?"

"Are you offering more than a one night stand?"

"No, but let's see how it goes."

"So, you are offering a one night stand?"

She pointed a finger at him. "You did say you're forgetful, right?"

"Hey, I'm a boxer. I've had the memory recall knocked out of me."

"You got a place here, in town?" Alicia asked.

"I'm staying at the Marriott. Would you care to tuck me in?"

"Is that tuck with a 't' or an 'f?'"

"Your choice."

"Uck has a lot of interesting variables."

"Does it?"

"Duck, buck, puck, suck ... as well as the obvious."

"Luck?"

Alicia stood up and grabbed his hand. "You said the magic word. Let's go."

Cory pulled out his phone. "I'll get us a taxi."

"That's okay," Alicia said. "I'll drive."

Chapter 24

Isaiah pulled into the parking garage of the Marriott. He found a spot not far away from the elevator. Yvette pointed to the parking bay across the aisle.

"That's our Voyager," she shouted. "Look at the license plate. EE. They're here!" She grabbed her purse off the floor. "Needed a car my ass. God doesn't give cars to people staying at the Marriott Riverfront hotel!" She pulled her phone out of the side pocket. "I'm calling the police." She looked at the screen. "Damn, no reception. I'm going to the front desk and have them call the police. Better yet, they should have a record of whose car that is and what room they're staying in. We got 'em, Isaiah. We got the bastards."

Isaiah dropped his head in despair. It was going to be tough to talk her out of this one. *What was Alicia doing at the Marriott? Maybe the car got stolen from her.* Yvette was right. Common car thieves wouldn't be staying at an expensive hotel. And strippers shouldn't either, unless ….

Yvette was out of the Volvo and blazing a hot trail toward the elevator before Isaiah even got the key out of the ignition. He arrived as the elevator doors slid back. He entered the elevator with his wife. She frantically pushed the starred button to take them to the lobby. Isaiah thanked God for the small mercy that Yvette didn't rant all the way up.

213

She was silent. Her face was a stone sculpture of determination. The elevator dinged and she didn't waste any time marching up to the front desk.

"I want to report a stolen car," she insisted.

The young girl looked stunned—and confused. "Excuse me? What was that again?"

"Never mind. Get me the manager. That Mr. Conrad."

"Yvette is this entirely necessary?" Isaiah asked.

"Yes, it is." Yvette stood tapping the toe of her high-heeled shoe on the white marble floor while she waited, her eyes roaming the empty lobby. Nearly empty.

A young couple emerged from around the corner. A white guy in his thirties with an attractive black girl, early twenties. They laughed and giggled as they made their way to the elevator. Once they stepped in the girl was hidden behind the guy.

Yvette nudged Isaiah, pointing to the couple. "Isn't that ... oh what's his name, you know, the boxer?" Her posture straightened, eyebrows furrowing. "It is! It's that dunderhead Cory Whats-his-face. What's he doing with a girl like that? He should be sticking—"

"What girl? I don't see a girl." Isaiah's head bounced from side-to-side trying to get a peek at the girl but couldn't see her—except for a dark brown arm. It was only his eyes that wanted confirmation. His gut already knew the story. With the Voyager in the parking garage and Cory Logan in the hotel with a dish of hot cocoa, it could only be a story of betrayal. He grabbed Yvette by the shoulders and turned her away. "Don't look. Pretend you don't see him."

"Why not? Don't you want to go over and see your buddy? Maybe he's found another way to help you raise a hundred grand or two."

"No, I don't. Leave it. I'm not talking to him after he let David Marsh down like he did."

"Well, maybe you *should* go over there. If nothing else you should find out why he's with a girl like that. But seeing those breasts I could venture my own guess."

He peeked again, but couldn't see her hidden behind Logan. "There's no girl there. And if there is, it's just two screwed up people screwing screwed up people."

Yvette laughed. Her rigid face had been replaced by a smile. "I've never heard you make a joke like that."

"Who was joking?"

***

When the elevator pinged, Cory and Alicia stepped inside. They turned around and faced the lobby as the doors slid shut.

"Oh my God," Alicia squealed. She hid behind Cory, peeking over his shoulder. "There's Isaiah. And that must be his wife. Oh my God, she's beautiful."

"Oh shit." Cory stood to cover her. The door closed and the couple began the ascent to the second floor. "What the hell are they doing here?"

Alicia pinched his bottom. "I'll bet the same thing we're doing."

"Why would he come to Savannah with his wife?"

"I don't know. He never mentioned to me he was coming to Savannah, but what the hey? A man should go places with his wife."

Cory's brows knitted together. "Why would he tell you if he was coming to Savannah?"

She shrugged it off. "I'm his favorite dancer?"

Cory faced her. "Yeah, right. Never mind. I don't want to know. Surely he's not going to duck into Dark Alleys while she's in town with him. I mean, why take the chance?"

"They used to live in Savannah. I'm sure they come back without him ever setting foot inside the club."

"Do you think they saw us?" Cory asked.

"I don't know. The woman was throwing stink eye our way. Have you ever met her?"

"Yeah, a few times, but it didn't go well."

"Oh?"

"Let's just say we don't see eye to eye on a lot of issues."

"Oh well, fuck her. No, I mean fuck me." She threw her arms around his neck and planted a deep kiss on him.

He replied with passion. When the elevator doors opened, he swooped her off her feet and carried her down the hall to room 225.

***

Mr. Conrad stepped out from a door from behind the reception desk and walked up to the counter. "Ah, Mrs. Hightower. I understand you wanted to see me. What can I do for you?"

"I'd like to report a stolen car. Well, it's already been reported stolen, but in their usual fashion, the police can't find it. But I've found it, and it's in your parking garage. In fact, it looks like the thief may be staying in your hotel." She flicked a finger toward the computer screen. "Look up and see what room the driver of a Chrysler Voyager, license plate

216

number one-six-nine EE is staying in? Just send the police straight to their room and get this matter settled."

Isaiah rolled his eyes behind his wife's back.

"I am sorry, Mrs. Hightower, but the hotel has strict privacy policies. I can't give out information about our guests."

"Fine. You don't have to give it to me. Give it to the police. Surely you have a policy to report a crime when it is reported to you."

"Of course we do, but—"

Yvette drummed her fingernails on the marble countertop. "Mr. Conrad, an upstanding member of the community is reporting a crime to you. A serious one. And one that has violated me personally. Now, either you—"

Conrad picked up a pen off the desk. "What was the number again?" He wrote 169 EE as Yvette repeated it. "Very well, madam. I will call the police and report the matter."

Yvette smiled. "Thank you, Mr. Conrad. If you need any more information, call me in the Presidential Suite."

"Of course, Mrs. Hightower. If there's anything else I can do, call the front desk. They will get in contact with me."

"Thank you." She dipped her head and walked toward the elevator—smiling. She liked this presidential treatment. It felt powerful. It felt right.

Isaiah took several steps with her before clicking his fingers. "You go on, darling, I should tell Conrad we saw it earlier too."

"Good thinking, baby. I'll wait for you by the elevator."

Isaiah made a brisk walk back to the desk and caught Conrad before he had disappeared. He got out his wallet, glanced to make sure Yvette wasn't watching, and pulled out a $50 bill. He slipped it over the counter to the manager. "Look, Conrad, my wife is writing a novel and is pulling a stunt for her market research. It's nothing more than a wild goose chase to watch the police in action. Cancel the call to the police. It's a hoax. I don't want her getting into trouble for wasting police time."

Conrad looked at the fifty bucks. "That's not necessary, sir."

Isaiah stuffed the bill in his own pocket. "If you insist, but cancel the call. If Mrs. Hightower asks, tell her the police came, they are investigating, but the thief is not staying at the hotel, and you can't talk about an ongoing investigation."

Conrad nodded. "As you wish, sir. We'll treat it as a presidential privilege."

"Splendid. One more thing, what room is Cory Logan staying in?"

"I'm afraid that's confidential, Mr. Hightower. You should know that better than most."

"No, it's okay." He glanced down the hall to Yvette who was admiring some artwork. "Cory Logan is a friend of mine. I need to talk to him. It's important."

"I am sorry, Mr. Hightower, but we have to respect *all* our guests' privacy."

"I really need to talk to him. We have some issues with a fundraiser he's working on with me. Something doesn't add up. If we don't get it figured out by morning, Josh McKinna could lose out on a terrific scholarship. It would be a shame. The kid deserves a break—you know, after you fired him and all."

Mr. Conrad momentarily dropped his head before re-engaging eyes with Isaiah. "Mr. Hightower, with all due respect, I fired Josh McKinna protecting your privacy. I ask that you respect other guests' privacy as much as I respected yours."

Isaiah nodded. "Of course. And I'll tell Josh his scholarship is not happening."

Conrad remained straight-faced. "Please give him my regards." He turned and left.

Isaiah hung his head in disappointment.

"Psst ..."

Isaiah looked up to find the receptionist motioning him toward her. He pointed to himself. "Me?"

She nodded and he stepped closer. "Did you say Josh McKinna is in trouble?"

"Yes, big trouble."

"That's a shame. I like Josh."

"Yes, me too. He needs help."

"And Cory Logan can help him?"

"If I can find him."

"I was never very good at math." She slid a piece of paper in front of her and wrote as she spoke. "Would you like to check my sums?"

She handed Isaiah the piece of paper.

2+2=5.

Isaiah smiled. "I'd say your sums look pretty good to me. Thank you." He turned on his heel and caught up with his wife, and they rode the elevator to the Presidential Suite.

Chapter 25

The Hightowers stepped out of the elevator and into the Presidential Suite. Yvette liked the fast track to the room without having to share her space with anyone else. She kicked off her shoes and enjoyed the soft, deep-pile carpet beneath her stocking feet.

Isaiah opened the door to the minibar. "Darling, would you like a vodka and tonic?"

His wife's ears perked up. "Are you inviting me to drink hard liquor? Paid for from an overpriced minibar?"

He nodded. "I told you I was going to spoil you this weekend."

"You don't have to get me liquored up to have your wicked way, that was already a given. But if you're offering booze with the deal, bring it on, baby."

Isaiah clicked his toy-gun finger at her. "You got it."

"Spoiling me?" she mumbled. "I feel like I've died and gone to heaven. Whatever you're on, keep taking it." She glowed.

"Great." Isaiah rubbed his hands together and pulled a glass forward. "Drat. No ice. I'll be right back." He grabbed the ice bucket and headed for the elevator.

"Don't be long," Yvette said as she headed for the bathroom. "I'm going to get ready. We're playing nudist camp when you get back." She giggled and closed the door.

Isaiah stepped into the elevator and hit the button taking him to the lobby. He transferred over to the elevator for regular people, then ascended to the second floor. His heart thumped a little harder as he approached the second floor. Except … what in the world was he supposed to do when he got there? Okay, Cory Logan was a loser. A proven loser, but he was still a professional fighter. A toned athlete who spent a lifetime training to hurt people. All Isaiah had on his side was anger. But he had plenty of that. Besides the money, was Logan stealing his mistress?

The elevator stopped on the second floor and Isaiah exited. His palms sweated. He worked to calm himself. He wasn't there to fight Logan. He was there to reason with him. *Give me my five grand and my mistress back and we'll forget the whole thing. My wife will raise the money for the foundation.* He ignored the "Do Not Disturb" sign and knocked just below the 225 plaque—then stood to the side of the peephole, out of view.

Muffled voices and the odd swear word resounded through the door, followed by a very clear man's voice. "Who is it?"

Should I announce my presence immediately?—No. "Housekeeping."

The door swung open. Cory stood on the other side of the door in gym shorts and shirtless. He leaned against the edge of the door. "Oh, Isaiah? You're a funny-looking maid."

"I need my five grand back."

"What? Sorry, man, but if you bet and lost, that's your tough luck. That's why it's called gambling. It's a risk."

"Yeah, but I was supposed to cash in on over thirty grand. You said you'd take that bozo out in the seventh, but bozo clowned you. I really needed the thirty, but I *have* to have the five back before Yvette finds out."

Cory bounced himself off the edge of the door and squared up. "Look, Isaiah, I'm sorry. Trust me, I don't like losing any more than you do. But it's not gambling if you get the money back no matter what. Hell, if I could get my stake back whenever I bet regardless of the outcome I'd pitch a tent in the lobby of the MGM Grand and bet on everything that passed. It doesn't work like that."

"You don't understand … besides, you got a couple mill even losing. What's five grand to you?"

"Five grand will buy me as much as it buys you. I'm not paying your gambling losses. Now if you don't mind …" He started closing the door.

Isaiah wedged his foot in the opening, craning his neck to look inside. "Wait. Let me see her."

"See who?"

"Alicia."

"She's not here."

"Of course she is. I saw her car downstairs."

"So you naturally assume she's with me?"

"Who else would she be here with?"

"Good question." He closed the door.

***

A naked Yvette greeted Isaiah when he stepped out of the elevator wearing nothing but a smile. "Welcome to Camp Yvette." She spread her arms over her head. Coupled with her long slender body,

222

and the shape of her arms, she did resemble the letter Y. A naked Y. "Does his majesty have any special requests?"

Camp Yvette was open for business. He smiled. His mood for lust didn't match hers, but he was sure her enthusiasm would be enough to carry them both through to the Promised Land. "Can you still do that merry-go-round thing?"

"You betcha. Just get me a slug of that vodka and I will amaze you."

"Oh, yeah, right." Isaiah looked in the empty ice bucket. "The ice machine was broken."

She sauntered over to him and put her arms around his neck. "Never mind. Maybe I'll have a drink later. For now, let the games begin."

She took off his shirt and placed her index finger in the middle of his neck, just below his Adam's apple. She slowly swanked around him, swinging her butt from side to side in exaggerated fashion. Each time she circled him, her finger dropped a little lower, leaving her fingertip to burn a trail of desire on his muscular body. She completed enough circles that her fingers finally rested on his belt.

She lowered herself onto her knees undid his pants. Isaiah's head fell back as he emitted a whimper of pleasure. He wondered where Alicia had got to, but for now, he would take his wife's gift and enjoy it.

Chapter 26

Yvette sat at the kitchen table adding up the cash and checks from her latest fundraiser, the treasure hunt. She had a feeling it was a good haul and it would help push her closer to her target. And a good thing too. Time was closing in. She needed the $40,000 by mid-August and it was already late July.

Isaiah was out networking with some of his colleagues helping her make the final push. She was proud of herself for what she had accomplished and was grateful for her husband's support. She needed that little extra thrust and she was glad she was getting it from Isaiah and not that obnoxious twerp, Cory Logan.

She added the treasure hunt funds to the money already raised from the speed golf, auctions, a fun run, and a flea market. She stared at the number on the calculator: 36,433.26. A warm feeling enveloped her. The numbers confirmed it; she was good. Just over three and a half thousand to go and she would ring the bell. She would have already had the money if the damn insurance company hadn't demanded that $5,000 Isaiah told her about. Imagine taking five thousand dollars from a charity for public liability insurance. They should have donated the coverage as far as she was concerned.

The insurance setback aside, the scheduled barbeque should just about put her over the top.

Isaiah would be proud of her. She couldn't wait to tell him. He'd heap praise on her. She'd heap her hot body on his, and they'd have amazing, earth-shattering sex. *Living the dream, girl. Living the dream.*

She put her pencil down when the doorbell rang. Walking across the wooden floor, she looked around to make sure the house was in order in case it was someone she wanted to invite in. She checked her watch. It was 2 p.m. Gloria would be up, not on the wine yet, and still able to drive. It was probably her.

She opened the door to two men in suits. White guys in suits. Mormons?

The taller of the two spoke. "Mrs. Hightower?" He flashed a badge. "I'm Detective Bexley and this is my colleague Detective Kennedy. We'd like to ask you a few questions."

"Is this about my car?"

"No, ma'am. We're from the Fraud Squad," Kennedy said. "It's about a fundraiser you held." He pulled out a flip-up notebook, glanced through some pages, stopping when he found what he was looking for. "On May 10th you sponsored an auction."

"Yes …" Yvette conceded.

"Some of the items, big-ticket items, were Troy Dugan autographed memorabilia. Namely a football and a jersey."

"Yes. So what? Is this a tax thing? Because it was for charity and I can prove it."

"That's not the issue, Mrs. Hightower," Bexley interrupted. "The question is, can you provide proof that they were authentic Troy Dugan signed items?"

Yvette's eyebrows pinched the top of her slender nose. "Of course I can. My husband got

225

them for me—or I should say for the David—
Foundation. Isaiah, Isaiah Hightower. Principal of
the Hilton Head High School and deacon of the
Hilton Head Evangelical Free Church. He knows
Troy and got him to sign it. Those items raised over
eight thousand dollars I'll have you know."

"We're well aware how much they raised
because that is the amount of fraud we're
investigating."

"Fraud?" Yvette's hands fell to her hips. "How
dare you."

"Mrs. Hightower," Kennedy said, "if you can
offer us some authentication that this was bonafide
Troy Dugan signed gear, then we'll look at the
investigation from a different angle."

"I have my husband's word. What do you
have?"

Bexley drew a deep breath. "The lady who
bought the jersey already had an autograph from
Troy Dugan. Apparently, she obtained it from him
in person at a Falcons game. Last week she was
setting up a ... shrine ..." He looked at Kennedy
smiling. "It looked like a shrine to me. Would you
call it a shrine?"

Kennedy nodded, himself smiling. "Yes, I'd call
it a shrine."

"Yeah, that's what I'd call it," Bexley agreed.
"She set up this shrine to Dugan and got all her
collectibles in one room, arranging them in this ...
shrine. Then she held up her autograph to the
signature on the jersey. They didn't look the same.
So she called us."

"Of course people's signatures don't look the
same on a jersey as they do on a piece of paper."

Bexley straightened himself, adding to his already towering height. "Considering the fan in question paid over seven thousand dollars for an autographed jersey, she has a right to get the real deal. We had our handwriting expert compare the two signatures and she agreed that they were not made by the same person. So we tracked down the gentleman who bought the football, and his was the same. A phony signature."

"Then I suggest you ask that Dugan character. Perhaps he had a broken hand when he signed it."

"We did contact Mr. Dugan and he can't recall those particular items, but he agreed that it didn't look like his signature."

"That's crazy. He must have been concussed. Talk to my husband. He'll straighten this whole thing out."

"Oh we will, ma'am," Kennedy assured her. "Even if we don't decide to press criminal charges, you will have to pay the money back."

"Criminal charges? Pay the money back? He's up for Citizen of the South! This is harassment. If you have any more to say, talk to my lawyer." She slammed the door in their faces.

The doorbell rang.

She opened it a sliver, staring the cops down with narrowed eyes.

"Can we have the name of your lawyer, ma'am?"

***

Yvette opened the fridge door, drug the box of Chardonnay forward, and decanted herself a large glass of wine. She would have preferred hard liquor, but it was difficult enough to get Isaiah to agree to allow wine in the house. He allowed her the rare and

227

occasional shot of the hard stuff, but he would never allow Satan's Swill within the confines of his castle as a matter of routine.

She moved to the patio at the back of the house. Besides her wine, she brought a bowl of olives and a calculator. She would have loved nothing more than to stare out to sea admiring the view and patting herself on the back for a job well done—and nearly complete. Instead, it was the calculator that held her attention. She repeatedly punched in the numbers 36,433.26 − 8,000. The result was the same every time. Then she would subtract 28,433.26 from 40,000 and there was the number that haunted her. An $11,566.74 shortfall with only two weeks to go and only one more event planned—and Meat and Eat wasn't going to raise that kind of money.

Isaiah came through the house singing out her name. He smiled when he discovered her on the patio. He reached inside his jacket pocket and pulled out a check.

"A thousand bucks from Diamond Danny Doyle." He kissed the check and laid it in front of Yvette. "That must just about put us there, doesn't it?"

"It would have done if I hadn't had a visit from the goon squad."

Isaiah's ears perked up. "I beg your pardon?"

"Where'd you get that jersey and football?"

"The donation? I told you, Troy Dugan."

"The Hilton Head police think otherwise. They said it was a forgery and want the eight grand back, and they're talking about charging you with fraud."

"What? That's insane. They can't do that."

"That's what I said. Apparently, the hormonal housewife who bought the jersey checked the autograph and it doesn't match up. I told them there must be some mistake and if they were going to make such ridiculous accusations they needed to talk to Ernie Simpson."

"You gave them the name of our lawyer?"

"They're setting us up, Isaiah. I can see it. Let's see if they want their eight thousand dollars back when Ernie threatens them with a lawsuit."

Isaiah studied the flagstone paving of the patio, not saying anything.

Yvette craned her neck to look up at Isaiah's lowered head. "We can sue them, right?"

"Curses to that Josh McKinna."

"What's Josh got to do with it?"

Isaiah gave himself a temple massage. "He knows he screwed up by not booking me into the hotel properly. So when I willingly forgave him, he was happy. When I offered him a scholarship, he was ecstatic. He asked me how I was going to raise money, and I told him one way was to have Troy sign a shirt and a football. He said Troy comes into Bubba Suds once a week to get his car washed. He said he'd get the autograph for me and save me chasing around for it. So I gave him the shirt and football."

"Why would he forge it?"

"Maybe Troy didn't show up and he was afraid I'd yell at him. I don't know. Or maybe he kept the real Troy stuff for himself and gave us fakes."

"You're saying they were fakes?"

Isaiah opened his arms. "Hey, the boy lied to me. What can I say?"

"You said you got them from Troy himself."

"No, I said that I knew Troy, and I didn't see the problem with using a middleman. It saved me a lot of time."

"Any chance you could ask Dugan for a real jersey and football then? If we have to give the eight grand back we'll never make our target."

Isaiah shook his head. "No, it would be too embarrassing."

"Why?"

"To admit the David Marsh Foundation forged his signature? No, that could destroy us. And another thing, we don't want Josh going to jail. He's a good kid and means well, just stupid."

"What about the scholarships? We won't have the money to send the kids to college."

Isaiah stroked his jaw. "We won't have enough money to send two kids to college. Josh McKinna screwed himself on this one. We'll pull his scholarship."

"What? But he's a—"

"Facebook friend, I know. But actions have consequences. He should have known that after the last stunt he pulled. No, we'll give the scholarship to the girl."

"I thought Lionel said you had to have a white person in the program."

"Maybe next year."

Yvette cocked her head to one side, looking unsure. "I don't think he's going to go for that, honey. You need to think about this. A white kid gets killed. Then a black man raises money for a black girl, in the name of the white kid. How's that going to look? And any money we have received from white folks might bring backlash."

Isaiah sighed. "You have a point."

230

"Put Josh back in the program."

"Yeah, yeah, sure, sure. But where the heck are we going to get the money?"

"I hate to say it, but pull the black girl."

Isaiah shook his head. "No, I can't do that. She has her heart set on this and she needs this opportunity to improve her life."

"What will you tell the police about the phony gear? I mean, they want to charge you!"

Isaiah stroked his chin. "I'll tell them I was sent an anonymous gift for help with the David Marsh Foundation. Apologize for accepting the gift at face value without checking the authenticity of the signature, but it never crossed my mind that people would deliberately donate fraudulent goods. Why would anyone do that? And we'll give the eight thousand back."

Yvette congratulated herself for getting to the bottom of it rationally and not going off half-cocked. After the mix-up with Isaiah's stay at the Marriott, she knew he'd have a logical explanation. Eight thousand dollars poorer, but happy to know that her husband wasn't behind the fraud. She knew better. He could still get the COTS award. She finished her wine and held her glass toward her husband. "Any chance of another glass of wine? It might help me think of something. Do you mind, darling?"

"If you must." Isaiah got up and took the glass into the kitchen, passing through the living room where the TV was on. He stopped and picked up the remote when he saw Cory Logan and Alexander Eubanks' pictures on the screen. He turned up the volume.

"It's official," the newscaster declared. "Charlie Gillettie, Cory Logan's manager, has announced that a Logan/Eubanks rematch is on. The fight has been in the making since they last met and the terms have now been agreed. The fight will take place at Madison Square Garden in New York."

"Well, I'll be," Isaiah muttered. He decided to pay Cory Logan a visit. He'd get some insight. And if Logan couldn't convince him he was in top form, he could always bet on Eubanks. The corners of his mouth turned up. "We'll get that scholarship money yet."

Chapter 27

"I need to see your pass."

"I don't have a pass," Isaiah explained. "I'm friends with Cory. He told me to come down and watch him train." Isaiah put his fists up, smiled, and moved his feet doing the Ali shuffle. "I might even teach him a few things myself so he wins this time."

"Sorry, pal. I have strict orders not to let anyone in without a pass. If you were friends with Cory, he would've sent you a pass. His training is confidential."

An argument looked futile. The guard, or bouncer seemed a more appropriate term, was twice the size of Cory and twice as mean. Isaiah would bet on him if he could get odds. The Hispanic Hulk stood with his arms folded, emphasizing his enormous biceps.

Isaiah turned, accepting defeat, and walked down the sidewalk toward the parking lot.

"Oh, hello, Isaiah."

Charlie Gillettie's British accent lifted his spirits—and she was still talking to him. Yvette may have blown it, but maybe he had remained in her good books.

"Hello, Charlie." He purposely sounded upbeat. "May I say how ravishing you look?"

"I bet you say that to all the boxing promoters."

He leaned in. "I have never ever said that to Don King. Nor would I."

She laughed. "What are you doing here?"

"I had hoped to talk to Cory, but the bouncer said no dice."

"Remind me to give him a raise. Not for keeping you out specifically, but for following my instruction. Cory needs to stay focused. I don't want him getting distracted during training. Apparently, he has a new fancy woman who wants more than his left jab, if you get my meaning."

His heart sunk at the thought that it could be Alicia. Did he really want to know? He was doing everything for that girl. Surely, if it was her with Cory at the Marriott, she would have come to her senses by now and was waiting for his call—which he silently pledged then and there that he would make soon. He would take her to Hawaii. He would get her the scholarship. And he would change her life. She never had a better lover than Isaiah. She said that herself. Besides, Logan was white. She would never entertain that for anything more than a novelty. He had to ask to satisfy his curiosity, and at the same time hoping to curb his jealousy.

"Is she a woman of color?" he asked.

Charlie touched his arm. "We're all people of some color, Isaiah. Even me."

That was good enough for him. Whatever happened at the Marriott was behind them. Logan must be dating a white girl. Nobody calls white people "People of Color" unless they are being ironic—or sarcastic. Good. Now he could forget it. He wanted to do business with Cory, but him stealing Alicia would be a deal-breaker.

"Besides," Charlie added. "I've never seen her."

Isaiah breathed a sigh of relief. If Cory was going around with Alicia he'd want to show her off.

She would be delicious arm candy for an egomaniac sporting image. It couldn't have been her.

"Other than that, how's his form?"

Charlie nodded. "It's good. He wants revenge. That's what he needs. Extra motivation."

"Excuse me for asking … I don't really know a lot about boxing, but isn't five losses kind of a lot for someone going for a championship? I thought challengers were always like thirty-three and oh or something. You know, undefeated."

"Luckily for Cory he's got a good manager." She exaggerated a smile. "He started his career at one and five. I was in the opposite corner managing the boxer who handed him his fifth loss. At that point, his career should have been over, but I saw something in him. I took a chance on him because I believed in him. I took over and he won his next twenty-six fights in a row. So he was twenty-six and oh under my management when he fought for the title. Okay, now he's twenty-six and one under me, but I got him a rematch. This time he's going to do it."

"You sound confident."

"I don't like losing. Neither does Cory. But at his age and record, if he doesn't take the title in this fight, he never will. He'll never get more motivation than he has right now. As long as I keep him off the women and the booze he'll be middleweight champion of the world. You can take that to the bank."

"Can I talk to the bank?"

Charlie looked at her watch. "Five minutes."

Charlie smiled at the bouncer as she and Isaiah approached the entrance. "It's okay, Pedro, he's with me."

The bouncer nodded and stepped to one side, letting them pass.

Isaiah soaked up the environment. The sound of leather hitting leather provided the musical backdrop. The stench of sweat—although not unpleasant—filled the gym. It smelled of determination woven into a graft of hard work. A voice in the back shouted instruction. "Keep your guard up."

In the middle of the gym, Cory laid leather on a punching bag while the trainer held it, shouting encouragement. "That's good, kid, keep it up. You got 'im. You got 'im. Don't let him play no head games."

Isaiah watched in awe as he stood a few feet away from a sweat-laden Cory. The punches sounded so much sharper from just a few feet away than they did when he sat in God's balcony. It made Isaiah shudder.

Cory faced Isaiah, perspiration cascading down his face.

"What brings you to my neck of the woods?"

"I wanted to wish you good luck with your rematch. How are you feeling?"

"Like the next middleweight champion of the world." He pushed some sweat off his forehead with his glove.

"Can we talk?" Isaiah asked.

Cory threw a glance toward Charlie.

"Oh, man talk, is it?" She flicked her hair. "Guess that's my cue to go powder my nose."

Isaiah smirked. "If you don't mind. It's just—"

Charlie held her palm up. "Don't worry, big man, but no more than five minutes. Cory needs to get in that ring and stay focused.

Isaiah nodded as she walked away. Cory led them over to a quiet corner of the gym where he took a seat on a wooden bench. Isaiah followed suit.

"So you feel good about this fight?"

Cory swiped at a beaded up sweat ball on the end of his nose. "I feel good about all my fights. We've covered this already."

"Yes, I know, but is this something I can bank on this time?"

Cory pointed at him with his glove. "Look, I'm going to do my best to win, and so is Eubanks. If you want to bet on me, fine, but I don't come with a money-back guarantee."

"I know you can't pick a round, or even guarantee a win ... but there is another outcome you can control, right?"

Cory pulled back, eyeing Isaiah with contempt. "If you're even thinking about suggesting what it sounds like, I'll put you in that ring right now and punch you until you're pronounced brain-dead." He glowered at the deacon.

Isaiah waved his hands halting the accusation, and hopefully calming Cory. "Of course not. I would never suggest—" He stopped himself. So the guy has a moral objection to taking a dive. Disappointing, but respectable "What makes you think you can take him this time? We know what happened last time you two met."

"That's right, and that gives me a purpose Eubanks won't have. Revenge. That's my motivation. What's his?"

"What's your strategy?"

"I'm going to play the long game this time. If an opportunity presents itself, I'm gonna flatten the son-of-a-bitch. But I'm looking at going the distance and getting the decision. I have more stamina than him. I can out dance him and hit more scoring punches. Going for the knockout is dangerous against someone like Eubanks. I learned my lesson. I'm gonna outlast him."

"So you think I should bet on a decision in your favor."

Cory smiled and shook his head. "You're really hooked on this thing, aren't you?"

"Me? No. It's for the children."

"Of course. Put it this way. I'm a five to one underdog. If you think I can win, don't bet any more than you can afford to lose, but you could increase your money five-fold if you just tick the box, 'Logan to win.' No other guesswork required."

"And you really think you can do it this time?"

Cory stood up. "My five minutes is up. Goodbye, Isaiah."

Isaiah stood up, touching Cory's arm to halt him another moment. "One more thing … I'd like to borrow your beachfront villa in Kauai."

Cory smiled, said nothing, and danced his way to the ring, shadow boxing along the way. He stepped between the ropes, still dancing in the ring as a warm-up for his sparring session.

Isaiah took another look at the challenger. Yes, he did look impressive—and confident. A $50,000 win would reap him the cash he needed for the foundation and the trip to Hawaii with all the trimmings with Alicia. And a bunch of flowers for Yvette.

All he needed was to get his hands on ten grand.

Chapter 28

"Yvette," Isaiah called out as he bounded into the house. "Yvette!"

"I'm in the laundry room," she answered.

He came in and gave his wife a quick peck on the cheek. "Good news. I found a way we can raise the money for the foundation."

"Great. What is it?"

"I bumped into Morris Schwartz, you know, the financial guy. He figures there's going to be a big surge in the bitcoin market. We need to get in there fast. We need some cash to invest. How much is in the foundation account?"

"Wait a minute." Yvette held her hand up. "Just slow down there, Hoss. You want to take money out of a charity account for bit what?"

"Bitcoins. It's all the rage for playing the market."

"Isn't that like gambling?"

"No, gambling is putting money on a horse."

"But it's still risky, right?"

"Life is risky, but we need money for the foundation. And quick."

"The police are still investigating the fraud case so I don't think we should be taking money out of the foundation to speculate on the market."

He stepped in and took her by the hands. "Look, Schwartz knows what he's doing. He has an oceanfront house and a Bentley. He knows the

239

market. We just need to ride on his coattails for a little while. We need to get the money from somewhere."

"Are you suggesting we use our money?"

He bobbed his head. "If we have to."

Yvette shook her head. "Uh-uh, no way, forget it. We are not risking our money to send two kids to cop school."

"How much do we need to hit the target?"

"Twelve thousand."

"Easy. When we recover what we put in, plus another twelve, we'll pull out."

"How much do we have to put in?"

"Ten thousand."

"Ten thousand dollars! Are you crazy? That will take the account down to eighteen thousand, then we need to make twenty-two grand to make bank. All for some bit ... bit ... bit shit—or whatever the hell it is?" She shook her head firmly. "No way, Jose. You'll just have to pull the black girl and that's that."

"I can't do that. I told you. Her mom's a crack addict and she needs to get a good job with decent benefits to get her into rehab. The police force looks after their own. She needs this job for a lot more than just money. It will save her family. This is the only way to get her in." He paused, letting guilt play on her emotions. And if that wasn't enough, "And would you please watch the language. The wife of a deacon shouldn't sound like a sailor."

Yvette pointed to her foot. "See that? Call me Sasquatch—and Bigfoot is coming down. No."

Isaiah stroked his wife's arm. "You know ... Morris is on the COTS board. I'm not saying that we can buy his vote, but if a man does business with another man, there's kind of an unspoken reciprocal agreement."

Yvette lowered her head. She hated the thought of pulling the black girl in favor of some white kid, even if it was Josh McKinna. But maybe they could make the money back with this bitshit. Isaiah was rarely wrong. And if he could get the COTS award, his name would look even better on a ballot. *Senator Hightower.* Then he could really get things done for the black community. She didn't like the game, but she certainly liked the potential. "Ten thousand dollars? Do you really need that much to make another twelve? Can't you do it with two?"

Isaiah shook his head. "That's not going to work. This is how you do it quick. If we only invest two thousand dollars we'll have to leave it there a long time—time we don't have."

Yvette sighed. "It sounds risky."

"Trust me on this one."

"I don't know. Maybe you should have Josh McKinna pay for it. I mean, really. Donating fraudulent goods. There should be a law against that."

"There is. And that's why I told the police it was an anonymous donation. Do you know what they'd do to a boy like Josh McKinna in prison?"

She shuddered. "It doesn't bear thinking about."

Isaiah gave her his sad puppy dog eyes.

"And you think this is the only way to get the black girl in?"

"Yes."

"And COTS …"

He moved in and stroked Yvette's arm. "Give me ten thousand out of the foundation and the

Citizen of the South will put back over twenty by next week." He raised his hand. "Promise."

A long silence followed.

She couldn't bear the atmosphere. "Are you sure about this?"

He remained serious. "No, but Morris Schwartz is."

"Okay," she sighed. "I'll go get the checkbook." Yvette stepped out to leave the room. "Should I make it out to Schwartz?"

"No, leave the payee blank. I'm not sure what name he trades under. I'll fill it out when I give it to him. Thanks, baby."

***

Isaiah called his bookie in Las Vegas. Just like Cory said, odds on a Logan victory were 5-1. He didn't ask for any variations. "Logan to win," he announced. "Anyway, any round."

He cashed the check in his name then wire transferred the money to his bookie in Vegas. Now he merely had to wait for the Logan/Eubanks rematch to collect his fifty grand.

The time passed tortuously slow until the fight. He couldn't think of a viable excuse to give Yvette as to why he may have had to go to New York, so a trip to Savannah to see Chief Webster to discuss scholarships was his next best lie. The truth he didn't tell her was that he would be sitting in Dark Alleys watching the fight with ten grand riding on the outcome.

To help pass the time until the fight he would hang out at the school to work on the upcoming year's curriculum. In between writing a memo to the custodian to seal up the hole in the boys' locker room that gave a bird's eye view to the girls' shower,

242

and requesting funding for more bleachers for the football field, he found time to call Alicia.

She answered on the third ring. "Hello, Isaiah."

"Hi, baby. How's my girl?"

"Depends. Are you going to yell at me?"

"Depends." He mulled over his next question. He didn't have any evidence, just doubt. He hoped she'd reassure him. "What's the state of play between you and Logan?"

"There is no state of play. I haven't seen him."

"So there was never any 'you two?'"

"Enough of the questions about my life without Isaiah. Why don't you tell me if there is ever going to be a life with Isaiah?"

"How about Saturday night. I have a late meeting then I can see you. We'll spend some quality time together."

"Just one night? Is that all you can spare?"

"For now. I'm still working on the trip to Hawaii."

"Are you sure about that?" she quizzed.

"Of course." There was some doubt as to whether or not he could still count on Logan's villa, but with the winnings, he could afford to splash out on a hotel if he had to. Isaiah played with the paper clip holder on his desk, poking his finger in through the magnetic hole. "Hmm ... you're not still working at Dark Alleys, are you?"

"Saturday?"

"No, I mean ever."

"Gee. I must have missed your big fat check last week. How's a girl supposed to eat?"

Pain pierced his gut. She was right. He couldn't afford to completely fund a mistress to the extent she wouldn't have to work, but he'd rather she wasn't teasing men to earn money. The temptation to have sex with them was too great—especially with meteorologists and men of the cloth showering her with gifts to bribe her affections.

He pushed his annoyance aside in an attempt to soothe her. "We'll talk Saturday, see what we can work out."

"Sure. Are we meeting at the Marriott?"

"You know what? I kind of like that Savannah Sleeper motel. It's cute."

"And more accommodating for a man having an affair." She exhaled a heavy breath. "Just to let you know … I ain't playing second fiddle forever."

"I'll make it up to you Saturday. If the meeting goes well I could have a big surprise for you."

"Bring it on, Daddy."

He smiled. "Call you Saturday." He hit the End Call button.

***

Isaiah passed through the curtain at Dark Alleys. He was relieved Alicia wasn't on stage, and he didn't see the Voyager parked anywhere. Perhaps his message of trying to better herself finally took root.

He made his way to the gambling hall, stopping at the bar to pick up a mineral water in anticipation of a long fight. He settled into the leather couch and found himself comfortable rather quickly. The young guy, William, who had first enlightened him to the world of boxing—and also the maître d at Luciano's—joined him on the couch.

"You here to watch the fight?"

"Too right I am," Isaiah confirmed. "So far I've won two and lost one with Logan. I'm expecting big things tonight. Big things."

"You're betting on Logan?"

Isaiah nodded. "I think it'll go the distance. Decision for Logan is my forecast, but I'll take a win any way he can get it."

"You don't think he's too old to be pulling an all-nighter?"

"No, I saw him working out. He's in top form." Isaiah leaned over and whispered. "And that's his prediction. He's going to ride him all the way to the final bell. That's his game plan."

"Good luck with that."

"What about you? You got a bet on?"

"Yep. I'm picking Eubanks. After the last fight, I just don't think Logan has what it takes. I got fifty bucks on the champ."

Isaiah patted his knee. "Hate to tell you this, friend, but you wasted your fifty bucks." He leaned back into the couch. "Nope, a Logan win."

William grinned. "Good luck, brother."

Isaiah had already finished his mineral water by the time the fight started. Although he had full confidence in Cory, a nervousness kept drying his mouth. He'd be fine once he won the money and was in Alicia's arms celebrating.

His attention turned to the announcer conducting the introductions. He scooted forward to the edge of the couch as excitement ran through his veins. Adrenalin had replaced the red blood cells. The bell ringing to introduce the beginning of round one produced a head rush. He went lightheaded and had to force himself to refocus. He'd have twelve rounds to sit through. It was no good passing out from the opening bell. He stayed on the edge of his seat as the boxers came out of their corners to face each other in the middle of the ring.

Cory led with a swift left jab that landed squarely on Eubanks' jaw. He looked good. He came to fight. Isaiah was pleased.

Eubanks was unfazed and countered with his own left jab that landed on the button. Cory wobbled. Eubanks followed up with a solid right to the body. A left to the head. A bombardment of body punches followed—then a right, a left, and a cosmic right to the temple.

Cory went down. He laid on the canvas like a bum on skid row. A crumbled, unmoving heap.

"No," Isaiah cried out. He rose and stomped his foot. "No, no, no! It can't end like this. Get up you low-life son of a dog." He punched his fist into his palm.

"Ten," the referee called, waving his arms over his head.

Eubanks danced a victory lap around the ring. Cory's doctor and trainer huddled over him administering smelling salts in an attempt to revive the fallen fighter. Eubanks halted his victory dance and stood over his opponent. A medical team jumped through the ropes and surrounded Cory.

After several moments, Cory moved. His legs jerked followed by his head and he sat upright. The medics helped him to his feet. Eubanks stepped over and embraced him, then quietly backed away to his corner—holding one arm in the air declaring himself the winner.

Isaiah felt like one gigantic bowel movement. Logan misled him again and now he was down fifteen thousand dollars because of him. He had nothing to give Alicia. The scholarship money for a second student was well and truly gone. And he'd have to come up with some incredible story about how Morris Schwartz didn't know what he was talking about and the bitcoin market crashed. Then he'd have to hope Yvette wouldn't go Googling bitcoins or call Morris Schwartz to give him a piece of her mind.

He left Dark Alleys, drove to the Riverfront Marriott, and checked in. After grabbing a mineral water from the mini-bar, he drew himself a hot bath hoping he could wash away the despair. While the bath filled, he sat on the edge of the bed and sent Alicia a text.

Sorry. Something came up. Can't make it tonight.

After hitting send, he switched the phone off. He went to the tub and lowered himself into the hot bath.

Chapter 29

A knock at the door awoke him. Isaiah looked at the clock in the hotel room. 8:05 a.m. It was too early for maid service. Surely it wasn't Yvette. She wouldn't have driven down unannounced—again. Would she?

He threw on his pants and wrapped a shirt around himself. He peeked through the peephole. There stood an angry-looking Alicia. He stared at the floor trying to figure out how she knew he was there.

She knocked again. Louder.

He swung the door open. "Alicia. What a pleasant surprise. What are you doing here?"

She put her hand on his chest, pushed him out of the way, and blitzed into the room. "I bet I'm a surprise. Who are you here with? Where is she?"

"What are you talking about? I'm not here with anyone."

"You better not be." She continued searching, storming into the bathroom, then retreating. She pulled back the long red drapes and looked behind the curtains.

"Seriously?"

Her angry faced hadn't dissipated. "I saw it in a movie."

His tone grew stern. "And where do you get off busting in here. If I had been in here with another

248

woman, it would have been my wife. How would you suggest I would have explained that?"

"You can cheat on me with your own wife in your own bed, but when you come to Savannah, Daddy, you're mine. And when you stand me up with an unexplained text, then don't take my calls, that's kicking one angry hornet's nest."

He held her by the shoulders. "Look, baby, I'm sorry. I lost a lot of money last night. Money I was going to give to you. You know ... to help with your expenses. I needed some time to come up with Plan B before telling you."

"How'd you lose it?"

"Bad investment."

"Does that mean Dark Alleys is my only source of income?"

"I don't want you to keep working there. I want you to better yourself."

She held her breasts. "Well, right now it looks like this is the only way I'm going to get fed. And what happens when I go to college? If you're not funding my private expenses, how am I supposed to eat? A girl needs stamina to study, you know."

"There's something else. There may not be enough money in the foundation for your scholarship. I was trying to raise the money another way, through the investment. But now that's gone belly up, I can't see how the foundation can manage it."

She took a step back and folded her arms. "So, you got it in my head that I *had* to become a cop, whether I wanted to or not. I *had* to quit working at Dark Alleys, whether I wanted to or not. And you don't want me seeing anyone else, but you won't put a ring on my finger. What the hell do you want from me, Isaiah?"

He held her by the shoulders. "Just a little patience, baby, I'll work something out."

She stomped her foot. "But why the hell did you stand me up?"

He stroked her arm. "I wasn't in the mood for you know what."

"I'm more than just a fuck toy, Isaiah. I have feelings, you know?"

"Alicia … don't use language like that. And that's not it."

She stood with her arms folded. Her lips quivered.

"How'd you find me anyway?"

"I took a chance. I figured if you were in Savannah, and if you weren't in the sleazy Savannah Sleeper, you'd be living high on the hog at the Marriott. I'm surprised you weren't in the Presidential Suite."

"What? How do you know—I mean, what's that supposed to mean?"

"Nothing. I'm just saying … I guess now I know where I stand. Thanks for the tits, Isaiah." She headed for the door.

"You still didn't tell me how you found me."

She wheeled around. "I can see that's the most important thing to you. Forget about hurting me, you just want to know how I uncovered your deception. Let's just say you can find out a lot from hotel staff when you speak their language."

"What's that supposed to mean?"

"Have you forgotten, Vice Principal Hightower? I took three years of Spanish in your school. I'm fluent." She smiled. "But I'm sure I won't need that skill if I talk to Mrs. Hightower. I'll spell it out in plain ole English."

He shook his finger at her as she walked away. "You better never—"

She walked out of the room and down the hallway. "Hell hath no fury, Isaiah."

***

Isaiah walked through the front door of his home on Vista Oaks. He prayed all the way home that Yvette hadn't received any phone calls.

"Hello, darling. How was your trip?" Yvette gave him a kiss.

Isaiah immediately appreciated her demeanor. Pleasant and unsuspecting. He could assume she hadn't heard from anyone. God answered his prayer. Perhaps Alicia was just venting temporary disappointment and she'd get over it. That would be Isaiah's prayer for Sunday—and he'd throw an extra ten bucks into the collection plate.

"Not as well as I had planned. I got mugged."

"What?" She raced over, took his head in her hands, and examined his face. "Are you okay? Did they hurt you? How'd it happen?"

He tried to calm her down with a few hand gestures. "I'm okay. It's the foundation that is going to suffer."

Yvette cocked her head to one side. "How's that?"

"Schwartz wanted the money in cash. He said he could save us a fortune in set up fees and his upfront commission if we paid with Bennys. So I agreed. That's why I had to go to Savannah. He has an agent there who deals with the cash transactions. On the way to his office, I got jumped."

251

"You got robbed again? First the car, now cash."

He cracked a smile. "Good thing we don't live in a mobile home, huh? They may have taken the house."

"This isn't funny." Her hands gripped her hips. "And why would you pay cash for such a thing? You never mentioned that."

"I told you, to get a better rate. And I didn't want you to freak out."

Her eyes narrowed. "Well I'm freaking out now."

"Don't worry. I reported it to Chief Webster and he's on the case."

"What are the chances of him finding the hoodlums? And if he does, what's the chances they'll still have the money on them? You did say there was more than one, right?"

He nodded. "Yes, three. Why?"

She stepped in closer. "I didn't think my man would give it up for just one punk." She stroked his chest. "Are you sure you're okay, baby? Of course I'm upset about the money, but you're the top priority."

He took her hands in his. "Yes, I'm fine. And you're right, the chances of them finding the perpetrators are pretty slim."

"What are we going to do?"

"We'll get it back somehow. The Lord looks after his own." Isaiah drew a deep breath. It was time to plant some seeds. "I happened to bump into the girl who was up for the scholarship. I thought it best to warn her that her place in the program was in jeopardy."

He studied his wife for a reaction. She looked calm, given the situation, and his revelation.

"Where'd you see her?"

"At church. After the incident, I found a prayer meeting. I wanted to pray for the misguided youths who robbed me, and of course, to get the money back. She was there."

"You're such a good man, Isaiah. Much more forgiving than I could ever be. But that's good. If she's a churchgoer she must be a forgiving person."

He shook his head. "I wouldn't say that. I told her and she did not take it well."

"What do you mean?"

"I told you how much she was counting on this scholarship."

Yvette nodded.

"For some reason, she blames me personally. She started shouting at me in church. It was embarrassing."

"You poor baby. You didn't need that. After everything you tried to do for her."

"Yes, I know. Just human nature, I guess. Anyway, she started shouting about how she was going to get even with me."

"Get even with you? What's that supposed to mean?"

He shrugged. "I don't know. Just … if you hear anything negative about me with regard to this girl, or the scholarship, ignore it. She may have just been blowing steam and nothing may ever come of it, but she was pretty mad. You know what young women in a rage can be like."

"Yes, I most certainly do." She wrapped her arms around him. "Don't worry, baby. I know my man and I'm going to look after you. And if that little madam wants to play games, she's messing with the wrong Hightower if she ever crosses swords with me." She held him tight.

Chapter 30

Chief Webster sat at his desk, rolling a pen between his fingertips. Isaiah sat across from him—sipping coffee.

"That's too bad about the girl," the chief said. "She just decided law enforcement wasn't for her, eh?"

"That's what she said."

Webster leaned forward. "But the white kid's still in, right?"

"Yes, yes he is. I spoke to him this morning and he's ready. We have the money for him and term starts next week."

"Are you sure you can't get the girl to change her mind? It took a lot of doing on my part, but the mayor finally warmed to the idea about this foundation and training cops on a scholarship. And he was especially keen on the boy/girl—black/white aspect of it all."

"That's what I've been doing for the past week. Then I came down again today to get her to change her mind. I stopped by her house but nobody was home." The truth was, Isaiah couldn't find her anywhere and she wouldn't return his calls. No one had seen her at Dark Alleys since they last spoke. He even made a special trip to her house, but no luck. He had no idea where she was.

"Too bad," Chief Webster said. "Anyway, I'll be there for the photo-op when the kid starts school."

255

"Me too."

"Why don't you bring your lovely wife? Yvette can always add a bit of glamour to an event."

Isaiah smiled. "I'll ask her, but I think she's busy."

"Tell her it would be a delight to see her if she can make it."

"Sure thing."

***

Isaiah locked the cruise control on at sixty-five for the trip back to Hilton Head. He was in no big hurry to get back home. He had little doubt that Yvette would have jumped at the chance to return to Savannah for the photo-op. She liked the town, she liked Chief Webster, and she loved having her photo taken. She would also love to quiz Webster about his progress on finding Isaiah's non-existent muggers. While the chief worked hard to bring the crime rate down in Savannah, Isaiah kept mythically pushing it up.

He pulled into the circular driveway noticing that the shrubbery looked a little untidy. He'd have a word with the gardener about that. Inside the house was immaculate as ever.

"Yvette," he called out.

"I'm in the kitchen."

He strolled past the couch taking notice of the central cushion with "Bless This House" embroidered on it. Yvette stood at the island, her hands in a mixing bowl.

"What are you doing?"

"Making chocolate chip cookies for the church social. If you're good, I might let you have one."

"Okay, how's this for good. How about I take you out for dinner?"

"That sounds very good. What's the occasion?"

"You're the occasion."

Yvette glowed at the suggestion. "Then may I suggest we have dessert back here? In the bedroom?"

He smiled. "I like the way you think, Mrs. Hightower."

Isaiah went up to the bedroom and had a nap while Yvette finished making the cookies. If Isaiah had his way they would have been out the door by five o'clock to catch the early bird special, but Yvette liked to dine later. It made her feel more European. At seven o'clock they hopped into the Volvo and headed to Rebel's Retreat Restaurant.

He turned north on Sylvan Street.

"Gosh, it's been ages since I've been down this street," Yvette commented.

"Yeah, me too. Maybe we should try to go out more often."

Yvette pointed across the street. "Oh look. That's new. What is it?"

The sign towered above the street. *Gentleman Gem's Gentlemen Club.*

"Oh my word, it's a strip club," Yvette gasped. "You'll have to do something about that. We don't want degenerates running around Hilton Head all … aroused. That's how sex crimes are bred. You're going to have to shut it down."

"Again? I don't know. It's not near the school and maybe they have a higher ratio of minorities dancing in there. It might be a tougher argument this time around."

Yvette screamed. Her arm waved wildly at the parking lot of Gentleman Gem's. "That's our car! The Voyager. Pull over, I'm calling the cops."

Isaiah sped up. "No, you can't. We'll be late for the dinner reservation."

"Blow the dinner reservation! I want those bastards thrown in jail. That's a family car they stole and they're taking it to a vagina drive-in. No. I'm not having it." She pulled out her phone and dialed 911.

"Please, Yvette. Put the phone away. We talked about this. We don't want any insurance hassles. Besides, I told you, I prayed about it. God told me they needed it worse than we did. And you don't want that piece of filth back now anyway. Let it go."

She stared at him then hit the call button anyway.

"Yes, this is a concerned citizen," she said into the phone. "I'd like to report a crime. It's taking place right now at Gentleman Gem's titty bar on Sylvan Street. They're selling drugs in there. And some of them don't have registrations for their cars. You better check it out." She hung up.

Isaiah looked at his wife, eyes wide, eyebrows raised. "What in the Oxford was that?"

She pushed her phone back in her purse. "If nothing else, that will at least kill their erections. They steal my car, I steal their fun." She smiled coldly and turned to look out the window at the passing boulevard.

"Must you be so vulgar?"

Isaiah shook his head in disbelief. Not so much at what Yvette had done, but the fact that Alicia was in town and making good on her word to use his gift to create her own wealth.

Isaiah tried to enjoy his chicken and dumplings at Rebel's Retreat but was distracted by the Voyager parked outside a strip club right there in Hilton Head. Yvette's determination to get the police involved added to his discomfort. He knew her. She wouldn't let this thing go. No doubt she'd be driving by Gentleman Gem's at every opportunity and even staking it out until she saw the person driving that Voyager. With Alicia being in the bar most nights, he presumed, Yvette would have plenty of opportunities to catch her.

His bigger concern was once Yvette confronted her, which in all likelihood she would one day, would Alicia spill her guts about their affair? She was sworn to secrecy inside the confines of Dark Alleys, but they were playing by a different set of rules now. Rules that made Isaiah very uncomfortable.

They left the restaurant and Isaiah exited left, heading down Clinton Avenue.

"Where are you going?" Yvette asked.

"Home."

"Why are you going this way? I want to go by that booby bar and see what's happening."

Isaiah groaned. "Probably nothing. This way's quicker."

"I'm in no hurry. I want to see if the cops are doing their job. We pay our taxes and they should be arresting scum—especially when they get a hot tip from a concerned citizen."

Isaiah knew a losing battle when he heard one. He turned down McAdams Way and cut over to Sylvan Street and begun the journey south. Gentleman Gem's sign came into view, but no police cars.

"Where are they?" Yvette screeched. "That's outrageous."

"They've probably already been and gone by now."

"But look." Her long slender finger pointed to the parking lot. "It's fuller now than before the raid." She reached in her purse. "I'm calling them and finding out what the hell's going on."

He placed his hand on top of hers. "No, you're not. If they trace that number back to you they're going to arrest you for wasting police time."

"Are you seriously trying to convince me that there are no drugs in there? There's a goldmine of arrests in that sleaze hall. Not to mention grand theft auto."

"Oh for crying out loud. Have you ever heard of probable cause? Police can't just go around shaking people down without justification."

"Tell that to all the African Americans who get gunned down daily by police in this country." She slammed her hand on the dash. "And there's the Voyager. It's still there! Stop the car. I'm going in."

"The devil you say. What are you going to do? Make an announcement?" He imitated speaking into a microphone. "Will the owner of a blue Voyager please step outside?"

"I might."

Next to the Voyager was a Ferrari. Cory said he had a Ferrari. That was too coincidental. Something was going on. Now he had motive.

"You're right, darling," Isaiah said. "I will get to the bottom of this. I'll drop you off home, and I'll come back."

"They might be gone by then. I want to come with you."

"No, this is no place for a lady. Things might get ugly. You never know what a drunk might do. But you're right. I have to do something."

She placed her hand on his thigh. "You will be careful, won't you?"

"Of course I will."

"Are you going to call the police?"

"If things get out of hand, but I'll get the lay of the land first."

She leaned over and kissed his cheek while he was driving. "You're such a hero. I know God has a special place for you in heaven."

They arrived back home and he escorted her in and went upstairs to change. He didn't want to ruin his best polo shirt if things did turn nasty. He slipped on a pair of worn jeans and a button-down shirt that should have found their way into the Salvation Army box at least a year ago. But they were suitable for fighting if need be. He was ready.

He kissed Yvette goodbye and headed for the Volvo.

Yvette wandered upstairs to use the bathroom. As she walked through the bedroom she saw Isaiah's phone on the dresser. She snatched it and ran toward the window, shouting for his attention. She could only watch as the Volvo glided out of the driveway and headed toward Gentleman Gem's.

Chapter 31

After shedding several layers of superfluous attire, Alicia gracefully reached behind her and pulled the string, freeing her thirty-four D's into action. She tossed the bikini top to one side bringing whoops of approval from the few dozen guys sitting at her feet by the raised catwalk. Cory discreetly adjusted his trousers under the cover of the overhang where his drink sat dripping with condensation. Enthusiastic gawks followed her around the platform as she slowly strutted, working her nakedness to earn another buck from lusting patrons.

Cory smiled. Alicia was different. She called and invited him to her new job. She said she wanted a familiar face in the audience for moral support. That made him laugh trying to connect some form of morality to a strip joint. But he liked her. A lot.

Now that he had retired from boxing, he didn't have to abstain from sex anymore like he did weeks before a fight. He also had plenty of time on his hands. Although he would have to live with the disappointment of never winning a world title, boxing had been good to him financially. He had no money worries, but loneliness could be an issue.

He wanted to spend time with Alicia. A trip to Hawaii might be what they both needed. He watched her dance on stage. She was fun. She was hot. Two vacation requirements. If they got on well in Hawaii, he would take it a step further. He could help her financially so she wouldn't have to strip anymore and he could be the sole beneficiary of her nakedness. He liked the idea.

He had trouble concentrating and going into a full fantasy mode because of the drunk next to him who wouldn't shut up. Cory had been throwing him death stares which would go unnoticed. But if the guy didn't stop with the wolf whistles and crude comments Cory was going to clock him into the next calendar year.

Alicia knelt in front of Cory. With cat-like prowess, she slinked toward him—her brown eyes staring at him, working to pull him into her world.

When she aimed her puckered lips at him, he reached in his pocket and threw a dollar on the stage. She reciprocated with a smile, which earned her another dollar. Cory didn't mind showing his appreciation by handing out dollar bills. The uneducated and uncouth might dub her a working girl. But she was an artist, although he seriously doubted Picasso's work could give him an erection like she did. It took a special kind of person to earn money taking their clothes off. Nice tits helped, but it was her confidence that intrigued him.

She winked at Cory. "Thanks for showing up. I can give you a private show later if you want," she whispered. "Your place?"

"Hey, sweetheart," the drunk next to Cory shouted. "You can fuck pretty boy there on your own time, right now you got a show to perform. Let's see that kitty-cat."

She scowled at the unshaven redneck. "Look here—"

Before she could finish, Cory was out of his chair. His clutch landed with a thud to the guy's chest as he grabbed the redneck by the front of the shirt. Cory pulled the derelict toward him. His six-foot-two-inch frame towered over the loudmouth still sitting in his seat. "She's working, dipshit, and doesn't need your comments. Now shut it and apologize to the lady," Cory demanded.

"I ain't apologizing for shit. And why don't you go fu—"

Cory's big right fist landed on the redneck's jaw. A loud crack echoed around the room, overshadowing Tina Turner singing "Private Dancer." He cocked his arm to deliver another blow. Before he could jab, a big Samoan grabbed him from behind.

"Come on, pal," the bouncer said, putting Cory in an arm lock. "Show's over for you. We don't want no trouble in here."

"Trouble? I was protecting the artist's dignity."

The Samoan laughed. "There ain't no dignity in this place, pal." The bouncer manhandled him through the bar and shoved him out the door and into the parking lot.

Cory stumbled landing face first on the crisply painted blue and white wheelchair logo in the handicap spot. His face scraped the fresh tarmac.

He covered his cheek with his hand, soothing the asphalt-inflicted pain. "Dammit!" He rolled over and stared up at Gentleman Gem's illuminated sign. "Rednecks R Us more like," he mumbled.

He got to his feet and brushed himself off, noticing he tore his pants and banged up his knee in the process. He limped over to his Ferrari and gently slid into the driver's seat. He sat wondering what to do next. He wanted to wait for Alicia, but how long would that take? He decided to give her an hour. Two if she didn't show in the first one.

He waited less than five minutes when from under the radiance of the sign over the front door, Alicia came out of the club and trotted toward the car—wearing sensible flat shoes and clothes.

She stood at Cory's driver's side window. She leaned in giving him a nostril full of Chanel perfume. "Are you sure you should be driving?"

"Course I am. Why?"

"I don't want you getting hurt—or arrested."

Cory smiled. "It's okay. I was only drinking Coke. I'm going home to get the hard stuff."

"Can I come with you? I could use some of the hard stuff myself—and I'm not talking about liquor."

Cory laughed. "A woman after my own heart."

"It's not your heart I want either." She winked. "I'll leave my car here if that's okay." She walked around to the passenger side and opened the door. "Can you bring me back in the morning?"

He smiled. "Not too early I hope."

Bright beams from an approaching car blinded them. The car stopped with the headlights trained on them. The driver's door opened. Isaiah stepped out of the Volvo.

"Well, well, well. What do we have here?"

Cory got out of the Ferrari. "You're not seriously here to try to get a refund out of me."

"If you want to make a donation to my cause, I might be a little more forgiving."

"Forgiving of what?"

Alicia moved away from the car and took a step toward Isaiah. "Don't tell me you're here because of me."

"What are you doing here, Alicia? You gave up the school, left Dark Alleys, and show up here in Hilton Head—working, I presume, in this glorified whorehouse."

Her jaw dropped. "Have you developed Old-Timers? You pulled the scholarship and wanted me to quit Dark Alleys. What the hell do you want from me?"

"I want you to have some respect for yourself," he shouted. "And for me."

Cory moved in between them. "Whatever is going on between you two—"

"Was," Alicia said. "There's nothing now. It's over, Isaiah. Go back to your wife. Leave me alone and I might not tell her."

"You wouldn't dare," Isaiah hissed.

Cory's gaze stayed on Isaiah. "It will be a miracle if Yvette never finds out about you two, but your best chance of her not finding out is to leave now—or I'll tell her myself."

"What?" Isaiah pointed back and forth between the three of them. "We have a bond, a contract, and a vow of silence. All of us. What happened between me and Alicia can never be discussed." He stared at Alicia. "Remember what happened to Jimmy?"

"What happened to Jimmy?" Cory asked.

Isaiah squared off with him. Nose to nose. "He ratted on another member of the club. The place lived up to its name. He was found in a dark alley. The case remains unsolved."

Cory bumped chests with him. "Are you threatening us?"

"If I have to, yes." He pointed at Alicia. "If you ever open your mouth about any of this you're going to find out what it was like to be Jimmy." He turned his attention to Cory. "And as a member of the club, one word out of you and you'll be dead too. I have connections."

Cory's went into his pre-fight pose. His eyes hardened and his jaw clenched. "Don't threaten me."

Isaiah lunged, taking a wild swing at him.

Cory blocked the punch then pushed him. Hard. Isaiah backpedaled trying to keep his balance but his feet couldn't keep up. He stumbled backward and hit the ground, landing on his tailbone. Rage engulfed him.

Cory pointed at the fallen deacon. "You leave us alone, Isaiah. If you lay one finger on Alicia I'll put you in a dark alley myself."

Isaiah reached inside the Volvo and pulled a gun out from under the seat. He got to his feet and aimed the pistol at Cory.

"Give me one good reason why I shouldn't blow you away right now. You cost me a ton of money because you can't fight. You steal my girl right out from under my nose after I introduced you to my private club. And now you threaten me?"

Cory took a stance. "You better dust me right now. Because if you don't, I'm going to shove that gun up your ass."

Headlights shone from an approaching car. The car stopped.

Cory moved toward Isaiah.

Alicia stepped in. "C'mon guys. Let's not—"

A shot rang out.

Alicia fell to the ground.

The headlights lit up her fallen body.

"No," Cory yelled. He huddled over Alicia's body, feeling her neck. He placed his hand on her face. "C'mon, Alicia, I'm going to take you to Hawaii. You can't die."

Isaiah stood open-mouthed, not saying anything, staring at her lifeless body. *Why did she move? That bullet was meant for Logan. What will people think if word gets out that Isaiah Hightower shot a black girl? I'll be destroyed.*

Cory sprung to his feet. "You killed her you son-of-a-bitch." He charged Isaiah and grabbed the gun from him.

Isaiah remained motionless. The state of shock kept him frozen, unable to speak or move.

Yvette climbed out of her Volkswagen Eos, stepping in front of the lights that shone on the three of them.

The cover of the night couldn't hide Yvette's shock. The whites of her eyes glowed in the darkness. "Isaiah?" she muttered.

Isaiah glanced over, then looked back at Alicia's unmoving body. He choked up but had to control his emotions. His wife was only yards from his dead mistress. He could only be sad for the death of a young woman, not a woman he cared about—for Yvette's sake.

Cory had the gun aimed at Isaiah. "Get back in the car, Mrs. Hightower. You don't want to see this."

"No!" she screamed at the top of her lungs.

Two men came out of the club and ran over to the scene when Yvette screamed.

"What's going on?" One of them asked.

Yvette pointed at Cory. "He's got a gun. He's going to shoot my husband."

The men circled Cory, their arms held at half-mast surrender. "Take it easy, bud. No one wants any trouble."

"This son-of-a-bitch just shot this girl," Cory declared, still aiming the pistol at Isaiah.

Isaiah deactivated his grief for the sake of survival. In a burst of supreme confidence, he advocated his defense. "I didn't do it," he declared. He pointed at Cory. "Look at him. He's the one with the gun. It was him. He shot that girl."

"You liar." Cory raised the pistol, aiming it at Isaiah's head.

Isaiah assessed the guys who came over. One wore a flannel shirt, jeans, and a belt buckle big enough to fry an omelet on. He looked like he could take Cory. Isaiah appealed to him. "Ask my wife." He turned his attention to Yvette. "You saw the whole thing, didn't you, Yvette. You saw Cory Logan shoot that girl. Tell them."

Sirens filled the night air, drawing ever closer.

"Tell them!" Isaiah shouted.

Yvette's mouth remained open but no words came out.

Screeching tires announced the arrival of a police car. Followed by another. Then an ambulance. The noise from the sirens wound down to a whimper before going quiet. Flashing lights bounced off the stars and shone back to earth, highlighting the tragedy.

Doors to the police cars swung open. Police officers emerged, peeking over the tops of the doors, guns drawn, aimed at Cory Logan.

"Drop the weapon," an officer barked.

Cory looked around, searching for divine intervention. When that didn't happen, he placed the gun on the ground and raised his hands.

Two cops raced in while the other one stayed behind the safety of his car door, still pointing his gun at Cory.

An officer grabbed Cory, wheeling the boxer around, and throwing him face first against the roof of his Ferrari. "You have the right to remain silent ..." he barked as he applied the handcuffs. With the suspect cuffed and Mirandized, the cop escorted Cory to the back of the police car and shoved him in.

The cop from the second car was on his own. He holstered his weapon and wandered up to Isaiah and Yvette. He spoke to Isaiah. "Hello, Brother Hightower. What happened here?"

Isaiah squinted, taking a moment to recognize the officer. He broke out in a smile. "Brother Thomas." The men shook hands. Isaiah turned to Yvette, cluing her in. "Brother Thomas is a fellow beacon shining deacon." He faced the cop. "Good to see you, brother, I just wish it was under different circumstances." He shook his head as if trying to piece together what had happened. "It's difficult to say what happened, I'm still in shock. I just pulled up and the white guy was attacking the girl, so I intervened. He took my gun and shot her."

"Your gun?"

Isaiah dipped his head. "Yes. I have a permit to carry. I can be a target."

"Of course. But why'd you pull the gun? Did he threaten you?"

"Not at first, but I recognized him. I knew he was a fighter. I wasn't about to stand toe-to-toe with him, so I grabbed my gun to scare him off—to protect the girl. He punched me in the stomach, took the gun, and shot the girl." He looked at his wife. "You saw it, Yvette. Didn't you?"

The officer looked at Yvette. "Did you see anything, ma'am?"

She held up Isaiah's phone, barely speaking above a whisper. "I just came down to bring my husband his phone."

"I need you both to come down to the station. You need to fill out witness statements. Secure your cars and come with me." He pointed to the squad car.

The Hightowers did as instructed and climbed in the back. The policeman shut the door and walked to the driver's side.

Isaiah rubbed his hands together. "Do you have a wet-wipe? My hands are all sweaty."

Yvette handed him a moistened towelette from the packet out of her handbag.

He wiped his hands and gave her back the used tissue. "Can you get rid of that for me, darling?"

She shoved it in her purse.

He patted his wife's leg. "With our testimony, we'll put Logan away for a long, long, time. He'll get what he deserves. You were right. He's a jerk."

Yvette stared straight ahead, saying nothing.

Chapter 32

Yvette sat on the padded bench for over an hour while the police took Isaiah's statement. She was pretty sure she saw Cory Logan corralled into another room. She had no idea what stories were being told in either room. She didn't want to either. She just wanted to go home.

A tall, dark, handsome man stood before her. Very tall and very dark. "Mrs. Hightower? I'm Detective Rison. Would you like to come with me?"

A detective? She found that odd. The cop who brought them in only spoke about witness statements. Surely they didn't have detectives doing simple admin work. She didn't want to talk in the first place, but now she was afraid of being interrogated.

She followed behind Detective Rison, taking notice of his highly shined shoes—even on the backs. They didn't look like they were very comfortable for running, which was what cops had to do, right? She judged his afro to be stuck in the last millennium. A good-looking guy like him should have been in dreadlocks.

She followed his non-verbal instruction of an extended arm and sat at the table where he aimed. He sat opposite her and opened a folder with several papers in it. *Several. Already? What the hell was going on?*

"Sorry to keep you waiting so long, Mrs. Hightower, but we've had conflicting stories from your husband and the other suspect."

"Suspect?"

"We're hoping you can shed some light on the situation for us."

"I really didn't see much."

Rison leaned forward and spoke in a hushed tone. "Before we get started, let me say how much I admire what you and your husband have done for the black community. And I've worked for Chief Webster in Savannah before coming here. He has always spoken very highly of your husband. Now …" He leaned back in his chair and raised his voice to a more natural tone. "I must advise you that our conversation will be recorded to ensure we get the facts correct. Is that okay with you?"

"Do I need a lawyer?"

Rison chuckled. "Not at all, Mrs. Hightower. You are not under suspicion for anything. We just need some verification."

She nodded.

Rison turned on the recorder. "Mrs. Hightower, can you tell me what you saw tonight in the parking lot at Gentleman Gem's."

"Not a lot that the police didn't see. They arrived shortly after I did."

"Okay, then let's try this. Where were you before the officers arrived?"

She drew a deep breath, her eyes zooming around the room before she spoke. "Our car was stolen last month. We saw it parked at this club place. My husband dropped me off at home because he said it was no place for a lady. Then he went back to see if he could find out anything. After he left, I noticed he didn't take his phone. So I took it to him."

"If your car was stolen, why didn't you call the police?"

"I did, but surprise, surprise, they didn't do anything."

Rison let out a frustrated breath. "What kind of car was it?"

"A blue Chrysler Voyager. License number one-six-nine EE."

Rison wrote it down. "I'll see what I can find out about it. Back to tonight, why would you take your husband's phone to him? I mean, if he was concerned for your safety, and wanted you to stay home, why would you go down there?"

"Because I was concerned for *his* safety. Maybe he would have needed to call the police. And by the looks of things, he should have."

Another cop joined them. He was more robust than his partner. Shorter, broader, and whiter. His suit wasn't as nice either. He approached the table with a confidence that looked like it had been gained by years of service. The gray hair may have added to her assessment of that.

"Mrs. Hightower. I'm Detective Bridge." He shook her hand. "We appreciate you coming in."

"I didn't have a lot of choice."

Rison handed Bridge the paper he had written on. "Teddy, could you check this out? The Hightowers' had their car stolen and it was at Gentleman Gem's tonight. See what you can find out?"

"Sure thing."

Yvette's eyes followed him out of the room, then looked back at Rison.

"Logan says your husband shot the girl, and your husband says Logan shot her. If you witnessed anything it would help clear this case up in a matter of hours rather than weeks."

"I didn't see anything."

"It was your husband's gun that was used. Regardless of who shot Miss Saunders, it was Mr. Hightower's pistol that fired the fatal shot. He admits getting the gun out of the car, but only to scare Logan. But simply by bringing the weapon out indicates that he was ready for a violent altercation. He claims Logan was attacking the girl. When he intervened, Logan threatened him. That's when he got the gun. A case of self-defense. Did you see anything to corroborate his story?"

"It was dark. I couldn't see."

Rison couldn't hide his eye roll. "This isn't helping, Mrs. Hightower."

She avoided eye contact with him.

"Did you know Cory Logan?"

She folded her arms across her chest. "I met him a few times."

"Did you like him?"

"I don't see that that's relevant."

"Everything's relevant in a murder inquiry."

"Then, no. I don't like him."

"But you don't dislike him enough to say he did it—regardless."

"What kind of person do you think I am? I don't lie about people to get them sent down just because I don't like them." She moved forward, staring Rison down. "I didn't see anything, and I'm done answering questions."

Detective Bridge returned and handed Rison a couple of papers. "Here's the details of the stolen car, and Detective Cunningham wanted me to give you this."

He took a few moments to read them. "Teddy, could you get us some coffee?"

"Sure. How do you like it?"

Rison invited Yvette to order.

"Black. How else?"

Rison smiled. "Make that two."

He directed his attention to the papers Bridge handed him. "Looks like we found the thief, or owner, of your car."

"Good. I hope you throw the book at him."

"There won't be any book throwing. She's dead."

"What? Who? She?" Her face went through an array of puzzled looks.

He tapped his pen on the tabletop. "Did you or your husband know the victim? The one Cory Logan allegedly shot."

"I don't even know who she was. I didn't see her face. She was dead when I got there."

"Alicia Saunders?"

She shook her head. "Never heard of her."

"She was the registered owner of the car."

"What? That's not possible. I mean, the car was stolen. Are you saying ..." A severe bout of dizziness swept over her. Things just weren't adding up, but as she knew, the police were often incompetent. There must have been some mix-up.

"It seems very unusual. In my twelve years on the police force, I've never known a common car thief to register a stolen car in their own name. She would also have had to steal the title as well and been a pretty good forger. And we couldn't find any record of it ever being reported as stolen."

"What are you saying?"

"I can't see clear evidence that it was ever stolen."

"Of course it was. Isaiah said—" She stopped. *How bizarre. There had to be a logical explanation.* "Of course it was stolen, but you know what? I'm not so sure we want to press charges. Isaiah said the thief had to be worse off than us to steal it, so we'll let God deal with her on judgment day."

"I'm glad you feel that way because it's kind of hard to press charges against a corpse."

Yvette folded her arms across her chest. "Glad I saved you the paperwork."

Rison reached over and switched off the recorder. "Mrs. Hightower, I'm going to be honest with you. Isaiah is being interviewed by Detective Cunningham. He may very well be innocent, but things are stacking up against your husband. He never mentioned anything in his interview about your stolen car. He said he went down there looking at ways he might get the club closed down on morality issues, which was always going to be a bit of a stretch. On top of that, he was the one who pulled the gun and he knew Cory Logan. And if this investigation leads us to find that he knew the victim and gave or sold her the car ... whew ..." He blew out an exaggerated breath.

Rison stared Yvette down, but she didn't return fire.

Rison continued. "There was no gun residue found on Mr. Hightower's hand. But, there was none found on Cory Logan's either. So it's your husband's word against a respected sports figure— and we know what their track record for getting off is. Unless you saw Logan pull the trigger, Mr.

277

Hightower is going to have a battle of epic proportions. And given his background, he'll find things exceptionally difficult if he gets a white jury. Do you understand where I'm going with this?"

Yvette sniffled, ran her finger under her nose, but didn't answer.

He pressed on. "Now, would you like to think again about what you saw or didn't see?"

Rison paused for a few moments giving Yvette time to reconsider her story, then reached over to switch the recorder back on. Yvette placed her hand on his, stopping him.

She spoke softly. "I think I best have a lawyer."

***

Ernie Simpson came into the interrogation room fifteen minutes after Yvette called him. He was already in the building talking to Isaiah, so it simply boiled down to a trip down the hall. When he came in, he asked Rison for five minutes of privacy with his client.

He sat next to Yvette and angled his thin frame toward her. "I couldn't take your call while I was in with Isaiah, but I got your message. What's up?"

She always liked Ernie. He was generous with his support of Ebony Evolution and often advised Isaiah on how to ensure he didn't cross any legal lines in his pursuit of righteousness against racial injustices. He had warned Isaiah that one wrong move and certain police officers would take delight in taking him out of the limelight.

Yvette stared at her hands clasped on her lap. "They want me to … well, I'm not sure what they want me to do—or say."

"It could be the truth they're after." Ernie pushed up his gold wire-rimmed glasses.

"I'm not so sure. I need time to think. Can you get me out of here?"

"What's your current status?"

"As far as I know I'm a witness who didn't see anything."

"Okay. That shouldn't be too difficult."

"How's Isaiah?" She asked.

"He's facing a good cop/bad cop duo. The white guy wants to stitch him up and the black cop is one of us. And he's senior."

"Will he get out?"

"Should do, but maybe not tonight. But remember …" He placed his hand on hers. "If they ask you anything, anything at all, you have spousal privilege. Not that's he's done anything, but you do not have to say anything about him to aid the police in their investigation. You're off limits if they go gunning for him. Don't talk about anything the two of you have discussed in private."

She nodded. "Thanks."

Rison returned and Yvette was free to go shortly after Simpson pointed out that she wasn't under any suspicion. The police had no right to detain a witness who didn't see anything. Rison wasn't so convinced that she didn't see anything, but Simpson won the argument.

***

Isaiah opened the door to their bedroom shortly after 11 a.m. the next morning. He looked exhausted. Yvette didn't look so good herself. She had been up half the night worrying about her husband. She got out of bed at 5:30 a.m. in an attempt to silence her mind. She tried to conceal the bags under her eyes with an extra packing of foundation, but they were still evident.

Isaiah walked across the room and threw his arms around her. "It's so good to be home, baby."

"What'd they say?" She asked.

"The lead detective believes my story, not Logan's. So they let me out. I can't leave the state until the investigation is over, but they think Logan did it—which he did. You saw it. You need to tell them—"

"I'm not sure what I saw, Isaiah. It was dark. I was disorientated. I didn't get a clear view of anything."

Isaiah sat down. "Is everything okay?"

She folded her arms. "Did you know the girl?"

"Who?"

"The stripper who got shot."

"The stripper? What are you talking—"

"Before we go any further, Detective Rison was very candid with me during the interview. He said the girl was the registered owner of the car. And as we know, you never mentioned to the police that you went to that Gem's place to find out who stole our car. You told them you were there on a morality crusade. Why would that girl be the registered owner?"

"Yvette—"

"And why were you arguing with that boxer anyway?"

"Yvette." He held her by the shoulders. "The girl was the one who was supposed to get the other scholarship. She did steal the car, and I found out."

"How the hell did she steal the car? Who is she? Holly Hotwire?"

"I might have left the keys in it."

"You what?" Yvette's face went ashen. "Oh, my gosh. That's why you didn't want to tell the police—or the insurance company."

He nodded. "I was going to tell them, but when I confronted the girl, she cried. She lives in Savannah but couldn't get back and forth to visit her sick mother in Atlanta. Then she said she couldn't accept the scholarship because she didn't have any transportation to get there every day. So I gave her the car."

"You gave her the car?"

He nodded sheepishly.

She raised an eyebrow. "Did you give her anything else?"

He sliced his hand through the air. "No. The car and the scholarship. That's all that girl ever got out of me."

"Then why did you even go down there if you knew the car wasn't even stolen?"

"I was going to give her a piece of my mind for lying to me. She was supposed to use that car to visit her mother and to go to school—not to drive to a job designed to excite men for immoral pleasures."

Yvette looked toward the heavens—giving God a pleading glance for hopeful assurance that her husband was telling the truth.

Isaiah saw it as a simple eye-roll of disbelief.

"Look, baby, it's a misunderstanding. I didn't know the girl was a stripper, and I didn't know Cory Logan was there. All I know is I showed up to tell her off, saw Logan attacking her, and I tried to defend her. He threatened me, then threw me to the ground. So I pulled my gun. He punched me and took the gun. Then he shot the girl because she was yelling rape. He wanted to shut her up. You were there. You saw it." He stroked her arm. "You need to tell the police I didn't do it."

"I'm not sure what I saw."

"You saw Cory Logan shoot the girl."

She stepped back. "Is there anything else I should know?"

"Yes, I think Cunningham is a Klansman and is trying to stitch me up. It's my word against a sporting icon, a white icon. Cunningham wants to take the easy way out and pin it on the nigger."

"Isaiah!" She stomped her foot. "Don't ever use that word. Especially talking about yourself. You've worked too hard to let trash like that escape from your lips."

He embraced her. "You're my only chance, baby. We've worked too hard to let Cory Logan put an end to everything we've done. We can't let him stop us from carrying on our good work." He lightly brushed the sides of her cheeks.

She wiggled out of his grip. "I don't know. Maybe."

He delivered one of his award-winning smiles. "Now, what did those gorgeous brown eyes see?"

Yvette dropped her head and looked at her watch. "I have to go. I'm meeting Gloria for lunch."

Chapter 33

The hostess escorted Yvette to the table. Gloria was already there, sipping Chardonnay, which alerted Yvette to the fact that she herself must have been *really* late. As soon as she sat down, Romeo appeared and poured her a glass of wine from the bottle chilling in the ice bucket by the table. The ladies ordered seafood salads and Romeo left them in peace.

"So what's up, girl?" Gloria asked. "You sounded distraught on the phone."

Yvette leaned in, whispering. "Forget about being sworn to secrecy, this has to be top, top, super top secret. Swear on your mother's life this goes no further than you and me. Ever."

Gloria pushed her fringe to one side. "You have my attention."

Yvette's face hardened. "I don't want your attention. I want your oath to God that this stays right here. Swear."

Gloria held up her hand. "I swear, I swear."

"I saw something last night I wish I hadn't." She took a solid gulp of Chardonnay. "I think Isaiah shot someone last night."

"What!"

Gloria's outburst drew looks of curiosity from other diners and a sharp reprimand from Yvette.

"Will you keep it down?"

Gloria spoke in a panicked whispered. "What do you mean he shot someone? Killed them?" She leaned in, halfway across the table.

She nodded. "We went out to dinner last night and when we were driving home we saw our stolen car sitting in the parking lot of that new strip club down on Sylvan Street. Isaiah dropped me off at home then went back there to investigate. But he forgot his phone, so I took it to him in case he needed to call the police. When I got there, he had a gun pointed at that boxer—Cory Logan. Then a girl ran between them, and Isaiah fired. Killed her. I saw it. I had the headlights right on them."

Gloria looked around the restaurant making sure no one was close enough to hear their conversation. "He shot a girl? On purpose?"

"I'm not sure. I think he was shooting at the boxer, but the girl got in the way. I couldn't tell. Then the boxer took the gun—or Isaiah gave it to him, I don't know which, but Logan ended up with it. That's when I jumped out. I screamed, and Logan said he was going to shoot Isaiah. Then the police showed up." She hid her face behind her hand, wiping away a tear.

"I can't believe it. Had you been drinking?"

"No! And if I hadn't seen it with my own eyes I wouldn't have believed it either."

"So what happened?"

"The police took us all down to the station. Isaiah said Logan did it. Logan said Isaiah did it. And the police asked me what I saw."

"What'd you say?"

"I told them I didn't see anything."

"So it's just his word against the boxer's?"

"Yes, but it was Isaiah's gun that killed her. Isaiah wants me to say I saw Logan shoot her. What am I going to do?"

They halted their conversation when Romeo returned with the salads. At Gloria's request, he ground some pepper on her salad. Yvette, in turn, shooed him away with the back of her hand.

Gloria restarted the conversation. "You cannot destroy his legacy. Isaiah Hightower has done too much good for too many people. I'm sure there was some justification. What did he say? Have you spoken to him?"

"He said the boxer was trying to rape the girl and he stepped in."

Gloria raised a hand in enlightenment. "Well, there you go. That's what happens when men go to those places. They get urges they can't control. It's a good thing you sent him down there or something bad could have happened."

"Something bad could have happened? A girl is dead!" She covered her mouth realizing she spoke louder than she should have.

"It sounds like a wicked thing was always going to happen, but at least Isaiah caught the bad guy."

Yvette shook her head. "Something's not right. Why not tell the truth in the first place? He didn't tell the police about the stolen car. He didn't tell me about the stolen car—or not stolen—whatever the hell it was."

Gloria shrugged. "I don't know. Maybe because he shot the victim instead of the perpetrator. I'm sure it was an accident, but it still doesn't look good, does it?"

"No, it doesn't, but something's not—"

Gloria clutched her friend's hand. "If a white guy accuses a black man of killing another Negro, who do you think a jury is going to believe?"

Yvette scrunched her face. "Who says Negro anymore?"

"A white jury trying to hang one." She patted Yvette's hand. "No. You have to stick up for your husband. You're duty-bound. You cannot let him go to jail. Tell the cops you saw that Logan guy pop the girl."

Yvette's jaw dropped. "What?" She expected support from her girlfriend, but an outright lie? "Gloria, a girl's life is over. I—"

"And there's nothing you can do to bring her back." She tightened her grip on Yvette's hand. "You love your husband, right?"

"Of course I do."

"Then you have to do whatever you have to do to protect him. Besides, this Logan is a professional boxer, right?"

"Uh-huh."

"So he's rich, right?"

"I suppose so."

"So he's going to use his millions and get himself a fancy suit to defend him. The suit will argue that rich white people don't kill people. If Logan doesn't get acquitted, he'll do a couple of years. Tops. Save your husband, Yvette. It's your duty."

It was as if God used Gloria as His spokesperson. There were no gray lines in her advice. It was a definitive "Save Isaiah" decree. And she had a point. Cory Logan would get off no matter what. He had the right colors—green money and white skin.

Yvette reached into her purse and took out the towelette Isaiah gave her after the shooting. She looked at the black smudges on it. She laid the tissue on the table for Romeo to clear up. "I suppose," she mumbled.

***

Yvette returned home and hung her car keys on the rack next to the front door. Isaiah was sitting on the couch in the living room. She plopped herself in the easy chair opposite him.

"Good lunch?" He asked.

"Yes, thank you."

"How's Gloria?"

"Supportive."

He squinted in puzzlement. "How's that?"

"She said I should support my husband. No matter what."

Isaiah smiled. "I always did like Gloria."

"But I already told the police I didn't see anything. What are they—"

"Yvette." He pushed forward to the edge of the couch. "You saw it. You saw the whole thing. Cory Logan killed her. Did he, or did he not, have the gun in his hand when you arrived? And he had it aimed at me. If you hadn't shown up when you did, I'd be six feet under and you'd be the Widow Hightower."

They stared at each other.

Yvette timidly shrugged. "I don't know. The light was casting a funny shadow. I'm not sure what I saw."

He moved over and held her by the shoulders, looking deep into her eyes. "Baby, I did not kill that girl. You have to believe me. You have to testify that you saw Logan shoot her. Whether you actually saw him do it or not, I did. I saw him do it. You have to believe me. Believe what your husband saw. If I don't get an eyewitness, you know they're going to pin it on me. I've ruffled a lot of police feathers with Ebony Evolution. They'd like nothing more than to get me out of their hair so they can go back to harassing black people without having to answer for their actions. Help me out, baby. Do it for all the people we help." Isaiah literally sat on the edge of his chair, waiting for his wife to respond.

She didn't look at him. After a few moments, she nodded slowly, then spoke in a hesitating whisper. "Yes, it's all coming back to me. I think I did see Cory Logan shoot the stripper."

"Are you sure?"

She looked Isaiah in the eyes. "Yes. I saw Cory Logan shoot that girl."

He moved in and held her tight. "Thank you, baby. Let's go to the police station."

***

Detective Cunningham stepped into the waiting area and summoned Yvette. Isaiah rose with her.

"Sit down, Hightower," the detective instructed him. "I need to speak to your wife on her own."

Isaiah dipped his head. "Of course." He winked at Yvette. "Do your thing, baby."

Cunningham led her down the beige corridor.

"I thought Detective Rison would be interviewing me," Yvette inquired.

"Naw, you got the good-looking cop this time."

He was paler than she thought he would be. Perhaps it was the contrast of his red hair that lightened him.

They walked into room three. Yvette sat down, clasping her hands on top of the brown veneer table.

Cunningham sat opposite her. He tapped the recorder. "Are you familiar with the procedure?"

She confirmed with a single nod.

The detective flipped on the recorder. "This is Detective Cunningham with Yvette Hightower. The time is 4:05 p.m." He eyed Yvette until she felt uncomfortable. "What triggered the sudden recollection? Did Mr. Hightower convince you to come forward?"

"I don't have to be here, you know. My lawyer said I don't have to tell you anything about my husband."

Cunningham stretched his long arms, interlocking his fingers behind his ginger hair. "No, you don't have to tell us about your private conversations. However, you will be summoned to appear in court as a witness. When asked under oath, you would be obligated to tell the court what you *saw*. You were a witness to a murder, Mrs. Hightower. That's not hearsay or privileged exclusion. What you saw was fact. The court demands that facts be presented by witnesses, especially when a man's life is at stake—be it your husband's or Mr. Logan's."

Yvette broke eye contact. She decided she didn't like Cunningham. Yes, she could see him in a pointy white hat. He must have given Isaiah a rough ride.

"It's good you're coming forward now" Cunningham continued. "If you stick to your story that you saw nothing, then suddenly remember events that could change the outcome of the case while sitting in the courtroom, I dare say that the prosecution would be inclined to charge you with obstruction of justice." He paused, letting his words resonate. "Of course, if you're here to save your husband's ass and fabricate events to corroborate his story, then that would constitute perjury in a court of law. Both crimes carry sentences of up to five years."

She cast her gaze toward the ceiling, looking bored. "Can we get on with this?"

He pulled himself up to the table and pulled a notepad in front of him. "Go ahead, shoot. What'd you see?"

"I pulled into Gentleman Gem's parking lot to bring my husband his phone. I saw a commotion. Fighting. My car headlights were aimed at three people. I recognized my husband, and I saw a man, a white man, Cory Logan, pointing a gun at a girl—an African American—and he shot her. Then Logan pointed the gun at my husband. I got out of the car and screamed. A couple of guys came out of the bar to help. Then the police showed up."

"You're saying Cory Logan shot and killed Alicia Saunders?"

"Yes."

"You seem pretty clear. What was so difficult about it before?"

"It was dark. I wasn't sure."

"But after spending the day with your husband, you developed a pretty clear picture. But it was still dark when the shooting took place. That didn't change. Are you sure it was Logan."

She nodded. "Yes."

"Which side was he on? Right or left?"

"Umm ... I'm not sure."

"Didn't you and your husband discuss possible questions that we might ask? Was the gun in Logan's right or left hand? How far away was the girl when he shot her? Did you see your husband with the gun? By his own admission, he did have it. Did you see Logan punch him and take it?"

"Stop!" Yvette buried her face in her hand and took several deep breaths. She composed herself and eyeballed Cunningham. "I saw Cory Logan shoot a black girl in the parking lot of Gentleman Gem's. That is my statement and I'll testify to that in court." She stood up, staring down at the detective. "Now ... if there's nothing else."

"If that's how you want to play it." Cunningham gave a weak salute with two fingers. "Thank you for your time, Mrs. Hightower. See you in court."

She turned on her heel and headed for the door.

"Oh, Mrs. Hightower ..."

She looked back.

"You best be ready for some tough questions on the witness stand. I know the accused's defense attorney. He's not as easy-going as I am. He's gonna grill you."

Chapter 34

Yvette noticed Isaiah was a different man since the shooting. He had always looked after her, but he was much more attentive in the days following the incident. He spent more time with her and was more tolerant of her Chardonnay sipping. He even bought her a small bottle of vodka for an occasional evening cocktail. When he did go anywhere, he would ask her if she wanted to come along.

Because he had been instructed not to leave the state until after the trial, he missed Josh McKinna's ceremonial first day at Chatham College. His disappointment at not being able to keep his promise and take her to Savannah was obvious to Yvette, but he kept to the confines of South Carolina and took her to Myrtle Beach instead. They had a wonderful weekend and their sex life had nearly reverted back to honeymoon frequency. And she had the promise of a trip to Hawaii after the trial.

The more she thought about it the more certain she became that it was, in fact, Cory Logan who shot the Saunders girl. She thought it was Isaiah who stood on the left, but it was Logan on that side. Isaiah confirmed it. She accepted it was her fault. If she hadn't sent Isaiah down there to try to find out who stole the stupid car in the first place none of this would have ever happened. She should have listened to him. Since she insisted on getting her own revenge, Isaiah felt duty-bound to talk to the girl and convert her to a path of righteousness. He even prayed for the Saunders girl and her family at mealtimes. That was the kind of man he was. Compassionate. She should have left it alone. God is fair and just. He'd send those responsible to hell in His own good time. She screwed up.

She stood in front of her closet looking at the choices of what outfit she'd wear to court the day after tomorrow. Isaiah concluded he should have a new suit for the trial and went into town to get new duds. She let him go on his own. He had impeccable taste but was a slow shopper.

The doorbell took her attention away from her wardrobe.

A tall figure stood at the entrance. She opened the door to Detective Rison.

"Good afternoon, Mrs. Hightower. May I have a word with you?"

Yvette hesitated. She liked Rison, but he was a cop—and cops knocked on doors of people they wanted to arrest, not help. But insisting on a lawyer at this stage might insinuate guilt—guilt she didn't have. Isaiah would be the next best obstruction. "Does my husband need to be here? Because he's out at the moment. You'll have to come back later."

"No, that's okay. I can speak to you, and you can tell your husband what we spoke about when he gets back."

She looked behind Rison and out to his unmarked police car. He was alone. She stepped to one side, a mute gesture inviting the detective in.

He glanced around in every direction, taking everything in. He even looked up at the vaulted ceiling and smiled appreciatively. "Nice place."

"Thanks."

They sat on the couch.

"I heard you gained memory of what happened."

She offered a silent nod.

"Good. I'm glad you're able to help. I was pleased to hear it."

"I think I was in shock when you interviewed me the first time. I had never seen anyone killed before. My subconscious must have blocked it so I didn't have to relive it at that moment. With the passage of time I got over the shock and regained my powers of recollection."

"Good. I just want to make sure you'll be ready for the trial. Logan has a lawyer, Bert Jones. One of the best in the business and he's ruthless on witnesses. I've faced him in court myself. He's a shark. He'll be coming after you."

Yvette bobbed her head. "That's okay. The truth has no fear."

"Neither does Bert Jones."

She warmed to Rison. He did sound as if he was trying to be helpful. "Who else will be testifying?"

"In addition to you and Mr. Hightower, the two men who came out of the bar and helped you. And some expert witness to explain the trajectory of the bullet, angles, and all that kind of thing."

"Is that normal? The expert thing?"

"Hmm ..." His face scrunched digesting the question. "This is coming from Logan's side so they're obviously going to dispute the angle Isaiah said he saw Logan shoot from. As long as the two of you have the same story, and saw the same thing, it'll be fine."

294

"Are you saying what I think—"

"I'm not saying anything. I shouldn't even be here, but I wanted to hear what jogged your memory." He stood up. "But … it might be a good idea if you and Mr. Hightower discuss in detail what you both saw. And hopefully, in court, your stories will be identical."

Yvette gave a nod of approval. "Gotcha."

***

Yvette wanted to make Isaiah his favorite dinner—scalloped potatoes with ham. She went to the pantry and discovered she didn't have enough spuds. She could have quite easily made spaghetti, but Isaiah had been through a traumatic ordeal and she wanted to please her man. A quick dash to the market and she'd be able to do that. And why not spoil him a little? After all, he did book her into the Presidential Suite in the most prestigious hotel in Savannah. He deserved a treat in return.

She got in her Volkswagen and flew down to Sam's Supermarket. She liked shopping at Sam's. The aisles were wide and stacked neatly and fully. Plenty of staff were always on hand to answer questions or to offer help. As she went through the vegetable section, she noticed a tray of Portobello mushrooms. She stopped in front of them for a moment. "Bitch," she uttered and moved on.

They always had several checkout lanes open and she was in and out in no time. She fished her keys out as she approached the car and hit the trunk release. The trunk lid was up by the time she got there allowing her to put the potatoes in without breaking stride. She rounded the back quarter panel.

Cory Logan stood opposite her driver's door.

Yvette jumped, placing her hand on her chest. "Oh my God. What are you doing here?"

"I followed you."

"Why aren't you in jail?"

"Because I haven't been found guilty of anything—yet."

"But ..."

"Oh, you must mean bail. Yes, wealth does have advantages."

Her heart pounded hard. She looked around the parking lot. There weren't many people around, but there were a few. She saw a big biker-looking dude. She thought about screaming, but the man standing in front of her killed the last girl that screamed in his presence. "What do you want?"

"I need to talk to you."

She pushed past him, reaching for the door handle. "I'm not talking to a murderer."

He grabbed her arm. "Please ..."

She looked in his eyes. The man holding her arm could kill or maim—in fact, did kill and does maim—but his eyes were soft. They were compassionate eyes that told a story of desperation—*desperate to save his own ass.* Cory Logan could rot in hell for all she cared. And she would give him a forty-year layover in prison before he got there. She shifted her gaze from his eyes and focused on his hand on her arm. "Get your hand off me," she hissed through gritted teeth. "You're already going down for murder. Do you want to add assault of a woman to those charges?" She reconnected with his eyes.

Cory let go of her. "Yvette, please, I'm begging you. You know as well as I do I'm no murderer. You're the only witness, and you know it was Isaiah who shot Alicia. I understand why you're doing it, but can you really live with yourself knowing you sent an innocent man to prison?"

"I saw what I saw."

"And you saw your husband shoot his mistress."

Yvette's eyes narrowed. "He did not have a mistress! She was some trash you tried to rape. He told me everything."

He smirked disbelievingly. "He told you everything, did he?"

"Yes, he did. And I was the one who sent him down there, I'll have you know. Trying to instill some morality into that place of ill-repute you seem so happy to frequent." She wagged her finger at him. "Not only is he a man of the people and a dutiful husband, he is also a man of God. He does not bang strippers and hoes."

Cory clasped his hands in prayer as much as a plea. "Yvette, please ... I know we don't see eye to eye—and I know you love your husband very much. I'm not going to drag his name through the mud because that will only make you hate me more than you do already. I'm just asking for the truth. Forget everything else. What is most important to you? The color of a person's skin or justice. Don't sleep next to a killer because you got your priorities mixed up."

"I can assure you, Mr. Logan, my priorities are exactly where they should be." She straightened her shoulders in a 'no fear' action. "Now, if you'll excuse me."

Cory stepped aside to allow Yvette to get into the car.

"You're the one who has to live with it," he said through the rolled-up window. He turned and walked away.

Yvette sat in her Volkswagen Eos and sobbed.

***

Isaiah waltzed into the living room looking dapper in his brand new blue checked Merino wool suit. He opened his arms and gave a twirl in front of Yvette. "What do you think?"

"Nice."

"Nice? I was going for fabulous."

"Okay. Fab."

"Is everything okay?"

"Detective Rison stopped by."

"Oh?"

"He wants us to rehearse our story."

Isaiah chuckled. "We don't have to rehearse. You saw it just like I did. Cory Logan gunned that girl down in cold blood. He was on the left of Miss Saunders when he fired the fatal shot. He's right-handed, remember? I tried to stop him, but it was too late." He leaned toward her ear. "You could say that you saw him punch me in the gut and take the gun from me if you wanted, but I wouldn't want you to lie if you didn't actually see that." Isaiah straightened himself up. "Other than that, the truth will send Cory Logan to jail and God will punish him as He sees fit after that. Right?"

"I guess so ..."

Isaiah sat next to his wife and put his arm around her. It was meant to be comforting, but it gave her a chill. "Look, darling, you were right. I should have never got mixed up with a low-life like Logan. He's barbaric, just like you said. We both saw it firsthand. I should have listened to you. I'm sorry." He delivered a kiss to the side of her head. "Now, with our testimony, Cory Logan will spend a long time behind bars. Who knows, maybe he'll find the Lord while in prison. That will be my prayer. Then, after the trial, you and I will go to Hawaii. The best hotel in the heart of Waikiki. Just what my girl wanted!" He ended on an upbeat note, lifting her spirits—a little.

"Yes, of course … We have our trip to Hawaii to look forward to."

"Yes, we do. We deserve it."

She didn't want to blow the trip to Hawaii, and she knew Cory Logan was a liar, but she wanted a little more reassurance. "And you didn't know the girl?"

"The dead girl? The stripper? No. Just what I told you. She was going to get the scholarship, so naturally, we talked a few times. And of course, we had the episode with the car, but no … I didn't know her personally."

"How did she get the scholarship? I mean, how was it that she came to your attention?"

"Oh, uh, she was one of the deacon's nieces. She had a lot of tough breaks in life and needed a second chance. The good deacon asked me to give her that chance. So I did."

She raised an eyebrow. "And the chief of police was okay signing a troubled youth up to be a police officer? I thought he'd be after stable, law-abiding people to uphold law and order."

"Look at Josh McKinna. He stole a police car, and I got him in." Isaiah stood up, his frustration beginning to show. "Did Rison pump all these questions into you?"

299

She traced her finger on the edge of the couch. "No, it's just if they ask me in court if there was any past history between you two, I need to know."

He laughed. "The only history you need to know was that I was trying to help an ambitious, but underprivileged girl get ahead in life."

She smiled and nodded. "Good. That's all I need to know. I thought Rison was full of shit."

Isaiah walked to the kitchen.

Yvette stayed on the couch well aware that he didn't challenge or reprimand her use of the word shit. *Very unusual.*

Chapter 35

Several reporters and photographers stood on the courthouse steps when Isaiah and Yvette arrived. Cameras clicked and voices shouted questions at the couple.

Dozens of people, many of them black, stood on the steps of the courthouse with placards and signs, most of them denouncing Cory Logan. One woman held a sign displaying the message "Black People Deserve Justice Too." Another read "Logan's Last Fight. Let Him Burn In Hell."

The crowd cheered wildly when Isaiah smiled and waved to them.

"We love you, Isaiah," different voices shouted.

A reporter yelled out to the Hightowers."Is this another one of your Ebony Evolution campaigns, Mr. Hightower?"

Isaiah stopped and faced the camera, clutching Yvette's hand. "This is not about black or white. This is a murder case that my wife and I were summoned to testify in. We are not here to campaign against injustice. We are here to see that justice is served. It doesn't matter what color the victim was, nor does it matter what color the perpetrator is. All that matters is that the killer is brought to justice." He tugged Yvette's hand and led her up the steps and into the courthouse.

Yvette developed a sudden hardening in her stomach. Harder than a knot, more like a stone. It felt heavy. Perhaps that's how justice felt. Like a two-ton granite burden.

They took their seats behind the prosecutor's table in the packed courtroom. Cory walked in wearing an immaculate gray pinstriped suit. The double-breasted cut showed his fitness and broad chest. His attorney looked equally as sharp in a brown suit with hints of maroon. His bronze skin suggested that when he wasn't in the courtroom he spent time in the Bahamas working on his tan—on a gazillion-dollar yacht. He and Cory sat at the defense table.

Cory looked antsy, Yvette thought. Strange for a fighter who stared death or brain damage in the face every time he stepped into the ring. She concluded this was a different kind of fight for him. An emotional one. Just behind his table sat his British bimbo. She was the one who had the fighter face on.

The bailiff quieted the murmuring crowd with an instruction to "All rise." He introduced Judge Alfred Hollingsworth as the presiding judge. A white-haired, dark-skinned man, pushing seventy and wearing large brown plastic-framed glasses, strolled across the platform and took his seat behind the judicial bench.

Yvette studied the jury. Six black and six white jurors. She was surprised Logan's hotshot lawyer allowed an even split.

The prosecution began by calling different police officers to the stand. Their testimonies didn't seem to have much impact with the jury—after all, they were there after the fact and only reported what was said while interviewing suspects and witnesses. It looked like it would be a simple case of Isaiah's word—and the testimony of any witnesses—against Logan's.

Then, the quest to send Cory Logan to prison began in earnest.

"The state calls Isaiah Hightower to the stand," the bailiff bellowed.

Isaiah squeezed Yvette's hand, then stood, and straightened his jacket. He marched to the stand. He was sworn in and took a seat in the richly padded chair in the witness stand.

Bert Jones shot to his feet. "Your honor, I'd like to ask the court that Mrs. Yvette Hightower be excused from the courtroom during her husband's testimony."

Judge Hollingsworth looked over his glasses at the defense attorney. "Why?"

"Your honor, the defense feels there may be some collusion between Mrs. Hightower and her husband. She changed her story at least once, and we are not convinced that her story is entirely hers. We believe she has been coached. Hearing her husband's testimony may simply give her a template to follow when it is her turn on the stand. The defense would like to hear her testimony without prejudice."

Judge Hollingsworth stared at the defense counsel without responding. He leaned back, resting his chin in the crook of one hand, drumming his fingers on the bench with the other. The courtroom waited for his response.

Isaiah raised his hand from the witness box. "Your Honor?"

The judge nodded respectfully toward Isaiah. "Yes, Mr. Hightower?"

"This ordeal has been traumatic for myself and my wife. The fact that we are co-witnesses is irrelevant. She's already given her statement to the police and will reiterate what she has said before, as will I. However, I need her here for moral support in having to relive the tragedy of that night. And I hope the court will allow me to give her my support when she is on the stand."

"Your Honor," Jones interrupted. "Mr. Hightower is an accomplished public speaker and used to the limelight. He gives vivid accounts of violence and injustices on a regular basis. I sincerely doubt he needs Mommy here to hold his hand."

People in the courtroom laughed.

Judge Hollingsworth's eyebrows knitted together. "Mr. Jones, Mr. Hightower is a respected member of the community and does not deserve to be ridiculed. And on a personal note, this court does not appreciate sarcasm."

The prosecutor stood up. "Your honor, the prosecution objects to the dismissal of Mrs. Hightower. The defense is suggesting premeditated perjury by the Hightowers which is in insult to a man of unstained character and his wife."

"Sustained," the judge ruled. "Counsel will refrain from suggesting improprieties by the witnesses and from using disrespectful language to those giving sworn testimony. Perhaps you'd like to offer Mr. Hightower an apology." Hollingsworth glared at Bert Jones.

Jones bowed toward Isaiah. "I apologize, Mr. Hightower. I meant no ill-intent."

Isaiah sat stone-faced, not acknowledging the apology.

"Good. Let's move forward," Judge Hollingsworth announced.

Yvette breathed a sigh of relief. She was pleased to be staying. She saw it clear as anything because she had the headlights on them. Cold-blooded murder—plain and simple. Still, she wanted to hear what her husband had to say.

She watched her husband in the witness box and noticed him throwing a smile the judge's way.

Tony Voss, the prosecuting attorney, paced in front of Isaiah several times before beginning his examination of testimony. He looked to be of mixed race, Yvette concluded. He was a handsome man and considered most of his genetic makeup came from the darker blood. That would account for his attractiveness. "Mr. Hightower, can you please tell the court the events that transpired on August 20th in the parking lot of Gentleman Gem's entertainment facility."

Isaiah adjusted his tie. "Certainly. I went to the club to gather evidence to make a petition to the court to close down this particular venue. I am the principal of the local high school and am concerned that these types of businesses can lead young girls astray. Easy money the uneducated way is not an example I want my students to see. It is inappropriate."

"How's that? Patrons must be twenty-one to enter, and the windows are blacked out. What harm can be done?"

"If teenage girls see women in their twenties and thirties arriving to work in expensive cars, they may want the lifestyle that accommodates that kind of wealth, even if ill-gotten. An easy way to satisfy their hunger for flashy cars is to prey on weak-willed, lust-filled men. And as we know from the events of that fateful night, lust can rage out of control, as it did for Cory Logan. He attacked Alicia Saunders to satisfy his own perversion which ultimately ended her life."

Bert Jones smacked his hand on the table. "Objection, Your Honor." Although he was a short guy, not more than 5'7", his voice boomed with all the bass of a marching band drum. "Perhaps the prosecutor would like to sit this one out and the court will simply listen to Mr. Hightower's monologue. Mr. Hightower is conducting the prosecution on his own. And as for injecting his own morality issues, may the court remind him that he is in a witness box, not standing behind a pulpit."

"Sustained. Mr. Hightower, as interesting as your conjecture may be, let's stick to the questions asked and forego any sermons."

Isaiah nodded. "Of course, Your Honor."

The prosecutor gave Isaiah an introductory gesture by opening his hand to him. "Mr. Hightower, please proceed with an account of what happened when you arrived at Gentleman Gem's."

"I saw a couple arguing in the parking lot. Well, I thought they were arguing at first. When I got out of the car, I heard the girl scream 'Leave me alone.' And the man said something like 'You're gonna get what you deserve.' Then he called her the 'B' word. So I got my gun and approached them."

"Why did you grab your gun?"

"He threatened me. When I stepped out, he said 'Get back in your car.' Then he called me the 'N' word."

Tsks of disapproval ran through the gallery, but no sense of outrage. As distasteful as it was, that was life in the South—even in the 21st century.

"Did he just?"

"Yes, he did. So naturally, I was alarmed, but I still had to protect Miss Saunders."

"And then?"

"The girl yelled rape. I think Logan must have seen I had a gun, but I'm no killer. I just meant to scare him off. I think he sensed that and he rushed me. He grabbed the gun, took aim at Miss Saunders, and fired. She dropped instantly."

"You said 'Logan.' Did you know him?"

"Yes. He was going to do a fundraiser for me but pulled out at the last minute. He said it wasn't in his best interest to do freebies. He said if he didn't get paid he couldn't do it."

"I see. Did you know the victim? Alicia Saunders?"

"She would have benefited from the money I was trying to raise to send young people to college to get a degree in criminology so they could join the police force. But we didn't raise enough money to send her this term. Perhaps if Logan would have helped with the fundraising like he said he would, we may have hit the target, and Alicia would have been in her dorm room studying instead of taking her clothes off."

Jones was on his feet again. "Objection, Your Honor. The witness is speculating on a wide array of issues and trying to put the blame on my client, which is not only misleading, it is slanderous—and he's off again on another morality crusade."

"Sustained," the judge deadpanned. "Mr. Hightower, let's stick to what did happen and not what might have happened. And I would remind you again for the sake of Mr. Jones, this is a courtroom, not a church."

Isaiah nodded silently.

"The bottom line, Mr. Hightower, is—you were there. Correct?"

Isaiah pointed at Cory. "I was five feet away from that man when he shot Alicia Saunders."

"Let the record show Mr. Hightower pointed to the defendant, Cory Logan. No further questions." Tony Voss sat down.

Bert Jones meandered over to the witness box. "Mr. Hightower, isn't it true that you placed bets on Cory Logan's boxing matches."

"I don't bet," Isaiah declared.

"Oh? Didn't you get a nice little windfall when Mr. Logan knocked out Ricky Rodriguez in the third round of a fight—just as he predicted?"

"No."

"And didn't you then lose fifteen thousand dollars on Logan's next two fights when he lost to Alexander Eubanks."

"No."

"In fact, you asked Cory for the money back that you lost while betting on him. And it was the fifteen thousand dollar sinkhole that kept Alicia Saunders out of college—"

"Objection," Tony Voss barked as he took to his feet. "Your honor, the defense is badgering the witness. Mr. Hightower has already said he does not bet, and he said it under oath."

The judge nodded toward Mr. Voss. "Sustained." He directed his gaze to Bert Jones. "Move on."

"But, Your Honor, Mr. Hightower—"

"I said 'Move on,' Counselor."

Bert Jones stood over the defense table rummaging through the paperwork. "If the court will allow, I'd like to address what Alicia Saunders told Cory Logan about her relationship with Mr. Hightower."

"Objection," the prosecutor barked as he rose to his feet. "It is inadmissible hearsay what Alicia Saunders may have said to Cory Logan. The prosecution cannot cross-examine her."

"Sustained. The jury will disregard," the judge instructed.

"And Mr. Hightower is not on trial here," the prosecutor continued. "The police filed charges against Cory Logan based on the evidence they had gathered, not Isaiah Hightower."

"Evidence concocted by Mr. Hightower and his wife," Jones argued. "And his testimony has marked differences from what he told the police just moments after the shooting."

The judge smacked his gavel in the wooden coaster. "This court is here to determine Mr. Logan's guilt or innocence, and Mr. Logan's alone. If he is found not guilty and the police have evidence against another suspect, then that will be a matter for another court." He addressed the jury. "Ladies and gentlemen of the jury, it is Mr. Logan on trial. No one else. It is up to you to decide *his* fate—no one else's. Are we clear?"

Several jurors nodded.

Jones continued in his booming voice, addressing Isaiah. "Other than through the scholarship program, did you know Alicia Saunders in any other capacity?"

"No."

"Are you certain? Records show that she was a student in your high school in Savannah, Georgia."

"It wasn't *my* school. I was merely the vice principal." Isaiah remained rock steady. "But, to answer your question, she may very well have been a student at Savannah High during my tenure. But if she wasn't a troublemaker, school-skipper, violent sociopath, or drug dealer, chances are our paths never crossed."

"Really? You only keep track of the students with discipline problems?"

"Those are the ones I would most likely see, yes. But okay ... I'll add to our chances of meeting. If she was valedictorian, a record-setting athlete, or an academic scholar, perhaps we would have met. If she was an average student who kept her head down, she would have flown under my radar like the other two thousand students at the school."

"Mr. Hightower, didn't you have an affair with Miss Saunders?"

Tony Voss stood. "Objection!"

Judge Hollingsworth raised his hand. "You don't have to answer that, Mr. Hightower." He dead-eyed Bert Jones with a stern warning. "May I remind Counsel, Mr. Hightower's morality is not on trial."

"Interesting." Jones headed back to the defense table. "I have nothing further, Your Honor."

Judge Hollingsworth engaged the prosecutor. "You may call your next witness."

"We'd like to call Yvette Hightower."

The judge looked at his watch. "Fine. This court will recess for twenty minutes. When we return, Mrs. Hightower will be on the witness stand."

Chapter 36

The Hightowers slipped into the foyer to catch a breath. Yvette was pleased to get the feeling of space around her. The courtroom felt claustrophobic simply sitting in the gallery. She imagined the witness box would feel like being confined by a straitjacket and sent to sea in a one-person submarine.

"That went well," Isaiah boasted. His broad smile reflected his confidence.

Yvette swayed nervously to and fro, her eyes wandering every inch of the marble encrusted building "So, this Saunders girl ... she was a student of yours?"

"Apparently." He shrugged. "But she must have been quite average. Average students don't catch my attention. And many students try to keep a low-profile, just like Alicia Saunders did. Makes sense, doesn't it?"

"I guess so."

Isaiah rested his hand on her shoulder. "Are you going to be okay?"

"I guess so, but I'm nervous as heck. That Jones guy scares me."

"Don't worry. Judge Hollingsworth won't let him crucify you." He winked.

Her eyebrows arched. "Oh?"

Isaiah leaned over and whispered in his wife's ear. "He's one of us."

Yvette's face scrunched. "What does that mean?" Her voice delivered a small squeak.

"Just tell the court what you saw—you saw Cory Logan shoot Alicia Saunders—and the judge will keep Jones off your case. Like he said, we're not the ones on trial here, Logan is." Isaiah straightened his suit jacket. "I have to go to the men's room. I'll be right back."

As he walked away, Gloria stepped into his vacated space. "You should be proud of your man. He held his composure well against that little twerp."

"Sounds like he had a little help," Yvette suggested.

"Of course he did. He had God in the witness box with him."

"I'm talking about the judge."

"What? They know each other?"

"Sounds like they exchange funny handshakes."

Gloria grinned. "All the better." She took Yvette by the hand. "You're doing the right thing, honey. We'll have Isaiah back on the battlefield fighting injustices by tomorrow." She delivered a supportive squeeze to her hand. "Do you know what you're going to say?"

312

"I think so."

"Fine. Stick to the least amount you can get away with. Logan shot the girl as soon as you pulled up. You didn't see who pulled the gun or any struggle to get it. Logan had it when you arrived, then bang. Then the cops showed up." She held her friend by the shoulders. "And plead the fifth on everything else."

"Won't that make me look guilty?"

"The less they hear, the better. You don't want that Jones guy twisting your words."

"No, we don't want that."

Gloria gave her a hug. "It's up to you to save Isaiah, honey. His reputation is at stake."

Yvette gave a slight nod and walked into the courtroom with Gloria. She held her head high. Her black and white dress hugged her slender frame. Isaiah returned from the men's room and took a seat next to his wife in the gallery. They hadn't been sitting for long when Yvette was called to the witness stand.

The butterflies took flight in her stomach as she made her way to the witness stand. She stepped into the wooden surround, not much bigger than a coffin. She raised her right hand as the bailiff secured the metaphoric straitjacket.

"Do you swear to tell the truth, the whole truth, and nothing but the truth, so help you God?" he asked.

"I do."

Jones was on his feet. "Your Honor, may I ask the witness one brief question before the prosecution begins?"

"You'll have your chance, Mr. Jones."

"But it is pertinent to the testimony she may be about to give. Just one brief question I'd like the witness to consider before answering questions."

Judge Hollingsworth looked at the prosecution. "Mr. Voss?"

Tony Voss stood up. "As long as it is brief and professional." He sat back down.

Jones nodded his gratitude at the latitude given. "Mrs. Hightower, has anyone advised you on the penalty for perjury?"

The prosecutor stood up and slammed his notebook on the table. "Goddamn it, Judge." He thrust his finger toward Jones. "He's basically calling the witness a liar and she hasn't uttered a word yet. His behavior is outrageous. I demand the court—"

Jones threw his hands up in mock surrender. "I apologize, Your Honor. I'll withdraw the question."

The judge shook his finger at Jones. "Counselor, one more stunt like that and I'll hold you in contempt." He addressed the jury. "The jury will disregard the inference that lies will play any part in the testimony about to be submitted and will accept Mrs. Hightower's account of what happened that night as gospel." He turned toward Yvette. "You do not have to answer that, Mrs. Hightower."

Yvette straightened her back. "But I do want to answer it, Your Honor." She set her steely gaze on Bert Jones. "Yes, I have been advised on the penalty for perjury. I have also been made aware of the consequences of obstructing justice. I am ready to give evidence, Mr. Jones, under the eyes of this court and under the eyes of God. As my husband said as we walked up the steps to this very courthouse, 'All that matters is that the killer is brought to justice.'"

Gloria smiled and gave her a little fist pump.

The prosecutor threw Jones a glance and a smirk before he began his questioning of the witness. "Mrs. Hightower, according to your statement, you were aware your husband was going to Gentleman Gem's nightclub on August 20th, correct?"

"Yes."

"And you were aware, as your husband has already testified, that he was there on a reconnaissance mission of sorts, regarding morality issues that may have been detrimental to the students he is in charge of educating."

"Objection," Jones shouted. "He's leading the witness."

"Sustained. Ask the question, Mr. Voss, without supplying the answer with it."

"You knew your husband was at Gentleman Gem's, didn't you, Mrs. Hightower?" Voss asked.

"Yes, I did."

"And why were you there?"

"To bring him his phone. He forgot it, and I thought he might need to call the police."

He frowned. "Indeed. A dangerous situation did develop, didn't it?"

"Indeed."

"When you arrived, you saw Cory Logan holding the gun, correct?"

"Objection," the defense barked.

"Sustained," the judge echoed.

"What happened when you arrived?" the prosecutor rephrased.

"I saw three figures standing in front of my headlights."

"Did you recognize them?"

"Yes. Isaiah, Cory Logan, and a girl—an African American."

"Did you have your window down? Did you hear anything?"

"My window was up, but I heard what turned out to be a gunshot."

"Was Cory Logan holding the gun?"

"Objection." Jones was sounding repetitive.

"Sustained." So was the judge.

"Did you see who shot Alicia Saunders?"

"Yes."

"Is he in this courtroom?"

"Yes."

"Can you identify the killer for the court?"

Yvette stared at Cory. He looked sad. Very sad. She expected to see some kind of hope in his eyes. Weren't boxers meant to hold supreme confidence in the face of adversity? How could anyone get into a boxing ring with a brut there solely to beat your brains out and maintain an unmatched optimism that you would kick his ass and reign supreme? But no. She saw a defeated man before the final bell. Their eyes locked. She wanted to look at Isaiah, but couldn't take her eyes off Cory. The butterflies had left. Forty years in the state penitentiary then onward to hell.

Voss cleared his throat. "Let the record show that Mrs. Hightower set her sight on the defendant, Cory Logan."

Judge Hollingsworth leaned toward the witness box. "I'm afraid we need verbal confirmation, Mrs. Hightower."

Yvette took her eyes off Cory and looked into the gallery. Isaiah and Gloria both gave encouraging nods to name the killer. The hope was on their faces, not Cory's.

The judge gave her another nudge. "Mrs. Hightower? We need an answer. Can you tell the court who shot Alicia Saunders?"

She drew a deep breath. "Yes. Isaiah Hightower."

A collective gasp sucked the air out of the room.

She looked at Cory. The painful grimace he wore five seconds ago had gone. Relief flushed his face.

"Mrs. Hightower," the prosecutor snapped. "Who shot Alicia Saunders?"

She didn't flinch. "Isaiah Hightower."

A surge of energy ran through the courtroom. Spectators pushed forward to the edge of their seats. So did the judge and jury.

Yvette looked at her husband for the first time since identifying him as the killer. She expected anger but saw shock. He sat open-mouthed with his eyes widened. Gloria hugged him sideways, her face buried into his shoulder, sobbing.

The prosecutor bolted to the judge's bench. "Your Honor, I'd like to ask for a recess."

"No chance," the judge barked. "Continue, Counselor."

The prosecutor drew a glass of water from the jug on his table. He took a large gulp then faced Yvette. "Mrs. Hightower, is it your testimony that it was your husband, Isaiah Hightower, who shot Alicia Saunders?"

"Yes, it is. I saw it with my own eyes. There is no mistake. Isaiah Hightower shot and killed Alicia Saunders."

Murmuring rippled through the courtroom before a silence of disbelief conquered the courtroom. Yvette felt naked. She sat in front of Hilton Head with her thoughts on full display to the public. She had no place to hide. She didn't know where to look. If silence was golden the courtroom just went double-platinum. She yearned for life to begin again.

"So, you lied to police officers," Tony Voss injected.

"I may have misled them, yes. And I apologize."

"'Sorry' does not excuse obstructing justice."

"Will committing perjury excuse obstructing justice?"

Isaiah sprung to his feet in the audience. "She's a liar, Judge. The woman's an alcoholic. She doesn't know what she is saying. She was drunk the night of the shooting and she's drunk right now. You have to disallow her testimony. I'll get her help. I'll send her to rehab." Isaiah frantically waved his arms over his head, addressing the jury. "The jury will disregard, the jury will disregard. You heard the judge. You cannot believe this woman. She has mental health issues!"

"Bailiff! Escort Mr. Hightower to a holding cell."

The bailiff grabbed a resisting and ranting Isaiah and led him out of the courtroom.

"You'll burn in hell, Yvette," Isaiah shouted as he was led away. "God doesn't abide liars!"

"No, He doesn't," Yvette mumbled, trying to console herself.

Gloria buried her face in her hands, crying uncontrollably.

Jones was on his feet. "Your Honor, in light of Mrs. Hightower's testimony, the defense request an immediate dismissal of all charges against Cory Logan."

Judge Hollingsworth nodded. "So granted."

Although the case was dismissed, Yvette remained seated in the witness box. She couldn't move. She was as stunned as everyone else in the courtroom. The confession was meant to separate her from her guilt. Whatever happened to "The truth shall set you free?" What a bunch of crap that was. She never felt worse in her life. She expected to find a relieved jury. A jury that did not have to make a crucial decision about a man's life. Instead, she saw anger. Twelve disconcerted faces staring at Satan's temptress. A woman who sold out her husband for a rich white guy. She wanted to yell, *I don't even like Cory Logan,* but hoped silence would bestow a certain dignity upon her.

She looked at Logan. Perhaps Gloria was right. His lawyer would've got him a light sentence. Maybe she should have lied for her husband. Bert Jones did rattle her with the reminder of perjury and she was afraid of prison herself. But ultimately, it was Cory Logan who turned her against her husband. How could she lie next to a murderer night after night? How would she ever have confidence that he wouldn't bump her off too if things got too sticky for him? Legacy be damned. She had to sleep at night. She wouldn't be able to do that next to a killer.

Chapter 37

Six Months Later

Yvette straightened the cushions on the sofa. She always enjoyed keeping the house tidy, but it felt odd over the past six months doing it solely for herself—not sharing the house with anyone else to appreciate it. But she did have purpose to keep it looking in tip-top shape—a sad reason, but a reason all the same. She stopped when the doorbell rang.

She checked herself in the hallway mirror en-route to answer the door. The image stood obscured through the patterned glass but she could see it was a man. A white man. It had to be a cop—or a Mormon. Then panic gripped her. Perhaps it was a prison guard there to tell her Isaiah had escaped from prison. She took a deep breath to steady herself. With trepidation, she opened the door.

Cory Logan swept his brown hair off his forehead. "Mrs. Hightower."

"Logan? What are you doing here?"

He pointed toward the sign at the front of the residence. "I heard you're selling your home. Where are you off to?"

She sighed. "I don't know yet. I have to sell it first."

"Are you staying on the island?"

"I got a year's probation for lying to the cops, so I have to stay in South Carolina. And my

probation officer is on the island, so logistically—"
She put her hands on her hips. "Why are we having this conversation?"

"Maybe I'm interested in buying it. Can I come in?"

"Viewing is by appointment only. You'll have to call my realtor and set it up."

"Yvette, please. I think we owe each other a conversation."

She rolled her eyes, but stepped aside and let him in.

He assessed the place as he walked toward the couch. "Nice place."

"Thank you." She invited him to sit down. "Why are you here? Really?"

"Have you heard from Isaiah?"

"He sent me a letter apologizing for what he said about me in court. And he wanted me to stick by him." Her eyes grew in intensity, staring at Cory. "Is it true what they said about him in court—you know, gambling? And what you said about Alicia being his mistress?"

His lips tightened. He nodded.

"Why didn't you tell me?"

"Would you have believed me?"

"No."

"That's why."

A silence hung in the air.

Cory chanced a glance at her. "So, are you going to stick by him?"

She shook her head. "The divorce papers are nearly finalized. I may not have known about the sneaking around, mistresses, and gambling, but murder is still a pretty big sin in my book. All I know is he'll be in an eight by ten cell for the next forty years. I need to get on with my life."

Cory remained straight-faced. "That took a lot of courage what you did. I know it couldn't have been easy, and I want you to know I'm grateful. You were my saving angel."

"Well, my halo feels pretty tarnished."

"You can still be an angel without a halo."

She smirked. "Then it looks like I answered your ad. Angel Wanted: No Halo Required."

"Yes, you did, and thank you." He smiled back. "Anyway, I'm pleased it worked out."

She let out an ironic chuckle. "I don't know about working out. I sent my husband to the slammer for life and my best friend wants me to burn in the hottest part of hell. She sees it that I betrayed him for some rich white guy."

"If only the world was colorblind. I'd like her to just see me as the rich guy."

She laughed. "Now there's a twist."

"So what's your plan?" Cory asked.

"Sell this, find a job, and start over. It's not going to be easy, but …"

"But if you're staying on the island, why sell this? It's a beautiful place."

She rubbed her thumbs across her fingertips. "I've always been a kept woman, Mr. Logan. I'm not sure what kind of job I can get, but selling hot dogs isn't going to pay the mortgage on this place. I have to be realistic."

"What if I can help?"

"Help how?"

"Pay off the mortgage for you."

"What? You can't do that."

"Excuse me, I can. I'm retired and I'm wealthy. I can do what I want."

"But why would you? You don't owe me anything. I've learned the truth is a free commodity, but it doesn't set you free."

"Yes, I do owe you."

"No you don't. Doing what's right shouldn't be ransomed."

Cory gave her a long, meaningful look. "My lawyer told me with two eyewitnesses I was screwed. That's why I came to see you in the parking lot at the market. I staked you out for days waiting to get a chance to speak to you alone. I had to make a last-ditch effort, hoping you might ... well, do what you did. Did my visit influence you at all?"

A tear dribbled down her cheek. She nodded. "Yes, it did. I never liked you, or your bimbo girlfriend, but I couldn't let an innocent man go to prison. Not even you. I've spent my life protecting victims, not making them."

Cory nodded appreciatively. "Perhaps I don't *owe* you anything, but I want to help. You have a beautiful home here. You should be able to keep it."

"So what? Do you buy it and I rent it from you?"

He shook his head. "No. I pay off your mortgage and you never have to hear from me again. Unless you want to."

"If you paid off the mortgage, wouldn't I be indebted to you?"

"No. We could call it square and start again."

"You mean like friends?"

He offered a coy shrug. "I'm not boxing anymore. And since I'm not fighting anymore, Charlie's not around. I get the impression those were the two things you disliked about me the most. Maybe this time it could be different."

"And if I still don't like you?"

"You'll still get your house. No strings attached."

Yvette smiled and stuck her hand out. They shook on it.

Yvette pursed her lips to one side. "About this string thing ... can we start with a thread and see where it goes?"

Cory smiled. "You're the one running the sew."

THE END

If you made it this far, I'm hoping it's
because you read the entire book and enjoyed it.
If that is the case, it would be very much
appreciated if you would help spread the word by
leaving a review on Amazon and/or
Goodreads.com
Word of mouth is more powerful
than any ad I can buy.

Thank you for your support

Travis Casey

Books by Travis Casey

TYLER'S TROUBLE TRILOGY SERIES

Trouble Triangle –Romantic comedy set in Hawaii. The first book of the series.

Oceans of Trouble –Trouble follows Tyler around the Western Pacific in this suspense novel.

Forbidden Trouble –Will Tyler find love in Scotland in this romantic comedy?

Southern Harm –Tyler takes a backseat to his son, Oscar, in this romantic suspense.

CAROLINA CALLING SERIES

No Halo Required – Righteousness yields to evil in this book of Noir fiction.

The Mayor's Race – Is her color alone enough to win office in this Political Satire

Dark Alley to Power – The third and final of the series. Political Satire/Noir Fiction

Made in the USA
Columbia, SC
12 January 2023

10125136R00180